DEFY DEATH

RILEY MALLOY THRILLER SERIES

BOOK 2

Judith A. Barrett

DEFY DEATH

RILEY MALLOY THRILLER SERIES, BOOK 2

Published in the United States of America by Wobbly Creek, LLC

2021 Georgia

wobblycreek.com

TAGGED BY DEATH is a work of fiction. Names, characters, businesses, places, events, locales, and incidents either are the products of the author's imagination or used in a fictitious manner. Any resemblance to actual persons, living or dead, or actual events is purely coincidental.

Edited by Judith Euen Davis

Cover by Wobbly Creek, LLC

ISBN 978-1-953-87013-1

DEDICATION

DEFY DEATH is dedicated to the colors brown and gray and to all the feral and stray animals that steal our hearts.

PREVIOUSLY . . .

RILEY

My name is Riley Malloy, I'm a vet tech, and I understand animals, which must be why people call me a "dog whisperer." After my employer abruptly closed the veterinarian clinic, I needed a job and a cheaper place to live that allowed dogs. I called my Aunt Millie for advice; she suggested that I move to my grandmother's cabin that was three hours away outside of Barton, Georgia, and told me about a veterinary hospital that had an opening for a good vet tech. I loaded my car with my belongings and Toby, a five-year-old, black and brown German Shepherd-Lab mix, who had been staying at the clinic for months while he waited for the man that had dropped him off to pick him up. Because my savings were running out and my apartment didn't allow animals, Toby and I headed to Grandma's cabin.

When I stopped at the veterinary hospital, Doctor Julie Rae Sorensen hired me after Pia, the current vet tech, and Amanda, the pregnant office manager, declared their enthusiastic support. Being in Barton was refreshing after the mean-girl atmosphere at my previous clinic. Doc Julie Rae, Pia, and Amanda are smart, kind, and funny.

My circle of friends expanded when a lanky deputy with greenish hazel eyes from a nearby county brought two sweet Yorkies and an irritable cat to the Barton hospital after their person crashed her car. One Yorkie was injured, and the cute deputy, Ben Carter, kind of stuck around when he wasn't at work after that. He helped me move from the cabin into town, laughed at my dumb jokes, yelled at me when a killer shot at me, and is my best friend, along with Toby. Ben became such a frequent visitor in Barton that our local sheriff hired him. In addition to being a stellar law enforcement officer, Ben is very knowledgeable about caring for animals because of the summers he worked with his veterinarian uncle. His uncle thinks Ben should become a veterinarian, and so do I.

My troubles started when I found threatening yellow notes too frequently for comfort. Even though I didn't know it, the killer was obsessed with me because I was the last person alive that knew his true identity after he murdered the others. When he attacked, I was ready. Grandma would have been proud.

BEN

Even though my uncle told me I had the natural talent to be a vet, I've always wanted to be a law enforcement officer. I loved my job, but working in my hometown, where I knew everyone, was awkward, and I knew it was time for a change when I saw Riley and her green eyes and golden copper hair. She was the prettiest girl I'd ever seen, and I'm lucky that she's become my best friend. It wasn't just those green eyes with flecks of gold, though, because she is also smart and nice, and I was in awe of the magical way she related to animals. She even understood "Psycho," the name I gave the irritable cat. If anyone should be a veterinarian, it's Riley.

I moved out of my apartment in Carson to Barton for the opportunity to work with the sheriff because he's the best in the state at understanding people. He offered me the job, so I could be closer to Riley. I suspect I'm not the only one who is glad her amateur detective days are behind her.

CHAPTER ONE

When Riley and Toby reached the veterinarian clinic, her eyes widened at Doc Thad's car in the back parking lot. He was their new veterinarian, and Claire, his wife, was learning the office manager's duties, so Claire could backup Amanda when she began her maternity leave.

"Doc Julie Rae's always the first one into work, Toby. Something's up." Riley carried the tray with the warm cinnamon rolls as she and Toby hurried inside.

The young, tall, slender veterinarian with a receding hairline hurried from the breakroom to meet them in the hallway. "I made coffee, and Claire's checking the messages from the weekend. I can't tell you how glad I am that you're here."

He smiled at the tray. "We'll get through the day after all. You brought your Monday cinnamon rolls."

Riley snickered. "Never knew I had a choice."

While they walked to the breakroom, Thad wiggled his eyebrows then continued, "You don't, as far as I'm concerned. We're in for a busy day. Doc Julie Rae called me yesterday. Charlie's elderly aunt in The Bahamas fell when she was cleaning her house roof gutters over the weekend, and Doc Julie Rae and their boys will go along with Charlie to help. Julie Rae will sit with their aunt at the hospital while Charlie and the boys catch up on all the maintenance and outside work. Amanda called a few minutes ago and told Claire she's on her way to her doctor's office. It's early for the baby, but not too early. Pia's going to be a little late because her son has an ear infection. If she can't get an appointment right away, she'll go to the doctor's office and try to be a walk-in. If Zach doesn't come in, let's buy some beer and lock the doors. When I was an undergrad, I heard beer and cookies were good; I'll bet beer and cinnamon rolls would be fantastic. You'll have to help me talk Claire into it, though."

Riley rolled her eyes as she set down the cinnamon rolls and poured their coffee.

"I better take a cinnamon roll and coffee to Claire since she's glued to her desk," Thad said; Riley and Toby followed him.

Claire was on the phone when Thad set her coffee and cinnamon roll in front of her. She glanced at him and held up her hand for him to wait then continued listening and writing. After she hung up, she said, "I've listened to all the messages, and there's nothing urgent to bring in right away. I'll call everyone back and set up appointments, but first I have news from Doc Julie Rae. They were at the airport, and their row was called to board when she remembered that a new veterinarian who graduated from the University of Georgia called her on Friday because he heard Doc had an opening. He's been working in Miami for three years, but his wife wants to return to Georgia to be closer to her family. Doc told him the position is filled, but she'd be interested in talking to him."

"I'm fired, right?" Doc Thad asked.

"Sorry, but you're out of luck, bud." Claire rolled her eyes then sipped her coffee and nibbled on her cinnamon roll.

"He's showing up today," Riley said.

"You're right, and Doc said we have to be nice to him." Claire smiled. "How did you know?"

Riley shrugged. "It's the worst possible scenario under the circumstances. You want more coffee?"

Doc Thad left for the coffeepot, and Claire said, "Poor guy is a bundle of nerves. He'll be fine when the clients show up because he'll have patients and be in his element."

Zach returned with Doc Thad with a cinnamon roll in each hand. One of the rolls was half gone. "Amanda called you, right?" Zach asked. "Mom called and wanted to know what we'd heard because her sister-in-law called to ask how her daughter was doing. I guess I'm the cousin designated to be the official family snoop."

Claire giggled. "We haven't heard anything yet. I'll be your informant." She glanced at her screen. "Our first patient of the day will be here in fifteen minutes. You're up first, Zach." She handed the client folder to her husband, then he and Zach headed to the first exam room to review the file.

After they left, Riley picked up the coffeepot. "I'll start another pot, and I want you to know I envy those two. Did you see how many cinnamon rolls they packed away? If I eat more than one, I'd go from what Pia and I call pleasantly curvy to downright roly-poly round."

Claire snorted. "I feel your pain, girlfriend. We hate boys, right?"

"Darn tootin'." Riley giggled and tossed her head as she headed to the breakroom.

After she started another pot of coffee, Riley returned to Claire's desk. A woman who sat in the reception area smiled at Riley; Riley returned her smile then grinned at the pug who smiled while she wagged her tail.

"Hello, Laverne. You're looking good these days. Are you feeling better?"

Laverne yipped, and Riley giggled.

"She's lost weight and is much more active. We take our walks every morning and evening. In fact, I've lost a few pounds myself." Laverne's person stood and raised her eyebrows as she peered at Claire and Riley.

"You look great." Claire handed Riley the file.

"Let's see how happy the scale is, Laverne," Riley said, and Laverne trotted along beside her while her person followed them.

"My friend asked me if I was still feeding Laverne egg like she told me, and I told her that Laverne was under Doc Julie Rae's supervision and on a special, prescription diet. When my friend told me that I was losing too much weight, I told her I was on a special diet too." She grinned.

"Your weight's good, Laverne." Riley lifted the pug to the examination table. "I'll check your ears. Are you getting enough to eat? Any stomach troubles?"

Laverne yipped, and Riley said, "Good news."

While Riley checked Laverne's ears, the woman said, "She eats all her food but seems satisfied."

"Your ears are fine," Riley said as Doc Thad came into the room.

"Hi, Laverne, Ms. Claire told me you're doing a lot better."

When Laverne lowered her head and whimpered, Riley laughed. "Laverne's feeling a little shy. She thinks you're nice, Doc Thad."

"Thank you, Laverne. That's the nicest thing I've heard all day," Thad said.

He read over Riley's notes and performed a quick physical exam of the old pug. "We can return to your usual annual appointment. Ms. Claire will make it for you." He rubbed Laverne's ear, and she licked his hand.

After Riley escorted her patient and the client to Claire's desk, Riley returned to the exam room. While she was cleaning, Doc Thad paused as he was entering his notes on the tablet. "I'm really sorry I outgrew understanding what my dog was telling me. I'd forgotten about it until you reminded me, and now I have great memories of spending time with him. When did you realize other kids didn't understand anymore what dogs and cats were saying?"

Riley sprayed the exam table with sanitizer then wiped it. "When I was nine, I learned my friend didn't know what her dog had said about going outside on the wet grass. When I asked her why she didn't, she told me she was too grown up for stuff like that. Now, that was strange."

Thad chuckled. "I can imagine it was."

When the room was clean, Riley returned to Claire's desk.

"Amanda called. Her doctor put her on bed rest. She was happy the baby's going to have a chance to grow more before he's born but annoyed about being stuck at home. We agreed I'd call her every morning and at the end of the day for updates. I did some fancy finagling to talk her out of calling her every hour." Claire rolled her eyes.

"That's good news." Riley smiled.

Claire continued, "I told Zach, so he could tell his mother then decided to let Pia and Doc Julie Rae know about Amanda when they call with their updates; I don't have time to spend my day on the phone reporting back to each one of them." Claire glanced at the day's schedule. "We have a brief lull before the next appointment. Would you watch the desk for me a second? I need a little stretch break that includes rescuing a cinnamon roll. I'll bring you one if you like."

Riley sighed then shook her head. "My round self says yes, but I'll limit myself to the one I already had which was actually two."

After Riley pulled the folder for the next patient, she checked her texts and read a new message from her Aunt Millie.

"Got a call from a Marcy. Wanted your address. Ok?"

Riley frowned at her phone. *I initially didn't want anyone to have my address because of Doc Truman, but he's dead.*

She returned Aunt Millie's text: "Did she say why?"

"Will check."

Riley furrowed her brow. *Why would a former work friend call Aunt Millie for my address when she has my phone number?*

When the office phone rang, Riley answered it.

"Hey, Riley. Are you filling in for Claire?" Pia asked. "We saw the doctor, and after we fill the prescription for Jackson's ear infection, we'll go home. I'll stay home with him until his fever's down, then if he's not up to going to school, his grandmother offered to take care of him. Jordy went with us to the doctor's office. When the receptionist made the mistake of telling me that Jordy couldn't be there, I gave her a full blast of my mama ferocity. I was up all night with my sick child, and I was exhausted. Do you think that's a good enough excuse? I think I owe her cookies or something. Her face got really red, but she didn't cry, so maybe she's tougher than she looks. I'm sorry I'm leaving you short-handed. Is everything okay?"

Riley filled her in on Amanda and Julie Rae.

"Oh, no. That leaves just you and Doc Thad," Pia said. "Wait, I think my fried brain just proved how tired I am because Zach's there and so is Claire."

Riley giggled. "We're doing fine, and you need a nap."

After Pia hung up, Claire returned with a cinnamon roll and a lukewarm cup of coffee; Riley rose to relinquish the receptionist's chair.

"I always try to catch the coffee before anyone throws it out." Claire sipped her coffee as she sat. "Ahh. Perfect temperature."

"My favorite too." Riley wiggled her eyebrows.

Claire snickered. "Thad shudders, so I thought vet people must be sensitive about coffee. I'm happy that I have a kindred tepid coffee drinker."

Riley told her about Pia's call.

Claire widened her eyes. "I'd have cried. Pia invented the mom glare."

Toward the end of the morning, Riley's phone buzzed a text from Ben while she cleaned an exam room for the next patient.

"First day, and I haven't been fired."

Riley grinned as she replied: "Good job."

Ben: "I need to find a place to live that allows dogs."

Riley's eyes widened then she tapped: "You can stay at the cabin, but what's wrong with Mr. Richard's house?"

Ben: "Talk later."

Riley frowned. *What is there to talk about?*

After the room was clean, she hurried to the front and was still scowling when she reached Claire's desk.

"It has to be Ben." Claire raised her eyebrows at Riley's sullen expression. "What's up?"

"Ben texted that he needed to find a place to live that allowed dogs."

"A place to live? I thought he was at your cabin and was going to move to Mr. Richard's house."

"I don't know what's going on, but he said we'd talk later. What does that mean?" Riley's shoulders slumped.

Claire shrugged. "I have no idea. It definitely doesn't mean that he decided to quit his job in Barton and leave, so nothing else is important. Let me know if we need to find him something else in town. I looked at just about everything here before we moved; house hunting is my new superpower."

Riley sighed. "You're right; he'll still be working for Sheriff Dunn whether he's at the cabin or in town. I have other things to stress about, like what do I pick up from the grocery store for dinner? Oh wait, it's his turn to cook tonight."

Claire laughed. "Now that you've mentioned food, how do we work our lunch breaks?"

"You, Doc, and Zach take your break first then I will. If a patient comes in with something that can't wait until Doc finishes his lunch, I'll ring Amanda's urgent break bell."

Doc Thad strolled to the desk. "Did I hear someone say lunch?"

Claire rose from her rolling chair. "Let's grab Zach. I packed your favorite lunch: a ham sandwich."

As they strolled to the breakroom, Doc said, "That's what you always pack."

"Because it's all you'll eat."

Riley reviewed the files that Claire had set out before she leaned back and stared at the cars that cruised past the animal hospital then picked up her phone, held her breath, and sent a text to Ben. "Will you be here for dinner?"

Ben: "Yes."

Riley exhaled and smiled. *Sometimes the direct approach works.*

When Claire returned, Riley put on her jacket and picked up her lunch before she and Toby went outside. While Toby explored the back parking lot and investigated the patch of grass, Riley ate her lunch. Before they went inside, Aunt Millie called.

"Just checking in. Did I catch you on your lunch break? I never heard back from Marcy. Is she kind of scatterbrained? It seemed like it when she called."

Riley raised her eyebrows as her aunt continued, "I might be unavailable for quite a while. I'm going to Europe for a conference then on to Southeast Asia. I'll be traveling light, so I won't be bringing anything back for you, but I might ship you something. Oops. They're calling for my plane to board. I'll see you in a month or two."

Aunt Millie hung up. Riley shook her head. *This trip must have come up suddenly. I've never heard her so rattled.*

Toby trotted to the door then turned to grin at Riley with his tongue hanging out, and Riley smiled. "You're right. Our lunch break is over. Time to go inside."

When Riley reached the front desk, Claire exhaled in relief. "I just got off the phone. We have a dog coming in that was hit by a car. The dog darted into the road and pushed a toddler out of the path of a speeding car, and the car hit the dog. The driver didn't stop, but a keen-eyed eleven-year-old girl got the license number."

A broad-shouldered, muscular man carried in a golden retriever with a deformed hind leg and blood from facial lacerations.

Riley hurried to the dog. "Hello, Gracie. We'll take good care of you. This way, sir." She led the way to the trauma room as she called out to Claire, "I need Zach and Doc to drop everything and come to the trauma room right away."

When they were in the trauma room, Riley said, "Give me one second to grab our rolling x-ray table, then you can set her down." Riley turned to the door as Zach rushed in with the x-ray table.

"Here we are." Riley pointed, and the man gently placed Gracie on the table.

"I'll have the x-ray ready for you," Zach said before he left.

Doc Thad came into the room as Riley leaned over Gracie and cooed then listened as Gracie whimpered. "I'm so sorry, Gracie. Doc Thad is right here. We'll take some x-rays, then we can give you something to help you feel more comfortable."

Riley turned to Doc. "X-rays first. Gracie's stomach hurts a lot."

Doc stayed with Gracie as Zach returned to roll the table to the x-ray room.

"We'll take the x-rays. Can you find out what happened?" Doc asked.

Riley nodded. "Sir, let's sit in the reception area. Can you tell me what happened?"

As they walked together to the front, the man said, "Gracie's my neighbor's dog. My wife and I were outside with our little Janelle when the neighbor's cat escaped from their house. It ran toward us and into the street, and Janelle said, "No, kitty," then darted into the street before any of us could grab her. I didn't even see the car, but

Gracie did. She raced ahead of me and flipped Janelle across the road. The cat's owner told me Janelle tucked into a ball and giggled as she rolled onto the grass."

The man shook his head. "That's our daredevil Janelle. The car slammed into Gracie and knocked her down, and the driver kept going. I couldn't believe it. My wife ran across the street and grabbed Janelle, and I scooped up Gracie. Another neighbor is bringing Gracie's owner here. If you don't need anything else from me, I'll go home."

"Gracie wasn't dragged?" Riley asked.

"No, it all happened so fast; I'm not sure where the car's bumper hit Gracie, but it might have been on her left. She didn't have time to get out of the way, and the car didn't swerve at all."

"Thanks for your help, and please give Janelle an extra hug from all of us," Riley said. As Riley hurried to the trauma room, she passed exam room two where Claire was talking with the client and stroking a cat as she placed him into his carrier.

When Claire glanced at her, Riley said, "Gracie's person will be here soon."

Claire nodded then picked up the carrier.

Doc Thad met Riley outside of the trauma room. "Her leg has a simple fracture. It doesn't appear to have been crushed by the tire like I expected. No broken ribs, and there's no signs of internal bleeding because her abdomen isn't distended or rigid, but I'd like for you to check."

Zach rolled Gracie back into the trauma room. He had placed a warmed blanket over her. "She was a little shocky, and her gums were pale; they've pinked up with the warm blanket."

Riley stroked Gracie's head. "I'd like to check your ribs to be sure nothing else is broken. Is that okay?"

Gracie whimpered.

"Thanks." Riley removed the blanket before she deftly traced Gracie's ribs with her fingertips then palpated Gracie's abdomen while she watched Gracie's face.

"Your ribs are sore because they're probably bruised, but your stomach is soft. That's good, sweet girl. Your leg has some cuts and is broken, so Doc Thad will bandage and splint it, and you'll feel more comfortable."

Zach returned with the rewarmed blanket, and Doc Thad asked, "Will you see if Gracie's family is here, Riley? Zach, we'll bandage the lacerations on her broken leg, then I'll splint while you clean Gracie's face and other lacerations."

When Riley reached the front area, her eyes widened at the crowd of people in the reception area. "Is everyone here about Gracie?"

After the group pelted her with questions, Riley held up her hand for silence. "Our hero, Gracie, has a broken leg, but it's a simple fracture. She doesn't have any signs of any other injuries. She's a brave, lucky girl. Who is family?"

Everyone in the group turned to look at an older woman who sat near the door. Riley smiled. "Come with me."

A man helped the woman rise, then Riley offered the woman her arm.

"Thanks," the woman said. "My knees are still weak; I was scared to death."

On the way to the trauma room, Riley told the client about Gracie's injuries. "We've cleaned the lacerations on her leg, and Doc Thad is putting a splint on her leg for now. He'll want to keep her overnight for observation, but she won't be alone. Do you know George, the retired animal control officer? He stays here at night and will call Doc Thad if he sees any problems. Doc Thad may put a cast on her leg before she goes home, but we'll know more tomorrow."

"I can't tell you what good news this is. I was afraid of the worst. I didn't see the car hit Gracie, but I ran outside when I heard all the screaming."

Riley helped the client to the trauma room, and Doc Thad smiled. "We put on Gracie's splint, and we're ready to roll her to a kennel where it's quiet, so she can relax. Do you have any questions for me?"

"No, Riley was very thorough." The woman returned his smile then hurried to Gracie and cooed. "Sweet girl. Janelle is safe, thanks to you. I'll see you tomorrow."

Riley walked the woman back to the front where the reception area had cleared except for one man.

"Thanks again, Riley." The woman squeezed Riley's hand. "Y'all are awesome."

The man offered his arm, and they left.

"This is the first time I've seen the three of you in action without Doc Julie Rae or Pia around, and you're an impressive, tight team," Claire said. "I understand now why Thad loves it here so much. Zach had given his client the sack with the medication before he left for the x-ray room, so I made sure she understood when and how to give the medicine, then I did the part I do best: I took her payment and made the next appointment. Oh, and I called George to let him know about Gracie. He'd already heard about it. I love small towns." Claire smiled. "I pulled the rest of the files for today. They're in order if you'd like to review them. We have a new patient coming in later this afternoon. I'll make sure to assign the patient to you. No sense in overwhelming Zach quite yet."

In the middle of the afternoon, when Riley returned to Claire's desk with a patient and client, a man in his thirties came inside and glanced around. He was average height and had brown hair and a neatly trimmed moustache and beard. After the client left, he approached Claire. "I'm Preston Ansell. Is Dr. Sorensen available?"

"Are you from Miami?" Claire smiled.

Dr. Ansell chuckled. "It depends. Are you a bill collector?"

Claire laughed. "I'm Claire, and this is Riley, one of our amazing vet techs. Riley, Dr. Ansell is the veterinarian from Miami that Doc Julie Rae expected. I'll tell Doc Thad."

Riley offered her hand, and they shook. She was taken aback at first by the strong odor of cigarette smoke. *I didn't realize how long it's been since I've been around a smoker.*

Riley returned his contagious smile. "Doc Julie Rae had to leave this morning to attend to an urgent family matter and left you to fend for yourself with her unruly staff. Dr. Thad Faraday is our recently hired veterinarian, and Zach is our newest vet tech."

Doc Thad strode down the hallway and extended his hand. "Thad Faraday," he said as they shook hands.

"Preston Ansell."

"Let's go into Doc Julie Rae's office to talk, then I'll give you a tour. You've met Claire and Riley?"

"Yes, I did." Preston Ansell followed Doc Thad to the vet's office. "The reception area is the brightest I've seen. Very cheerful."

Claire rose to peek out the front window. "I don't see a car, but I thought his wife was coming too. We'll have to grill him."

When the next client came in, Claire handed Zach the folder that he'd read earlier, and Zach led the client and the growling cat to exam room two. "This is just a follow up, Dexter, on your weight. You're looking a lot better. Are you seeing your groomer regularly? I keep meaning to ask you if she's married."

"She comes once a week," the client said. "He does look a lot better, doesn't he? We don't know if she's married, but we can sure find out. You aren't married?"

Claire snickered. "Zach connected with a matchmaker. What was Dexter complaining about?"

"You don't want to know what Dexter said because he has a trash mouth, but he may be mellowing; he wasn't nearly as rude as he was the first time we saw him."

Dr. Ansell came to the reception area. "Doc Thad is examining a patient. Do you have a few minutes to talk, Riley?"

Riley glanced at Claire who said, "Ten minutes."

"We could go to the breakroom," Riley said.

After they sat at a table in the breakroom, Dr. Ansell said, "Doc Thad told me you're one of the most talented vet techs he's ever worked with, so why aren't you a veterinarian?"

Riley laughed. "Did Doc Thad put you up to that?"

Dr. Ansell grinned. "He might have said something. How do you like it here? Didn't you move from a larger town?"

"I don't have any family except for an aunt who travels out of the country, so the larger town was fine for a first job, but it was impersonal. I love Barton because I have a support system, and the staff here is remarkably knowledgeable and skilled which is more than I can say about my previous employment."

Dr. Ansell raised an eyebrow. "That's an interesting comment. I've grown tired of the incompetence around me to the point that I was worried it might rub off them and onto me."

"I understand," Riley said. "It was hard to do what I knew was right in the face of the sloppy shortcuts I saw until I decided that was their style not mine. It made it easier for me to get through my day, but as I withdrew from the group, I became more isolated."

He shook his head. "You could be talking about me. My wife's family lives in Atlanta, so we thought another big city like Miami would be fine, but it wasn't, at least for us."

Riley narrowed her eyes. "Has she always lived around Atlanta? This is definitely not a city, and it's true that everyone knows your business. It isn't for everybody."

He chuckled. "Evy is an author. She'll be right there with them knowing everyone else's business."

"Really? What does she write?"

"Historical fiction, which makes Barton a big plus for her. She says the area is steeped in intrigue, romance, secrets, and betrayal and just waiting for her to uncover their stories."

I smiled. "I like her already. What other questions do you have for me?"

"Do you think the practice could support three doctors?"

"Absolutely. With a third doctor here, Doc Julie Rae can expand her practice, for example, to include farm visits; it's something she'd love to do but does now only for emergency cases." Riley rose. "Time for me to get back to work."

Preston followed her. "I called Evy earlier. She may already be here."

When they strolled to the front, Claire and a woman with short, spiky, dark blond hair were chatting at Claire's desk.

"I see you've met Claire," Preston said. "This is Riley."

Riley hurried to the desk, and the woman hugged Riley. "Nice to see another short well-padded person whose scrawny bones don't poke out," she whispered.

Riley snickered. "Well-padded is an excellent description."

"Evy's a hugger." Claire giggled.

"I hope that's okay." Evy peered at Riley. "I forget that not everyone is. However, it's an excellent way to bond with a friend or stop your enemy from killing you with a sword, and since you don't have a sword, you must be a friend."

Riley grinned. "I'll have to remember that. Do you have a sword?"

Preston rolled his eyes as Evy said, "Actually, I do. It's important to understand the enemy."

Claire laughed. "If you decide against working here, Doc, leave Evy with us. I'll let Doc Julie Rae know you've been here when she calls. I have your card, so I can be intermediary, if necessary."

"Thanks, Claire. We'll be around for the next few days while we check out the area and visit nearby state parks," he said.

After Doc Thad and Riley had finished the annual exam for a two-year-old pit bull mix, Hector, Riley strolled with Hector and the client to Claire's desk. Doc Thad motioned for her to follow him to the breakroom.

"What do you think?" he asked.

"From a staff perspective, Dr. Ansell will fit right well with our diverse group. He asked how I liked it in Barton and if the practice could support three doctors, which I thought were good questions."

Doc Thad nodded. "He asked me the same questions. I asked about his typical cases in Miami, then we talked about the typical cases here. So, from a professional standpoint, he's knowledgeable. I'll give a couple of friends from college a call."

"Are you afraid Doc Julie Rae will tell you to decide whether she should hire him?"

"Exactly." He shook his head. "I don't know why that scares me."

"I'll help however I can," Riley said.

He exhaled. "You already have. After years of school, all of this is new to me; it helped that you zoomed right in on what was nagging me."

He squinted at her as he headed to examine his next patient. "Are you sure you aren't a people whisperer too?"

Riley snorted. "I'm positive. I'm totally clueless when it comes to figuring out Ben."

On her way to the desk to check for the next appointment, Riley's phone buzzed a text.

Ben: "Okay if I cook at your house?"

Riley rolled her eyes then replied, "Sure."

When she reached the front desk, Claire was scribbling notes while she was on the phone. "Got it."

Claire hung up and referred to her notes. "Doc Julie Rae only had a minute, so I had to write as fast as I could to be sure I didn't forget anything. Thad and I need to check her house after work because Charlie couldn't remember if he left the back door unlocked. They have a foster dog scheduled to come to their house tomorrow, so I have a call to make. I'll have the dog come here instead, then we'll need to figure out what to do about the new dog that Kenny and Freddy decided to call 'Chuck' because he'll be their chuck wagon dog. Doesn't sound like a temporary foster to me. He is the runt of a German Shepherd-Airedale Terrier litter. She wants Thad to decide whether to hire Preston Ansell. Thad's going to break out in a rash when I tell him. I'm supposed to tell Amanda she's fired if she tries to come to work." Claire grinned. "I'm going to tell Pia that's her assignment." She tapped her notepad. "That's it."

Riley smiled. "Good. No assignment for me."

Claire grimaced. "I can't believe I forgot to write it down; I'm glad you mentioned it. If Pia comes back by Wednesday, you're supposed to take Doc Preston to Lindsey's to examine a horse. Doc Julie Rae doesn't think he has any equine experience, and she wants to throw him a curveball. Now, that's it. I'll call Pia and Lindsey to set it up then schedule Doc Preston to come in Wednesday. I'm not supposed to tell him the plan, so he'll be going with you in whatever he's wearing. Did you know our boss was so devious? Thad will be happy to hear he'll have another data point for his decision. That man loves his data."

Riley snickered as the next client came in. "Doc Julie Rae is a complex person."

At the end of the day, Claire held up her hand. "We survived all day."

Riley, then Zach smacked her hand as Doc Thad joined them.

"What are we celebrating?" he asked.

"We survived the entire day," Zach said.

"Worth celebrating. Glad I wasn't the only one who had doubts a time or two," Doc said.

Claire went over her notes from her conversation with Doc Julie Rae. When she reached Riley's assignment, Doc Thad chuckled. "Doc Julie Rae is an evil genius, isn't she?"

"Exactly why we love her," Claire said. "I've called Pia and Lindsey, so the stage is set for Wednesday. I'll call Doc Preston tomorrow. Let's blow this joint before we're caught. Thad and I will lock up. Y'all go on."

"I'll straighten the breakroom before I leave. It'll take me just a second," Riley said.

Zach stayed to help her. "What did you think of Dr. Preston Ansell?" Zach asked as he sacked up the trash.

"I thought he'd be a good addition to our staff. What about you?"

"I don't know what I expected, but I was relieved that he wasn't overbearing like all my instructors were. I really like it here, and I was afraid a new doctor might rock the boat, so in spite of all my insecurities, I think he will be a good addition too." Zach grinned.

Riley chuckled as she finished wiping down the table and counters. "I think we all were worried about a new doctor messing up our team."

"I'll carry out the trash," Zach said.

"Let's go, Toby." Riley and Toby hurried to her car.

As Riley pulled into her driveway, she stared at her porch. *There's a package by the front door.*

CHAPTER TWO

"What do you think, Toby? Do I call Ben?"

When Toby whined, she relaxed. "You're right; it is a cat carrier. What's it doing on my front porch?"

She climbed out of her car and opened the door for Toby, who dashed to the porch and sniffed the carrier. As Riley strode to the door, the cat hissed, and Toby yipped before he trotted to her and nuzzled her hand for a reassuring rub.

Riley scratched behind his ear. "The cat does sound cranky."

She picked up the note on top of the carrier then gasped when she read it.

"Listen to this, Toby. 'Riley, take care of my cat for me. I called your aunt for your address, but she didn't get back to me yet. I remembered you were in Barton because who could forget that? I don't have your phone number anymore because I purged all my old numbers. I'll pick up the cat and the carrier later. My mother bought the carrier for me, so be sure to take good care of it. Marcy. p.s. I stopped by your office to drop off the cat but decided it was better to leave it at your house after the people at the gas station told me where you live. Will send you my address in an email.'"

I never knew Marcy was such a jerk.

Riley peered inside the carrier. "No wonder you're cranky. You don't have any water, and your collar seems a little thick for you. Is it too heavy? Let's get you a drink then I'll check you for fleas. Are you feral?"

The cat hissed.

Riley unlocked the door and nodded. "Your ear's notched. That's why I asked. No offense meant. I'll get you some water first. Glad you had a food lady who took care of you and the other cats and dogs, but I'll still check for fleas after you've had a drink."

Riley filled a small bowl with water; when the brown and gray cat drank the bowl dry, Riley frowned as she refilled it. "You were really thirsty." While the cat drank a little more, Riley jotted down a list of the cat supplies she needed.

Riley wrapped the cat in a towel before she checked for fleas. "What's your name, pretty girl?"

The cat meowed, and Riley said, "Princess is the perfect name for you, and you have absolutely no fleas."

Princess hissed as Riley put her back into her carrier when Riley's phone rang. *Good, it's Ben.*

"I just got off work. I'll go to the grocery store then be right there; is there anything I need to pick up?"

"I can't think of any groceries I need, but Marcy from Pomeroy dropped off a cat at my house, and I need cat supplies. Could you pick up some cat food for Princess while you're at the grocery store?"

"What about a cat box and litter?" Ben asked. "Isn't that a priority too?"

"It is." Riley rolled her eyes. *Sometimes I forget about Ben's veterinary skills.* "She needs a new collar. She's wearing one, but it's heavy, like a dog collar, and it must be uncomfortable. I have a list of some other things too, but the rest can wait."

"Got it. See you soon."

Riley grabbed a sweater before she and Toby went out back. While Toby investigated to make sure no intruders had been in his yard, Riley relaxed on the porch and gazed at the white clouds until Toby was ready to go inside.

When Ben's truck pulled into her driveway, she hurried out to help.

Ben handed her a small sack. "This is her new collar. I'll come back for the heavier groceries after I take in the cat supplies."

After they unloaded the truck, Ben placed ice cream in the freezer and the produce and dairy items in the refrigerator before he knelt next to the carrier and peered inside. "You're a pretty girl, Princess."

Princess purred in agreement.

"Here's the letter from Marcy." Riley handed him the note.

He rose then frowned as he read. "She never refers to Princess by name, and she seems more interested in the carrier than the cat. She's supposed to be a vet tech?" He sneered. "Princess is ours now. There's no way Marcy can have her back."

Riley nodded as she filled the cat box with litter then set it near her pantry near Princess's carrier. "That's exactly what I think."

While Ben opened the carrier door, Toby lay next to the carrier, then after the door was open, Princess peeked around the corner at Toby. When Toby whined, she strode out of the carrier with her tail in the air as she circled the kitchen then marched to the cat box.

Riley dished up food for Toby and Princess while Ben removed the clunky collar and replaced it with the teal cat collar before he handed the dog collar to Riley.

"That collar is really pretty on you, Princess. I'll take the old one to the office. Collars are handy to have around." Riley stuck the dog collar into her backpack.

What are you cooking?" she asked.

Ben turned on the oven to preheat then washed his hands. "Chicken quesadillas with salsa and salad."

"Sounds good."

"I want to hear about your day." Ben dropped ice cubes into two glasses then filled them with sweet tea.

Riley sat at the table to watch him cook and sipped her tea while she told him about Julie Rae, Pia, Amanda, Gracie, Dr. Ansell, and Evy. In the middle of her long story, he joined Riley at the table.

He shook his head. "One of these days, I'll ask about your day, and you'll tell me it was boring." He smiled. "Of course, then I'll know you were kidnapped by aliens, and I was talking to your replacement robot."

He rose and checked the chicken he'd put into the oven to bake before he washed then diced the tomato for a salad.

"What about you?" she asked.

"Let's eat first." He smiled as he pulled out the chicken and placed it on a cutting board.

While he shredded the chicken with two forks, Riley stared at his back. "If you'll turn around, I won't be burning a hole in your back with my eyes of fury."

He turned around and hugged her. "Everything's going to be okay as long as you keep those eyes of fury charged."

Riley told him Evy's theory of hugging, and Ben chuckled as he returned to shredding chicken.

"How can I be irritated when you're so funny? What can I do?"

"I need some chopped onion for the quesadillas, and you could pull the salad together, if you like. How does Charlie do everything at once?"

"He is amazing, isn't he?" Riley peeled then cried while she chopped the onion.

Ben stood behind Riley and wrapped his arms around her while she chopped the rest of the onion and the tears flowed.

"You poor thing," he said. "It's been a terrible day."

Riley giggled. "I'll get even with you somehow. How long have you been planning this?"

He hugged her tighter. "Oh, a couple of months."

Riley raised her eyebrows and turned to face him. "We're talking about two different things, aren't we?"

"Yes." He bent down and lightly kissed her forehead then gazed at her and smiled.

She leaned against him and wrapped her arms around him then snickered. "I still have my knife."

He released her and sighed then stepped back and smirked. "I know, but you won't stab me because we haven't had dinner yet."

Riley waved her knife and turned back to her onion. "And you still have to tell me how your day was."

Ben grabbed a handful of onion and dropped it into a pan to sweat while Riley packaged up the rest of the chopped onion and put it in the refrigerator.

After Riley made the salad, she asked, "What else can I do?"

"We need forks, knives, and salad dressing." Ben set the first quesadilla in the hot pan to brown the tortilla and melt the cheese. When one was finished, he put the next one in the pan until he had four quesadillas browned and ready to cut into quarters.

"Almost forgot the salsa." He turned to the refrigerator.

"On the table," Riley said.

"Then we're ready to eat."

Riley ate one of the quesadillas while Ben ate two. "What do we do about the extra quesadilla?" Riley asked.

"Wrap it in foil. It's great rewarmed for breakfast."

After they cleared the table and washed dishes, Ben said, "Let's go out on the porch."

Riley put on her sweatshirt before she went outside, and they sat while Toby roamed.

"Did you notice Princess was becoming more comfortable and venturing farther away from her carrier?" Ben asked.

"Tell me about your day," Riley said.

Ben exhaled. "The hot water heater at Richard's rental house failed sometime over the weekend, and it was completely flooded when he checked it this morning. After he shut off the water to the house, he went to the sheriff's office to tell me about it. He called me a little later this morning and told me the insurance was going to pay for the damage, except it may be months before it's repaired because contractors are slammed with work, and materials are scarce right now. He's going to return my deposit. I love the cabin, but our plan was for it to be a place we'd go for a relaxing weekend because I need to be living in town. I have to be available to cover a shift as on call back up for the night shift, and I can't if I'm at the cabin."

"Wow," Riley said. "Do you have a shift to cover this week?"

"Of course. I'm on call tomorrow night."

"Stay here. I'll sleep on the sofa, and you can sleep in my bedroom."

"No, I'm not kicking you out of your bedroom. I can sleep on the sofa."

Riley snorted. "Have you noticed how not tall I am? I can lie flat and stretch out on my sofa. You try it."

Ben laughed. "You're not tall, and I'm not short. I could stay with Zach."

"You'll have the same argument with him. He's not tall too."

"Fine. You're cuter than Zach; I'll stay here."

Riley jumped up and danced. "I win!" Toby howled then grinned.

"I feel like such a loser." Ben lowered his head then side-glanced Riley, and she laughed.

"I'll call Helen." Riley went inside, and Ben followed her.

When Helen answered, she said, "I was just about to call you. I heard about Richard's house earlier. Can you look at something this evening? Maybe in thirty minutes?"

"That's perfect," Riley said.

"It's a smaller house, but it's furnished like yours and only a block away from your house."

After Helen gave Riley the address, she hung up.

"Helen may have known about your house before you did. She's found a house a block away from here for us to look at in thirty minutes. What else happened today?" Riley asked.

"Well, this could turn out to be really good. I don't know. Let's sit on the sofa."

Riley leaned against the arm and sat with one leg tucked under her, so she could face him. "Well?"

"Mom called me; my uncle talked to Doc Julie Rae."

"That could only mean trouble." Riley narrowed her eyes.

"You're right. The two of them want us to go to UGA veterinary school next fall with full scholarships. Mom told me they must belong to the UGA veterinarian underground. She handed the phone to Dad because he wanted to talk to me. He told me the applications are due now, so both of our applications will come to your address because I was in the middle of moving. Dad told me that both of us might want to use Mom and Dad's address on the applications because we're not quite settled yet and acceptance letters will be going out next week. He reminded me that we could decide about attending after we hear whether we've been accepted, and he and Mom would fully support our decisions, whatever they are. What do you think?"

"I don't think the vet underground will give up. If we apply, the pressure's off, and we'll have time to think."

Ben nodded. "Exactly; we need time to think. What if we're both accepted, and you hate me next summer?"

"If we both want to go, we can, and I'll be the most obnoxious classmate you could imagine."

"Eyes of fury?" Ben grinned.

"You got it. Let's go look at a small house."

As they headed toward the door, Toby followed them, and Princess scooted into her carrier.

"Be good, Princess. We won't be long," Riley said.

As Ben pulled out of the driveway, he asked, "Are you sure Princess will be okay? We don't need to go back and close her carrier?"

"She'll be fine," Riley said. "Turn right at the corner."

When they pulled up to the house, Helen was waiting for them on the porch.

Riley stared at the peeling, faded paint and the sagging gutters. "What do you think?"

Ben whistled low. "The yard is mowed, and the backyard is fenced, but the house is a little rough."

"Understatement," Riley mumbled as she climbed out of the truck while Ben opened the back door for Toby.

"I'm glad you didn't drive off at first glance," Helen said with a twinkle in her eye. "She's seen better days, that's for sure. Come inside but watch that loose bottom step."

When they went inside the house, Riley's eyes widened. "Are all the rooms painted dark purple?"

"Heavens, no. The bedroom's painted black." Helen flipped on the lights. "The electrical was upgraded to code."

"What about the water pipes?" Ben asked.

"Upgraded to code, no mold or termite damage, and the roof doesn't leak. She's got good bones, as they say; she's just ugly as sin." Helen laughed.

"This is one of your houses," Riley said.

"Sure is. I bought it two years ago. The updates and repairs have been slow, but I started with the basics. I put in a new central air and heat ducting system this past summer and a new heat pump for heating and air conditioning. The kitchen's nice, even the paint color because I painted it myself this last summer after the new air conditioner was installed. I have a painter lined up tomorrow to paint the rest of the interior. I may have somebody who will paint the exterior next month."

"Gutters are sagging," Ben said.

"Yes, they need to be secured and cleaned out." Helen led the way to the small kitchen.

"Before I show you the kitchen, this is the dining room and utility room combo." She strode to a bifold door and opened it. "Full sized washer and dryer fit in here. I'd like for you to notice there are two faucets for the washer, so you'll have hot and cold water."

Riley snickered. "Fancy."

"It actually is. I can't tell you how many houses I've seen that had only a cold-water faucet, but you had to climb behind or on top of the washer to know that, which I did."

"For me, a washer and dryer in the house are a luxury. I've spent many hours carrying my clothes to a common laundry room then hanging around while I waited for the next machine or for my laundry to finish," Ben said.

Helen stood back, so the two of them could go into the kitchen.

"New countertops and cabinets, and new appliances. It's a tiny kitchen, but it's nice," Riley said.

Helen nodded. "It's for a solo cook, that's for sure. It had a door on it, but I removed it. Can you imagine trying to cook in this tiny space pre-air conditioning with the door closed? At least, there were no stinky cooking odors to offend the delicate dinner guests back in the day."

As Helen led them to the bedroom, Riley peeked into the bathroom. "This bathroom is beautiful and huge."

Helen chuckled. "I think it's bigger than the kitchen. My contractor ripped out everything because nothing was salvageable. The cabinets and fixtures are new; can you tell we used the same cabinets as the kitchen? Cheaper that way. The floor's ceramic tile; it's the same as the kitchen. The rest of the floors in the house are the original wooden floors. They were under at least three layers of linoleum and carpeting which protected them for years from any wear." She flipped the light switch. "This is the bedroom. The closet's tiny. I didn't want to make it any bigger because the room's fine for a queen-sized bed but wouldn't be if it were any smaller."

Ben strolled around the room then stared at the ceiling. "Do the stars on the ceiling glow at night?"

"I'm afraid they do," Helen said. "I've seen stars in kid's bedrooms, and I realize it's a matter of taste, but this really creeps me out."

As they returned to the living room, Helen continued, "By the way, remind me never to buy another house that needs so much work. I totally underestimated the amount of time and the cost to bring the house up to an acceptable level for habitation. It doesn't have a fireplace or garage and has absolutely no resale value, even with all the work I've had done."

Ben smiled. "There you go with your arm-twisting, hard-sell talk, Helen."

She laughed. "Can't help it. It's how us shysters are wired. I'll have furniture for it next week. I bought it after I confirmed the painter's availability. If you can hold off for a week, it's yours, if you want it. I'll give you four months free rent including the utilities if you'll reattach and clean the gutters and take care of the other minor repairs that you find. I'll provide a good ladder. I have a lawn service for all my properties, so that will continue to be my responsibility. If you find a major repair, let me know, so I can put it on my priority schedule."

"Wow. That's generous," Ben said.

"No more than I do for my property managers who take care of my apartments. Can you hold off for a week?"

Ben looked at Riley, and she nodded.

"I think so," he said. "Can we look at the backyard?"

Helen tapped her forehead. "I'm slipping. I should have had you come in the back. It's the best part of the house, next to the bathroom."

When they went outside, Toby followed them. Riley gazed at the porch and scanned the yard. "The backyard is huge, and the wide porch is beautiful. Is it new?"

"No, I power washed it and was shocked at its excellent condition. The outdoor ceiling fan is new, but the chain link fence has been here for a long time. Do you approve of the yard, Toby? The two large trees are oaks. The three smaller ones are peach trees. This yard is larger than any of the others on the block because it includes almost half of the backyard of the property behind it. There must be a story there, but I don't know what it is."

After they went back inside, Helen said, "I made you a key. If the furniture comes in earlier than I expected, I'll let you know. Take the key; if you decide you don't want it, call me, and I'll pick up the key from you."

Ben accepted the key. "Thanks, Helen. This is a real lifesaver. You've turned it into a nice little house, and it's around the corner from Riley."

She nodded. "I thought that would be a nice bonus."

On the way back to her house, Riley asked, "What's the plan?"

"Let's check on Princess."

"What time does your on call start tomorrow?"

"As soon as day shift is over."

"Why don't we go to the cabin this evening and pick up two days' worth of clothes for you? You can hang up your uniforms, and they won't get wrinkled from being in your truck all day."

"I hadn't even thought about that. Richard's house really knocked me off kilter. What about Princess?"

"I'll ask her and Toby if they want to go. If Princess is tired of car rides, Toby might stay with her to keep her company. He's a softie when it comes to girls."

"So am I, old man." Ben glanced at Toby. "Riley, you talk like they're actual humans."

"Of course, they aren't. People aren't nearly as nice."

Toby whined, and Riley rolled her eyes. "Fine, except for you, Ben."

Ben grinned. "Thanks for the support, Toby."

Toby bounded to the front door, then they all went inside. Princess was stretched out on the oval rug in front of the cold fireplace. She yawned then stalked Toby while he drank at his water bowl. She barreled into his back leg, and he swung his head around and yipped at her. She trotted closer and lay next to him, and he continued drinking.

"Did he just tell her one minute?" Ben asked.

"Something like that," Riley said. "We're going to be gone for a while. Do you want to stay or go?"

Toby ambled to the fireplace rug with Princess at his side, then he flopped down, and she snuggled next to him and purred.

"We'll be back after a while." Riley joined Ben at the door.

On their way to the cabin, Ben said, "It's really convenient that you and the dogs and cats understand each other."

"I'm pretty sure they understand other people too, but people have forgotten how to listen."

"The more I watch, the more I'm starting to pick up on cues," Ben said.

While Ben packed his clothes, Riley stacked a set of sheets, a pillow, a blanket, a quilt, two towels, and a handful of washcloths to take along. "I don't have any extra linens or towels at my house. The cabin's better outfitted for guests than I am."

"We can spend the weekend here to pack up the rest of my things," Ben said. "I'm ready to load up."

At the end of the driveway, Ben hopped out of the truck and closed the gate. On the way to the house, he asked, "Are you sure this is a good idea? Aren't you worried about what your neighbors will say about my truck being parked at your house all night?"

Riley stared at him then picked up her phone. "Hi Pia. How's Jackson?"

She listened and giggled while Pia talked then said, "Ben's house in town fell through, so he's going to stay with me until one of Helen's houses is ready for occupancy next week."

After Riley listened, made affirmative noises, and snickered, she said, "Her name is Princess."

She nodded while she listened to Pia then smiled as she hung up. "Jackson's fever broke, and Pia might be at work tomorrow if it stays down. She already knew about Richard's house, Helen's house, and Marcy dropping off Princess on my doorstep. She'd heard you'd probably stay with me until Helen's house was ready, was glad you'll be in town, and fighting mad about Princess. You feel better?"

Ben snorted as he parked in the driveway behind Riley's car. "Much."

After they unloaded the truck, Ben hung up his uniforms, and Riley stacked her bed linens on the coffee table and put the extra towels and washcloths in the bathroom.

"Ready for dessert?" Riley asked.

They took their ice cream to the back porch and watched the brilliant red sunset until the mosquitos chased them inside. Riley made her bed on the sofa then stretched out to read, and Ben found the old series of Westerns on the bookcase.

"These are classics," he said. "I read them years ago."

"They were Grandma's favorite books. She read them to me every summer until I was old enough to read them myself, then I'd read to her."

Ben picked up the first book and settled into the chair to read. After a half hour, he asked, "Are you wearing your inside holster and pistol to work?"

She shifted onto her side to face him before she answered. "Most of the time, but I forgot today."

"Do me a favor: don't forget." He resumed reading.

Riley didn't realize she'd dozed off until her book fell to the floor with a thud. *Why am I on the sofa?*

When she opened her eyes and glanced across the room at the chair, Ben grinned.

She smiled. *That's right; Ben's here.*

"You woke me up too. Must be time for bed." Ben placed his grocery slip into his book to mark his place then strolled to the sofa and bent down to kiss Riley goodnight. She smiled then rolled over and snuggled down for the night with her pillow and blanket. He took Toby outside then turned out the lights before he headed to the bedroom.

CHAPTER THREE

Millie stared out her hotel window at the crawling headlights and taillights on the streets below and the illuminated skyscrapers of the Paris skyline against the dark sky.

She checked her watch and frowned. *What time is it on the east coast of the US? I have brain fog from jet lag.* Her chuckle was hollow. *Afternoon sometime, maybe four o'clock. I should have heard something by now.*

Millie sat at the small desk and studied the menu. *I need to order room service before the kitchen closes.* She sighed as she picked up the hotel house phone and placed her order in fluent French then returned to the window and watched a light mist float on the water in the distance.

When her cell phone rang, she immediately picked up.

"About time," she growled.

"You want to orchestrate these bozos? Be my guest. Marcy went to Barton today with a cat before they caught up with her in Pomeroy. She was quite chatty and quick to point the finger at you. Marcy claimed she gave the information to your niece. Is that convenient or inconvenient?"

"Damn. See what Riley has, but I don't want her hurt."

"Right."

After they hung up, Millie ran her fingers through her hair and narrowed her eyes. *If he can't follow directions, I'll need to replace him. Inconvenient all around.*

* * *

He tossed his half-smoked cigarette onto the ground and crushed it into the dirt with his heel as he sneered. *Millie's getting soft. A takeover will be easy, but first, Riley Malloy needs to be removed from the equation.*

He made his call.

CHAPTER FOUR

The next morning, Riley woke to the tantalizing aroma of fresh coffee and the whine of the faucet when Ben turned off the shower. When Ben left the bathroom, she took her turn and hopped into the shower. After Riley dried off and blow-dried her hair, she scurried out of the bathroom and to the bedroom with a towel wrapped around her; Ben stood at the kitchen table while he made sandwiches. Riley dressed before she beelined to the coffeepot.

Ben pointed to the cup he had poured for her. "It's cooled the way you like it. Your lunch is in the refrigerator. I have to dash." He hurried to the door. "Toby and Princess have been fed; don't let them lie to you. Your turn to cook tonight."

Riley giggled as Ben drove away from the house then checked her email. *Nothing from Marcy.* She shrugged as she powered down her laptop. *Typical Marcy.*

After she pulled out the lunch sack from the refrigerator, she said, "Princess, I'm going to work, and Toby goes with me. You can go too, but you'll have to stay in your carrier or in a kennel. If you stay here, you'll be alone all day. Your choice."

Princess hopped onto the sofa and curled up before she closed her eyes.

"Enjoy your day." Riley stuck her holster with her pistol inside her jeans before she and Toby left.

It was still dark. The low-lying fog made the streets eerie, and the cold, damp air chilled her like icy fingers on the back of her neck.

When they reached the employee parking lot, George's car was the only one in the lot. Toby growled, and Riley shivered and peered at the thickening, soupy fog as she climbed out of her car. "I think the fog's creepy too. I need to remember to wear my sweatshirt in the morning. Our nights are getting colder."

Riley flipped on the lights after they were inside then found George at Gracie's kennel.

George smiled. "I'm not surprised that you and Toby were the first ones in. After you all left yesterday, I used the sling to help Gracie go outside for her pee break, and we've already been out this morning. Gracie slept comfortably last night and has had breakfast. Best nighttime companion I've ever had. Be careful today. Something's brewing; I can feel it in my bones."

After George left, Riley and Toby checked on Gracie who was chewing on a new toy. Toby yipped, and Gracie grinned.

"I'm glad you're feeling better too, Gracie. We'll see you later."

On the way to the breakroom, Riley said, "I'm not a bit surprised George's arthritis is bothering him. Grandma used to always complain when the weather was damp and cold."

Before she finished making the first pot of coffee, Doc Thad and Claire hurried inside.

"I have to pull out a warmer coat. This light sweater isn't enough in the mornings." Claire hurried to her desk while Doc Thad put their lunches in the refrigerator then poured Claire's coffee and took the cup to the front.

When he returned, he said, "Before you get all flustered, we already know Ben's staying at your house until Helen's other house is ready, so you don't have to worry about how to tell us. So, how's Gracie?"

Riley snickered. "She's fine. George took her out last night and again this morning for her bio breaks, and she's had breakfast."

"After you check in with Claire, let's examine Gracie."

Riley strode to the front, but Claire was still listening to messages and taking notes. Claire had already pulled the folders for the morning's appointments, so Riley reviewed them in order. After Claire hung up the phone, Riley said, "Give Zach the first patient because our fourth patient may be a little complex."

"Got it, thanks. We didn't have any emergencies overnight; is that unusual? I'll call everyone back and schedule appointments. You and Doc Preston are scheduled to go to Lindsey's tomorrow morning at ten-thirty. I'm still waiting for Doc Preston to return my call. I'll ask him to be here at ten."

Riley picked up fresh bandaging material then joined Doc Thad at Gracie's kennel.

"Hi, Gracie, how are you doing?" Riley asked.

Gracie yipped then grinned.

Riley smiled. "You do have handsome men taking care of you. I'm glad you're feeling better."

Doc Thad gently palpated Gracie's injured leg. "You still have some swelling. I'd like to remove the bandaging while Riley holds your leg for me."

After Gracie laid down her head and relaxed, Riley opened the door and knelt next to her then supported her leg while Doc Thad unwrapped the bandaging.

"Can you lift it a shade higher?" he asked then carefully slid his hand underneath her leg. "Good, it's dry."

He quickly and skillfully wrapped the gauze around her leg. "There you go. It's looking good, Gracie. We'll check it again tomorrow morning."

After Riley gave Gracie a treat and closed her kennel, she and Doc Thad strolled to Claire's desk.

"Do you think she can go home tomorrow?" Riley asked.

"Probably."

When they reached the desk, a woman in her early forties, with a stylish haircut, was complaining in a loud, jarring voice to Claire. "I'm in town only one day, and my Queenie needs her bath, her toenails clipped, and her special arthritis pills. Don't tell me again that you can't work her in because I can see you sitting and doing absolutely nothing."

She tapped her foot and exhaled in disgust. "Typical Georgia small town practice. Slow and incompetent, but if you're too busy for her bath and nails then just give me her medicine."

She crossed her arms. "And be quick about it. You might have all day, but I don't."

Riley approached the woman and smiled. "How have you been? I haven't seen you since Doc Truman's. I thought your dog was off those terrible pain pills that hurt her stomach, and I know you wouldn't be taking them."

The woman's eyes widened; she rushed toward the door and mumbled, "You have me confused with someone else."

"What was that all about? Did you really recognize her?" Claire asked after the woman drove away.

"Never saw her before, but she was using the typical tactics of a drug seeker: all bluster. Did you see a dog? Her suppliers must be drying up. Call Amanda and ask her if we call the sheriff or the DEA, and how we warn the rest of the vet practices in our area."

"Interesting, I didn't see a dog. I definitely learned something today; I'm glad you were here." Claire picked up the phone to call Amanda.

"I knew about drug seekers," Doc Thad said, "but she's the first one I've seen in action. It really was a show, wasn't it? I wouldn't have given her the special pills for Queenie, but I don't care to think how loud and abrasive she would have become."

Riley nodded. "We had quite a few come into the clinic in Pomeroy. Dr. Truman insisted on talking to them himself and took them to his office then escorted them out the back door. I thought he was being very sensitive to the staff. In retrospect, he probably sold them their special pills."

Claire hung up the phone. "Amanda will make the necessary calls for me. If you hadn't chased her off, Riley, I would have escorted her out the back door then beat her up."

"Yes, dear." Doc Thad chuckled. "We know you'd have taken her to the breakroom, poured a cup of coffee, asked if she felt safe, counseled her on the dangers of drugs, and called for an intervention."

Zach hurried to the desk from the back, and Riley snickered as he spoke. "Sorry I'm late, and I have no good excuse because I overslept after I stayed up too late trying to finish a book. Did I miss something?"

"Yes." Claire handed him the folder for the first patient. "First one's yours, Zach."

"Is that my punishment? I don't get to know what was funny?"

Claire smirked as the first client of the day used two hands to bring in an extra-large carrier.

Zach peered inside the carrier. "Hello, Dexter. I thought it was you. Are you back for another checkup?"

Dexter growled then hissed.

"Tell me about it, bud. I feel the same way about going to the doctor."

The client sighed. "His groomer is on vacation this week, and he's been out of sorts for two days. I don't know if I can survive the rest of the week."

After Zach took the carrier from the woman, she dropped onto the nearest chair. "Thank you. I'll wait here."

"Come with us, Riley?" Zach asked.

Riley followed Zach and Dexter, then after they were in the exam room, she asked, "What are you so cranky about today?"

Dexter meowed.

"No shots, and we're not going to take your temperature. I'll ask." Riley turned to Zach. "If Dexter behaves, will you rub his ears?"

"Only if he behaves." Zach lifted Dexter out of the carrier and placed him on the scale.

Riley peered at the scale. "Wow, Dexter. You're close to your normal weight."

"Time to rub your ears." Zach placed Dexter on the exam table and rubbed his ears while Dexter purred.

"Anything else? Ready for your client?" Riley asked before she left to see if her patient had arrived.

"Dexter and I are ready, thanks."

"How's it going with Dexter?" Doc Thad met her in the hallway.

"His weight's close to normal, and Zach is rubbing behind his ears."

"I'll tell Claire it was just a weight check. We have a walk-in."

"Zach would like his client to join him in the exam room. I'll take the walk-in patient to room two," Riley said.

"I'll take the client to Zach, then I'll join you."

A woman with blood on her shirt and jeans held a one-year-old black and white cocker spaniel on her lap as she applied pressure to the puppy's paw with a pale pink sweatshirt. Blood seeped through the cloth and dripped onto the floor. A young woman in her late teens stroked the puppy and spoke softly to her.

"We were at the park, and Piper must have stepped on some glass. She yelped, and when I looked down, her foot was flowing blood. I pulled off my sweatshirt and held it against her paw to try to slow the bleeding."

"I have Piper's folder." Claire handed it to Doc Thad before he approached Dexter's person and smiled. "Zach would like to discuss Dexter with you. Come with me."

"I'll take Piper," Riley said, and the woman released the puppy as Riley gently lifted Piper off the woman's lap.

Piper whined until Riley cooed a soft tune; the puppy relaxed.

After Riley and the puppy were in the exam room, Doc Thad came in then pulled back the sweatshirt. "Bleeding has slowed. After you clean the cut, I'll stitch it up."

Riley cleaned Piper's paw, then Doc Thad sutured and bandaged it.

While Riley placed a cone on Piper, Doc Thad said, "She can go home."

Riley dropped the sweatshirt into a plastic bag then carried Piper to the reception area. "Piper can go home with you. Doc Thad wants to see her tomorrow; be sure to keep her foot dry. The cone will keep her from licking or biting her stitches. Ms. Claire can make your appointment."

Piper whimpered.

"I'm sorry about the cone, Piper," Riley said.

While Claire and the woman discussed appointment times, the sheriff parked in front then strode inside. The expression on his face was stormy, and Riley's eyes widened as the back of her neck prickled.

His mouth was tight as he spoke. "Are you available, Riley? I'd like to speak with you in private."

She gazed at him in dread. "Did something happen to Ben?"

"Ben's fine. He wanted to come with me, but we're too short-handed to double up. Where can we talk?" the sheriff asked.

"We can use Doc Julie Rae's office," Riley said.

After they reached the office, the sheriff closed the door behind them "You might want to sit."

He waited until she was seated in the visitor's chair. "The sheriff's office in Pomeroy reported a murder late last night. Ben said that you knew Marcy Nichols."

Riley stared at the sheriff. "Marcy was in Barton yesterday. I didn't see her, but she dropped off her cat at my house and left a note. I can't tell you what time, but I'm guessing it was in the middle of the afternoon. Princess was thirsty."

"That's what Ben said. Do you mind if Ben goes to your house and picks up the note?" the sheriff asked.

"That's fine. He has a key to the house."

The sheriff nodded, then his face softened. "Were you and Marcy close?"

"Not really. We had tentative plans to meet not long after I left Pomeroy, but she had another commitment. In fact, I was surprised to find the cat carrier on my porch and even more surprised when I read the note."

"I don't have any details about her death, but I'll call the sheriff after Ben picks up the note." Before he left the office he narrowed his eyes. "Be careful, Riley. I don't know where you might fit in, but I have a bad feeling."

You and me both, Sheriff. Riley breathed in then exhaled to shake off her cloud of unease as she hurried to the front desk.

"Did the sheriff tell you about the murder in Pomeroy?" Claire asked. "Pia called me after a friend of hers called her. Pia said the news about the death of a vet tech definitely shook up the veterinarian world and has spread statewide." Claire furrowed her brow. "Does this mean Princess will be a permanent resident in Barton?"

"I guess so. I'll have to talk to her to see if she'd rather live with someone that has other cats, but I think she and Toby are buddies, and she's a good girl. Toby and I don't mind having another roommate."

"I'm not sure you've mentioned Marcy Nichols. Were you friends?"

"We ate lunch together every day for three years. She went out every night with her crowd, so we were basically work friends. I was too busy with work and school to do any socializing and actually never had the taste for the noise and jostling of egos, so she was the only person I knew."

Riley's phone buzzed a text, and after she read it, she said, "Ben wants me to call him."

"Go ahead. Our next appointment is in five minutes."

Riley returned to Doc Julie Rae's office and called Ben.

"I wanted to be sure you're okay," he said. "I'm at the house. Is it okay if I go inside?"

Riley rolled her eyes. "I'm fine, and of course, it's okay. That's why I gave you a key, so you wouldn't have to wait for me."

"Pretty lame excuse to call you?" Ben snickered.

"You could have called to ask me what I planned to cook tonight; that might have been even more lame." She giggled.

His tone changed. "Be careful. See you this evening."

Toby nudged her hand.

"Ben's worried, but right now, I'm more worried about what I'm going to cook tonight. I'll ask Claire for some ideas. Life was simpler when it was just you and me. You'd have your food, and I'd have cereal or toast and ice cream."

Toby yipped, and Riley nodded. "We'll take Ben over simplicity any time."

Claire grinned as Riley and Toby returned from the breakroom and pointed at the fluffy brown dog under her desk. "This is Kenny and Freddy's dog, Chuck. He's a German Shepherd and Airedale terrier mix and is the runt of the litter, according to the rescue group, and not quite a year old. He's definitely a sweet guy."

When Chuck rose, Riley said, "I'll grab a leash for Chuck and take him and Toby out back for a break, but I'm sure I won't need the leash because Toby's a great trainer."

Toby yipped, and Chuck followed Riley and Toby to the back door. Riley watched while Chuck raced around the parking lot and tried to barrel into Toby then laughed as Toby sidestepped, and Chuck tumbled when he tried to make a fast turn.

After Chuck settled down enough to relieve himself, Riley strolled to the door and whistled for Toby, and Chuck ran alongside the older dog. When they returned to Claire's desk, Riley said, "Chuck's still a puppy, but he's been housebroken. He'll be a great dog for Freddy and Kenny."

Claire smiled as Chuck returned to his private cave under her desk. "Our last appointment for this morning is in twenty minutes. I'm still not as good as Amanda at the timing for appointments, but I've decided that a little extra time is better than not allowing any time between patients."

"I'm pretty sure Amanda does the same. It's been convenient to have the cushion for our emergencies and walk-ins."

Claire turned toward the front door, and her eyes twinkled as she smiled. "Here's one of my favorite walk-ins."

Riley grinned at her tiny, five-year-old doppelganger who skipped inside the clinic; Claire laughed. "Hello, Mini-me. It's nice to see you."

Maddie's mother, Tamara, patted her baby in the carrier and smiled. "Mini-me wanted to talk to Ms. Riley about Princess."

"We need privacy, Ms. Riley," Maddie said.

"We can go to the breakroom. Bring your mommy. She's good at keeping secrets," Riley said.

Maddie narrowed her eyes and pursed her lips as she examined her mother. Tamara raised an eyebrow and met Maddie's gaze.

Maddie nodded. "She'll guard us. Mommy's fierce."

Toby rose then led the way to the breakroom. Mini-me accepted Riley's hand and skipped alongside Riley, and Tamara chuckled as she followed them.

Maddie sat at the table and swung her legs as Riley and Tamara joined her; Toby flopped at Maddie's feet.

Maddie glowered. "If somebody left a cat at our house, I wouldn't know how to take care of it."

"I understand. Ms. Claire has a good booklet you can take home with you to read and study. Cats need food and water, just like we do, but their food has to be cat food; people or dog food would make them sick."

"No giraffe food either," Maddie said.

Riley glanced at Tamara, who shrugged.

"Correct, no giraffe food." Riley matched Maddie's serious demeanor. "Cats go to the bathroom..."

Maddie interrupted. "Just like us and cows."

Riley nodded. "So, they need a special place to go to the bathroom. What else do we like to do?"

"Dance." Maddie jumped up from her seat and twirled then bowed as Riley and Tamara applauded, and the baby cooed.

"You're exactly right," Riley said. "Cats need exercise just like we do, and they like to play and be around their people."

Maddie nodded. "I like to be with Mommy and Daddy." She looked at Toby. "Toby likes to be with you and me."

"Are we ready to ask Ms. Claire for the booklet about taking care of cats and dogs?" Tamara asked.

"Yes." Maddie marched out of the breakroom with Toby following her.

As Riley and Tamara headed to the front, Tamara smiled. "Thank you, Riley. She's been obsessing about Princess being left on your doorstep. When I suggested that we talk to you, she told me Ms. Riley knows everything."

Riley grinned. "You're pretty smart yourself."

Tamara chuckled. "Sometimes I feel like I have to scramble to stay ahead of your mini-me."

"Mommy, Ms. Claire gave me a book. It has pictures and everything. I said thank you because that's polite."

After Maddie and Tamara left, Claire said, "Maddie is the sweetest thing ever, and Tamara definitely has her hands full. Your mini-me is always thinking."

When the next client came in, he carried an old, overweight French bulldog.

"Hello, Collette. Are your feet bothering you again?"

The man said, "Her feet are fine, thanks to Doc Thad."

"Are you still giving her the medicine for her itchy feet?"

"No, I told my landscaper what Doc Thad said, and he changed the chemicals he uses on the yard. Collette's feet stopped itching, but she's developed wheezes just like my mother who had congestive heart failure. My mother took two tablespoons of honey every day, so I added honey to Collette's dog food, but her wheezes are worse."

Riley picked up Collette's folder. "Come with me, Collette, and I'll take a look at you."

Collette lumbered along at Riley's side to the exam room.

When Riley placed Collette on the scale, she said, "Your weight is up. Do you feel okay?"

Collette growled.

"I'll let Doc Thad know about the honey and that you're not taking your walks anymore." Riley listened to Collette's heart. "Your heart's strong, but you definitely have wheezes."

When Doc Thad came into the room, Collette yipped.

"Nice to see you too, Collette," he said as Riley handed him Collette's records.

Doc Thad listened to her heart and lungs. "It's definitely seasonal allergy time. I think there's a pollen floating around that's causing those wheezes. The honey's not helping." He furrowed his brow as he read Riley's notes. "No more walks and the honey most likely caused the extra weight. Do your legs or feet hurt at all?"

When Collette whined, Doc Thad looked at Riley.

"Not a bit. She misses her walks."

"Time for some client teaching," Doc Thad said.

Riley asked the client to join Doc Thad in the exam room. "Will Doc Thad give her some heart medicine?"

"He'll explain his findings," Riley said.

When Doc Thad asked about the walks, the man said, "When we went outside, her wheezes were worse, so we stopped taking our walks." He bit his lip. "I've put on a few extra pounds too, but it's worth it to help Collette be more comfortable."

Doc Thad nodded. "Makes sense. Her wheezes are most likely from a seasonal allergy that most people call hay fever. I'll prescribe something for her hay fever then after tomorrow resume her walks. Start with once a day for a week in the mornings, then you can increase it to twice a day. The honey is too much sugar for her. Sometimes a little local raw honey might help allergies, but for Collette, she's not ready for the extra sugar."

"I didn't know it was supposed to be raw honey. I've been putting it in my hot tea at night too. It makes my tea sweeter than I like it, but I thought it might keep me from getting congestive heart failure."

"You might want to talk to your doctor about your concerns," Doc Thad said.

"I can do that; my annual appointment is in two weeks," the man said.

"Riley will get Collette's medicine, and I'd like to see her back in a month." Doc Thad stroked Collette's back then patted her before he left.

After the man made his appointment and paid Claire, he reached down to pick up Collette. "Don't pick her up," Claire said. "You might strain your back, and every short walk will help her feel better."

"I don't want to hurt my back." He clipped her leash onto her collar before they ambled to his car.

Doc Thad cleared his throat.

"Don't say a word." Claire glared at him. "I couldn't stand to see him treat her like she was a sack of potatoes."

He raised his eyebrows. "I was just going to ask if you were ready for lunch. It's time, isn't it?"

"I'll staff the desk, Claire. Take Zach with you, and I'll ring the bell if I need help," Riley said.

When Claire hurried off to find Zach, Doc Thad whispered, "I need a bell in the breakroom in case I need help."

After Doc Thad left for the breakroom, Riley read through the afternoon's files. When her phone buzzed, she smiled at the text from Ben.

"Call when it's lunch."

After Zach had eaten, he joined Riley at the front. "Claire told me what was funny in trade for the reason I talked to the client about Dexter. I won't charge you. I taught her how to rub Dexter's ears the way he likes."

Riley snickered. "Smart. Now Dexter won't be cranky just so he can come to the clinic for you to rub his ears."

Zach grinned. "That's one job I don't mind delegating."

Claire returned. "Doc Thad went to his office to catch up on some paperwork. I'll take back my desk now."

After Riley rose, she said, "It's my turn to make supper tonight. If it was just Toby and me, he'd have his usual, and if I couldn't think of anything, I'd have cereal. I'm stuck."

"Have you ever cooked salmon? I have a recipe that walks you through every step. It's super easy and doesn't take long at all. All you need is salmon, pepper, and olive oil. You'll be a star if you add a salad and jasmine rice with peas; I'll send you that recipe too."

"How long will it take me?"

"No more than forty-five minutes. I'll write a shopping list for you, and you'll be good to go."

"That sounds fancy," Riley said. "Are you sure it isn't for an experienced cook?"

"You'll be fine," Claire said.

"You're a lifesaver." On the way to the breakroom, Riley said, "Let's step outside, Toby." After she put on her jacket, they went out back. While Toby roamed the lot, Riley called Ben.

"How was your morning?" he asked.

"The highlight of our day was when Mini-me came to visit. She'd heard about Princess and had to know what to do in case somebody left a cat at their house. Claire gave Maddie a booklet."

"Blooming veterinarian?" Ben asked.

"I didn't think about that, but I'll bet you're right. How about you?"

"I finished reading all the procedures and took a couple of tests; this afternoon, I'm going to help the sheriff with one of his two current investigations. I'd say I'm glad things are back to normal, but I feel like this is the eye of a hurricane, and we're about to get hit from the other side."

Riley stared as a car crept past the animal hospital then turned toward where she was at the back of the building. She stepped behind the fence that hid the trash bins as the car with two men in it continued its slow pace past the building. After the car turned at the next corner, it sped away.

"Are you there? Is something wrong? You were quiet," Ben said.

"I thought I saw something. I guess I'm more jittery than I'd like to admit."

"I don't think you're jittery. I think you're on high alert. If you call nine-one-one, the sheriff and I have already planned to race to wherever you are, and I will win."

Riley smiled. "That's actually comforting, thank you."

After they hung up, Riley and Toby went inside, and Riley pulled out her lunch sack from the refrigerator. She unwrapped her sandwich, and the tears welled up.

She sniffled. "Ben made me a peanut butter and banana sandwich, Toby. I didn't know he knew it was my favorite. That's the nicest thing anyone's ever done for me."

Doc Thad strolled past the breakroom from his office and stopped. "Are you okay, Riley? It's okay to tell me to mind my own business."

"I'm fine." She brushed at the tears that kept rolling down her face. "Ben made my favorite sandwich for my lunch."

He groaned. "Don't tell Claire, or I'll have to do something nicer. I don't need that kind of pressure right now."

Riley grinned when he chuckled as he hurried away. After she finished her lunch, she threw away her trash and cleaned the table and counter before she hurried to the front.

"We have a busy afternoon. I've slid in a couple of new appointments, so put on your skates and fasten your seatbelt because it's going to be a rocking and a rolling kind of day."

Riley's eyes widened, then she laughed.

Claire tossed her hair. "It sounded more poetic in my head."

* * *

Toward the end of the day, Riley said, "Your predication of a busy afternoon was completely accurate. I could have used some skates a time or two."

Claire smiled. "I finally heard from Doc Preston. He'll be here tomorrow at ten. Evy went to Atlanta to visit her folks, so she won't be with him. Amanda called, and she's bored, which means she's doing fine. Doc Julie Rae called Thad. She's hoping they can return by the end of the week, but we'll have to see how it goes. Thad may have forgotten to tell you that he called three old classmates and his favorite professor to ask about Doc Preston; he's only heard back from his professor who couldn't place Preston Ansell, but he did say the name was familiar. Thad was a bit surprised because the man remembered everyone's name who had ever been in one of his classes. Of course, like Thad said, we all get a little forgetful at times, and the professor's been teaching for over thirty years. Can you imagine how many students that would be? Anyway, the professor will review his records." Claire turned back to check the schedule.

"What about Pia? How's Jackson?" Riley asked.

"Don't tell Thad I forgot to tell you." Claire rolled her eyes. "Jackson's driving her crazy because he feels great, so if he is still fever-free in the morning, he'll go to school; otherwise, he'll go to his grandma's. Pia will be here in the morning either way."

"We're working on getting back to normal. Is there something I could do to help you?"

"I'm all caught up. I have your recipes and shopping list in a folder. Do you want it now?"

"Don't give it to me until time to go home because I'm afraid I'd leave it."

Claire nodded as the phone rang and a client with two preteen boys came inside. The older boy held a carrier in his arms.

"Last patient," Claire whispered.

Riley picked up the folder and led the client, the boys, and her patient in the carrier to an exam room. Riley peeked into the carrier as the guinea pig sneezed then coughed.

"Albert's been sneezing and coughing since yesterday," the woman said. "When it became more frequent, I called to see if we could come in, and Ms. Claire said we could."

"We won't stress you any more than we have to by reaching into your carrier, Albert. We'll wait for Doc Thad."

When Albert squeaked, Riley asked, "Is he eating and drinking his usual amount? What about pooping?"

The boys giggled and repeatedly whispered, "Poop," while they elbowed each other.

"Settle down, boys, or you'll have to wait in the reception area," the woman said. "Albert's not eating much at all and drinking very little. His elimination is almost nonexistent."

Riley smiled. *Elimination: good word to know.*

When Doc Thad came into the room, Riley said, "Doc, Albert the guinea pig has been coughing and sneezing since yesterday. No appetite, drinking very little with no elimination."

"Elimination." The younger boy giggled. When his brother shrugged, the boy shrugged too.

Magic word.

Doc Thad peeked at the sneezing, coughing guinea pig. "Let's treat his upper respiratory infection. Are you comfortable using a medicine dropper?"

The woman nodded.

"Good," Doc said. "Try that first, but if he refuses, call tomorrow; otherwise keep an eye on him, and if you don't think he's improving, call."

"Thank you, Doc Thad," the woman said, and the boys echoed, "Thank you, Doc Thad."

"I'll get Albert's medicine then be right back," Riley said.

While she and Doc Thad strolled to the medicine room, he whispered, "Elimination?"

Riley snickered, "The mom taught me that; poop causes rampant giggles."

"I love this job." He grinned.

Riley returned to the exam room with Albert's medicine then walked with the woman and the boys while the older boy carried Albert. After they left, Riley said, "Claire, did you know saying poop causes uncontrollable laughing?"

"I certainly did." Claire smiled. "I was a teacher. What word did the mom use to correct your poop error?"

"Elimination." Riley giggled.

"Ah. The word that sets off the older crowd, I see." Claire snickered. "I'm laughing with you, not at you, by the way."

"What's so funny?" Zach asked.

"Elimination," Claire said, and she and Riley laughed.

Zach stared at them then left to sanitize the rooms, and they laughed harder.

"I'll lock the front door then help Zach." Riley wiped her eyes.

After Zach and Riley sanitized the rooms, Zach went to Doc Thad's office while Riley checked on Gracie. She and Toby sat with her until Doc Thad said, "Gracie is doing great and will be fine to go home tomorrow with a splint. George is here, so you and Toby can be off duty. Zach thinks you and Claire are nuts. I agreed with him."

As Doc Thad and Riley headed to the hallway, Claire and Chuck met them. "We've decided Chuck will go home with us until Kenny and Freddy return. Here are your recipes and your shopping list, Riley. Call me if you have questions."

While Riley went into the grocery store, Toby took his position to stand sentry at the door.

When Riley looked over her shopping list, she smiled. *Claire is awesome. She even listed the items by aisle.*

After Riley zipped through the aisles and the ten-items-or-less line, Toby was in his same spot. He stared at the store exit door and growled. Riley turned to look, but no one was there.

"Let's go, Toby." Toby stayed close to her side as she hurried to the car. As she pulled out of the parking lot, she asked, "What was all that about?"

He growled again then barked.

"I didn't see a bad man or anyone at all, but I'm glad you did. You must have scared him off." Riley tapped her fingers on the steering wheel. "This isn't good. Do I tell Ben?"

Toby whined.

"Of course, I'll tell Ben; I was just thinking aloud. He'll understand we weren't skittish."

She peered at her gauges. "I'm down to a half tank. I don't have time to stop because I need to be cooking. Maybe Ben and I can go after we eat. No, that won't work because Ben's on call tonight. We can wait until tomorrow after work because he's cooking, but if he's up all night and has to work his day shift, maybe we should have a contingency in case he's exhausted. I'll talk to Claire in the morning."

When she pulled into the driveway, Ben had parked his sheriff deputy's cruiser in his spot next to hers. After Toby leapt out of her car, Riley gathered her groceries, then her heart sank when Ben dashed out of the house.

"Got a call." He stopped and stared at her then shook his head before he rushed to his cruiser. "Don't wait for me. I'll text you as soon as I can."

He pulled away and hurried down the street without turning on his lights or siren.

Princess met them at the door and meowed at Toby. He flopped down on the floor and she sat at his head and purred.

Riley placed the groceries in the refrigerator and texted Claire.

"Ben left on a call. What do I do about supper?"

"Cook it. If he comes back in time to eat, great. If he doesn't, prepare his plate in a pie pan and cover it with foil. Warm up in the oven when he returns. Or fix two plates and eat ice cream now."

Riley giggled. *Claire is smart.*

After she fed Princess and Toby, Riley read and reread the recipe then washed her hands, took a big breath, turned on the oven, and made the salad before she chopped an onion. She added a handful of the onion, per the recipe, and a half cup of rice to a heated pan with drizzled olive oil. She stirred until the rice looked different to her before she added three-quarters of a cup of water. *I guess that's what translucent is.* After the rice came to a boil, she turned down the burner, stirred in the partially thawed peas, and covered the pan before she set the timer.

Riley exhaled. *Wonder how long I've been holding my breath?* She patted the two pieces of salmon with a paper towel to dry them then peppered each piece before she put them into a heated frying pan with olive oil. *I need a second timer.*

She pulled out her phone and set a timer for the fish while she set the table for two.

"I'm an optimist, right, Toby?"

When the three minutes were up, she flipped the salmon and cooked the other side for three minutes then placed the salmon on a baking sheet and slid it into the hot oven.

After six minutes, the timer went off for the salmon then less than a minute later, the timer went off for the rice, and Toby yipped.

"Good timing," Riley said as Ben burst into the house.

"Smells amazing. I'll change to another shirt, wash my hands, and be ready to sit at the table."

While they ate, Ben said, "This is really delicious. It was nice to come home to a hot meal."

"Thank you." Riley smiled.

After they ate, Ben said, "I'll take care of the dishes. You've earned a few minutes off your feet."

When the dishes were in the dishwasher, Ben dried the last pan he'd washed by hand then set up the coffeepot for their morning coffee before they sat together on the sofa. Ben put his arm around Riley, and she rested her head on his shoulder.

"How was your afternoon?" he asked.

"Steady stream of patients. I did learn something. A woman and her two preteen boys brought in their sick guinea pig. I made the mistake of asking whether the guinea pig, Albert, was pooping as he normally did."

"You said 'poop' in front of two preteen boys?" Ben snickered.

"I didn't even give it a second thought." Riley shook her head.

"Poop was totally hysterical to them, right?"

"They quoted me repeatedly and punched each other every time."

"I can see it." Ben laughed.

"Their mother tried to help me out when she spoke of elimination," Riley said.

"Wait, she actually said elimination?" Ben asked then laughed.

He continued to interrupt her by repeating what she just said and laughing as she told him about elimination, Claire, and Zach.

"Doc Thad told me that Zach thinks Claire and I are nuts and so does Doc Thad."

Ben hugged her and laughed. "Can't say I blame either of them."

Riley gazed at his face and smiled. *Ben is exactly the kind of friend to have around.*

Ben leaned down and kissed her. When he sat back and met her gaze, she smiled; as he cradled her cheek with his hand and leaned forward again, his radio went off.

"Arrgh," he grumbled as he dashed to put on his uniform shirt and his utility belt then raced to the door. "Don't lose my place," he called out as he hurried to his cruiser.

She furrowed her brow as she touched her lips lightly with her fingertips. "That was a little awkward but sweet. I shouldn't read too much into it, after all, good friends kiss, right, Toby?"

When she reached to rub his ears, Toby lightly licked her hand, and she hugged him and kissed his head. "Yep. Good friends kiss."

After she made up her bed on the sofa, she changed to her nightclothes then relaxed on the sofa with a book. When she kept dozing off, she turned on the porch light and the light over the stove then turned off all the other lights and worried about Ben.

CHAPTER FIVE

When Toby whined, Riley woke and stretched then frowned. *The porch light and the light over the stove are still on.* She picked up her phone that she'd set on the end table next to the sofa and stared at the time. *It's five-thirty. I slept all night.*

"I'm so sorry, Toby. I fell asleep and didn't take you out." She stumbled to the back door; when she opened it, Toby dashed outside. She squinted at the pot on the stove then rolled her eyes. *I'd forgotten he'd set up this morning's coffee after supper.*

She turned on the stove and opened the refrigerator. *Ben packed my lunch for today. He didn't wake me up when he came back.*

While Toby was outside, she checked the bedroom. *No Ben.* She shook her head. *He made his bed, but I don't know when he left.*

Riley dressed quickly then stuck her cell phone into her back pocket, so she wouldn't forget it. She folded her sofa sheets and blanket then put on her heavy sweatshirt, slid her holster inside her waistband, and poured a cup of coffee before she joined Toby outside. The silence of the still-sleeping neighborhood was broken by a low, distant rumble; the light breeze turned to a brisk, cold wind.

Riley frowned. *The weather forecast didn't mention any rain today and certainly not a storm.*

When Toby nosed the door, they went inside; she fed him and Princess. She refilled her cup for a quick sip. When she pulled out her lunch sack from the refrigerator, she stared at the sack and snorted. Ben had written on the side of the sack: "Eat a real breakfast."

She quickly scrambled an egg and popped a piece of bread into the toaster. When the bread was warm, she canceled the toast and folded the bread like a hot dog bun and spooned in the scrambled egg.

"We're going, Princess. You're welcome to go with us, if you like."

Princess stared at Riley then turned her back to return to her grooming.

Riley snickered. "That's clear. See you after work."

While Toby waited at the door, she grabbed her lunch sack, and they dashed to her car as the rumbles became louder.

When she backed out of her driveway, a streak of lightning lit up the dark sky. As she drove toward the end of their block, the wind grew stronger, and small, leafy branches from nearby trees skittered across the road. She counted until the loud crash of thunder interrupted her at three seconds. "It's getting closer, Toby. We'll have to hurry if we want to stay dry."

Riley turned on her wipers and finished her egg sandwich before she left her neighborhood, and Toby whimpered with each of the more frequent rolls of thunder. Before she reached the animal hospital, she turned the wipers to their fastest setting. When she reached the employee parking lot at the back of the building, a flash of lightning and a loud boom of thunder directly overhead startled her, and Toby whimpered then barked.

Riley shuddered. "It's going to be a nasty day."

When she parked, a nearby lightning strike blinded her. She blinked and stared at the darkness that engulfed her car, and the rain became heavier. *We need to get inside.*

After she grabbed her lunch sack and climbed out of her car, she quickly slammed her door as Toby snarled and barked in a frenzy then frantically scratched at his side window. She scrambled to open his door, but a blow on the side of her head knocked her to the ground, and the sudden silence terrified her.

She sprung to her feet and felt a satisfying crunch when her fist connected with the bulbous nose directly in front of her. Blood streamed down a large man's face as he clutched his nose.

She instinctively threw up her left arm to protect her head when a thin man swung a heavy club at her from that side, but she collapsed from the excruciating pain when the club slammed against her arm. She rolled away from the heavy boot aimed at her ribs and took cover under her car.

The rain became a deluge as a set of hands grabbed her feet before she could roll to her stomach to crawl away, and she kicked and struggled to free her legs as the large attacker pulled her out from under her car. She bent her knees when she was clear of the car and kicked against the man's knees as hard as she could, and her attacker lost his grip. She flipped to rise, but a kick to her stomach slammed her against her car, and another blow to her head turned her world black.

* * *

Doc Thad peered out the window while Claire finished preparing their lunch for the day. "The rain's so heavy I can't see our driveway," he said. "If I weren't worried about Riley being alone at the animal hospital, I'd suggest we wait until daylight to see if the rain slows down before we leave."

"I'm ready." Claire sacked up their lunches, clipped the leash onto Chuck's collar, and grabbed her umbrella.

They dashed to their car, and Claire chuckled after she closed her door. "I'm not sure how much good the umbrella did. I'm soaked, and I smell a wet dog."

Chuck yipped. Doc Thad turned his windshield wipers to the highest setting and pulled away from their driveway. He leaned forward to peer at the road. "I might as well be driving without the wipers for all the good they're doing."

"It's crazy to drive in this rain," Claire said.

"At least we don't have to worry about hitting another car. When I was a kid, I tried to run as fast as I could when it was raining hard. My theory was if I ran fast enough, I'd run in between the raindrops and stay dry."

Claire chuckled. "Sounds logical to me. Don't tell me if it didn't work."

"My running practice in the rain actually paid off when I made the track team in high school, but I never told anyone how I trained." Thad grinned.

When they reached the parking lot, Claire peered at the two cars. "George is still here, and Riley made it safely."

"That's a relief," Doc Thad said as he pulled next to Riley's car and squinted at the movement in the window.

"Toby's still in her car. Take Chuck inside, Claire. I'll let Toby out then be right there."

Claire and Chuck dashed to the back door and went inside. Doc Thad rushed to Riley's car and heard Toby's frantic barking over the storm. As he opened the back door of the car, Toby leapt past him, tore away into the rain, and disappeared.

Doc Thad raced to the building as Claire opened the back door.

"Riley's not here," she said.

"Toby ran off. Call nine-one-one. I'm going to see if I can find Toby."

Doc Thad jumped into his car then lowered both front windows while he crept slowly from the parking lot to the main road and around the block before he returned to the building and slammed his hand on the steering wheel. *I can't see anything.*

When Thad stepped out of his car, the wail of a siren approached the animal hospital, and he waited in the rain for Ben.

CHAPTER SIX

The fast-moving vehicle jostled Riley as it traveled on a rough road, and the floorboard hump bit into her side with every bump. She listened in relief to the muffled rattles and the muted whine of the tires. *I can kind of hear.*

She opened one eye and bit her lip to keep from moaning. *My other eye must be swollen.* She was on her side, and her good arm cradled her head. Her left arm, head, face, and ribs hurt. It was daylight; the rain had slowed to a steady shower.

A man asked, "When do we dump her?"

"We'll be there soon," the driver said. "Is she still unconscious?"

Riley closed her eye.

"Yeah. Can't tell if she's breathing."

"Doesn't matter," the driver said. "She won't be soon; doctor's orders."

"What do you mean? The boss ain't a doctor," the passenger said.

"It's a figure of speech. Forget it."

I thought I'd hear something helpful. How helpful is it to know they plan to dump me, and I won't be breathing anymore?

"How can you see where you're going in this rain?" The passenger lowered his window then raised it. "It's raining into the car. Can I smoke without the window being down?"

"No, the rain will quit; you can wait."

"Easy for you to say. You never smoked," the passenger grumbled.

"Let it go," the driver growled.

"My nose is still bleeding, and my knees hurt. I'm getting nauseous."

"Yeah, well, I'm getting tired of you complaining."

When the driver slowed, the passenger asked, "Is this where we dump her? Whose shack is that? Are there snakes here?"

"This is it, but I'm not sticking around long enough to check for any snakes. What do you care about the shack? You planning on staying? You can if you want to; I'm leaving."

"You better not leave me here." The man's whiny voice rose in panic.

When the back door opened, Riley willed herself to be limp as rough hands dragged her out of the car then through the wet grass.

"Grab her feet," the driver said. "We'll toss her into the water on the count of three."

"Into the river?" the passenger asked as he picked up her legs.

"What did I say?" the driver growled. "Ready? One, two, three."

Got it. Dumping me into the river. Pick a deep part where there are no rocks, please.

When Riley sailed through the air, she took in a breath and held it as she splashed into the icy water and relaxed as she sank.

I don't want to drown. She kicked her feet. *My feet aren't bound.*

She stroked with her arm and put her feet on the bottom of the river then bent her neck back to look up. *Light! I've either drowned, or the river isn't very deep. Hope they're gone.*

She bent her knees, kicked to the surface, and gasped for air when she cleared the water then floated on her back until her panic subsided. She listened. *Car's gone.*

She stroked with her good arm to navigate and kicked her way to float toward the riverbank. When she was in shallow water, she stood then waded as close as she could to the land before she jumped toward it and landed on her face. Riley struggled until she pulled herself out of the water then sat and shivered in the rain. *I have to find shelter before I become hypothermic.*

She pulled off her boots and emptied them of river water before she struggled to her feet. *Where's smoker man's shack?*

She gasped at the blurry landscape in front of her. *My eyesight's terrible.* She slowly turned around. *A blurry something.* She made her way through the tall grass to the dark object, and as she neared it, tears slipped down her cheek in relief. *It has a roof; I'll be out of the rain.*

She stumbled inside then sat against a wall. *Good, it didn't collapse on me.* She struggled to pull off her sweatshirt, but the effort was too much, and she closed her eye. *I can't go to sleep because I'll die.* She leaned back and relaxed. *Maybe it's dry in heaven.*

* * *

Ben swerved into the parking lot and raced to Thad. "What happened to Riley?"

"I was on my way inside."

"Let's go."

When they reached the door, Claire jerked it open. "George didn't hear anything. The storm was too loud."

"Ben, we don't know what happened to Riley," Thad said. "It took us longer than usual to get here in the storm. Her car was out back, and Toby was still in her car and frantic to get out. I opened the door, and he ran off into the storm. I couldn't find him."

Ben frowned. "Toby's gone too? He must have gone to look for her."

Ben pulled out his phone. "Still nothing from her; I'll check her car. For now, I'd rather the news not get out that Riley's missing unless the sheriff has another idea. He'll be here soon."

Ben pulled out his flashlight and strode to Riley's car. He swallowed hard when he saw her soaked lunch sack on the ground but shook off his dread and searched inside the car for her cell phone. *It's not in her car.*

He removed her backpack from the passenger's side floor before he closed the car door. When he searched around outside her car, he found the drag marks from under her car to the driver's door and a dent in the door. More drag marks led from the car to the far corner of the lot, and his heart sank. *They dragged her away.*

The sheriff parked behind Ben's cruiser as the rain slowed to a light shower. "You've been up all night, Ben. After you leave here, go home and get some sleep then call me, and I'll give you your assignment."

"I have to find Riley," Ben said.

"That's your assignment, but you have to get a few hours' sleep first to think straight. So, what do you have so far?"

Ben told the sheriff about Toby missing, searching for Riley's cell phone, and the drag marks.

"When I called her cell phone, it rang to voice mail after one ring."

"It's turned off. Does she usually do that?"

"No, during working hours, she silences any rings but leaves it on to buzz for calls or messages."

"We'll get her cell location records; maybe we can see where they took her. Show me the drag marks you found," the sheriff said.

After Ben showed him, the sheriff said, "This tells me she tried to get away from them. She may have been knocked down and rolled under the car. Her plan would have been to let Toby out the passenger's door."

Ben nodded, and the sheriff continued, "She wouldn't have left willingly, but it's still troublesome to see that they dragged her away."

Ben bit his lip as he nodded again then cleared his throat. "Doc Thad, Claire, and George are still inside."

"I'll talk to them; you go home and sleep. I should have the cell phone records by early afternoon, and you can analyze them. We want to keep this quiet." Sheriff headed to the back door.

"Right." Ben climbed into his cruiser and went home.

When he opened the door, Princess meowed.

"I'm sorry it's just me too, Princess."

On his way to the bedroom, Ben picked up Riley's pillow; after he climbed into bed, he held her pillow close and inhaled her fragrance before he fell asleep.

It was early afternoon when a repetitive scratching woke Ben from a nightmare during a fitful sleep. Princess jumped onto the bed and meowed.

"I'm awake." Ben stumbled to the front door, and when he opened the door, Toby collapsed on the porch. Ben cried out, "Toby, are you okay?"

Toby raised his head then took a few steps into the house. Ben grabbed a towel from the bathroom and rubbed Toby to dry him off.

"You stink, boy. We'll give you a bath later, but I'll bet a long drink and breakfast will perk you up. I'll bring your water bowl to you."

Ben placed the water bowl in front of Toby, and Toby drank it dry. "You were thirsty. I'll refill your bowl, so you can have more after you've rested a bit."

Princess raced to Toby and lay next to him.

Ben sent the sheriff a text: "Toby came home."

Sheriff: "Good news. On my way with cell locator records."

After Ben sent the same text about Toby to Doc Thad, he made a sandwich and poured a tall glass of iced tea. "I feel better with you at home, Toby. We'll find Riley."

The sheriff knocked on the door then let himself inside. "Toby, you're a sight to behold." The sheriff sniffed. "Where have you been? You smell like a swamp."

Toby grinned.

"Care for some tea, Sheriff?"

"Don't bother. Let's look over these records."

As they pored over the records, Ben said, "They were traveling fast. They must have had a specific location in mind. Looks like they drove north near the river then stopped around ten or so. Am I reading that right?"

"Something like that. Then nothing since ten thirty. They could have run over her phone or thrown it into the river."

"I could search for her here for starters." Ben pointed to the last location on the record.

The sheriff nodded. "That's five hours from here, but it fits the timeline if she was abducted no more than a half hour before Doc Thad and Claire arrived at the clinic. This is totally outside my expertise, and I might be misinterpreting, but this is from a single tower. It may be up to a half mile or more off."

Ben finished his sandwich and drained his glass. "Still a smaller area to search than the entire state."

Sheriff's brow furrowed. "It doesn't mean she's there though."

"Right, it's just the most likely location where her cell stopped transmitting."

Toby whined.

Ben smiled. "Yes, you can go too, after you have breakfast. Is it okay with you if I take my truck instead of the cruiser, Sheriff?"

"Probably a good idea. The cruiser is a fast car with power under its hood, but it's not great on backroads. Pack water, food, blankets, and first aid supplies for when you find her, and keep me posted."

Ben nodded, and the sheriff strode to the door. "You're not a civilian, Ben. You're working on the clock, so don't get revenge into your head."

The sheriff stopped after he opened the door, and when he turned, Ben took a step back at the sight of the sheriff's stormy face and the fire in his eyes. "Leave that to me. I'm close to retirement anyway."

Ben's eyes widened, and after the sheriff left, he exhaled. *I have to find Riley, then we'll have to find her kidnappers before the sheriff does.*

Doc Thad called Ben. "Thanks for the update. We've been slammed with clients, or I would have called earlier. Good thing Pia came to work because Claire, Zach, and I had a pact to close the office if Pia couldn't make it. We expected Preston Ansell today, but he called Claire at nine and told her that he had a conference call he'd forgotten about and would reschedule later. Worked out for us. Claire is cooking dinner for four. She's optimistic. Call when you're ready for your supper, and she'll heat it up."

"Claire is a rare jewel. Tell her she doesn't need to do that."

"No way. Tell her yourself." Thad chuckled.

Ben smiled. "Tell her it's more likely to be breakfast but no promises."

"I can tell her that; otherwise, she'd stay up all night waiting to hear from you. You don't intend to return until you find Riley, do you?"

"Damn straight," Ben growled.

Ben emptied one of his duffel bags and filled it with two quilts, first aid supplies, and a change of clothes for Riley. He zipped up the bag then reopened it and added a change of clothes for himself.

He hurried to the kitchen and poured cold sweet tea into a thermos. After he made sandwiches, he put them into an insulated picnic bag. Ben frowned at what he'd packed so far. *Might need a little more.*

After he added crackers, cheese slices, and apples, Bene put the thermos, six bottles of water, food and treats for Toby, and the insulated bag into a box then stuck the locator record into a side pocket on his backpack.

He and Toby went out back for Toby's break. *Riley might be chilled. I need hot tea for her.*

He went inside and heated a pan of water then poured the boiling water into the thermos he found on a top shelf over the sink. He dropped four tea bags into a plastic bag and added a large mug. When he opened the back door, Toby rushed inside.

Ben asked, "I'll leave your dinner out for you, Princess. We might not be home until tomorrow morning. If we'll be any later than that, I'll call someone to feed you and check your water."

Princess flicked her tail then licked her paw.

He refilled her water and placed her food for the evening in her bowl. "Okay, we'll see you later."

Before Ben pulled away from the house, he looked at the coordinates again. "If they made any stops along the way, Toby, they would have been very brief. Let's go straight to the last coordinate, then we can decide whether we want to retrace their steps or continue in the same or even a different direction." Ben took a breath then exhaled. "Actually, I have no idea what we'll do; all I know is that we have to find her."

CHAPTER SEVEN

Riley moaned. *Sun's out. I'm still soaked.* She struggled to her feet and held onto the wall with her right arm inside the sleeve, so she wouldn't touch anything like a spider or a lizard.

When she stepped outside, she squinted in the bright sunlight then smiled. *Not blurry.* She closed her eyes and soaked up the warmth of the sun as she leaned against the building.

I have to be dry. Sweatshirt off first. She held her left arm close to her side with her right arm then clutched her right cuff with her left fist and held tight while she struggled to pull out her right arm from its sleeve. A Bob White whistled its support. When she freed her arm, she was breathing hard, and Bob White whistled.

"Thanks, Bob; that was tough."

Next, she eased the sweatshirt past the deformity on her left arm then slid it off. She limped to a small, nearby tree and hung her sweatshirt on a branch then tugged away her scrub top from her skin. She kicked off her boots then leaned against the tree. *Jeans after I've rested.* She lowered herself to the ground by holding onto the tree trunk, and Bob White whistled.

"Bob, I'm going to rest one minute." She closed her eyes. *Love the warm sunshine.*

Riley felt ants crawling on her legs and brushed them off then struggled to her feet to move away from the ant hill before more ants attacked. "Remember the survival rule of three, Bob? I can survive three minutes without air, three hours without shelter, three days without water, and three weeks without food, except I don't believe that food part."

Riley's stomach roiled, and waves of nausea dropped her to her knees. She retched, then her stomach ejected its watery contents. After a second wave of nausea, she had trouble catching her breath between her choking bouts of gagging and dry heaves.

When the spasms slowed, she wiped her mouth with her scrub top then removed it carefully without moving her left arm more than was necessary. *I threw up mostly river water. Just as well, I suppose.*

Bob White whistled.

"Come on, now, Bob. You're supposed to look away discreetly, but thank you." She rose to her feet and held onto the tree in case another round of nausea hit then hung her scrub top on another branch.

Bob White whistled his distinctive call.

"You're right, Bob. I might as well dry my jeans too."

When she unbuttoned her belt then her jeans, she felt her holster. "Guess what, Bob? They didn't search me. Now, I'm embarrassed that I was abducted by incompetent kidnappers."

Crows cawed as they harassed a hawk in the nearby woods.

"Have you noticed everybody's a critic, Bob?"

She made a crude rack with fallen branches under the tree then pulled out her pistol, unloaded it, and set the pistol on the branches, so it would be above the grass. After she removed her ammo from the cartridge holder, she set her ammo on the holster to dry.

"Supposedly, my pistol may shoot in an emergency without having been carefully disassembled, dried, and cleaned after being submerged, but I'd rather not be in a position that would require me to rely on it, Bob."

Bob White whistled his agreement.

When she bent to remove her jeans, she gasped from the sharp rib pain and quickly straightened up to relieve the pain and catch her breath. *I'll have trouble putting them back on, but if I don't take them off, I'll be chilled tonight.*

"I vote take off the wet pants and deal with putting on dry pants later. Any dissenters?"

All the birds were quiet. She loosened her belt and pushed her jeans down as far as she could then held onto the tree while she stood on the hem of her right leg with her left foot. After she cleared her right leg, she shifted her weight, but a stabbing pain in her right knee caught her by surprise. *I'll bet I twisted my knee when the thug grabbed my feet and pulled me out from under my car.*

Riley held onto the tree while she eased herself to sit on the ground, so she could take off her jeans. When they were off, she whistled a Bob White tune, and her feathered friend answered.

"Thank you, Bob," she said. When she hung her jeans in the sun, her cell phone fell to the ground.

She picked it up and frowned. "It's either off or completely dead. If I turn it on and it's wet, the circuits will fry. I'll give it a while longer to dry then see if it works, Bob. I'd give anything to be able to send a text to Ben, but I don't have much hope that it will work."

She looked at her socks. "You're next but not until my pants are dry, and I'm wearing them. The rest of you get dry."

She examined the grass and the nearby ant hills. "I'll explore the shack while my clothes dry."

Dry clothes probably fall under the shelter rule. She found a branch on the ground that would work as a walking stick and walked with halting steps to the dilapidated building.

After she was inside the shack, the sunlight streamed through the window openings and the cracks where the caulk between the boards had crumbled away, and the large golden orb webs sparkled in the light. The room where she had taken refuge had a wooden floor and an old woodburning stove in the back corner. She examined the stove and opened its door to peer inside. *Jackpot. An old tin can.* Its stovepipe chimney was intact, as far as she could see. *Might be a possibility if it's cold tonight. I have wood; all I need is fire.* Riley rolled her eyes.

As she made her way to the next room, she stepped cautiously around the broken floorboards. The second room was smaller than the first, and a rusted iron bed with ornate head and foot frames was against the wall near the door; across the room from the bed were two doors with broken hinges. She peered inside the door closest to the back part of the shed and coughed at the noxious odor from the toilet with a broken lid, a missing seat, and sludge in the bowl. The shower drain looked plugged with slimy grime, and the small, stained sink contained an unsightly oily goop with dark chunks. *I'll continue using my outside potty spot.*

She moved to the second door and found a small closet. Ripped unidentifiable clothing was in a corner. She reached to pick up the pile but pulled back her hand at the sight of the dried rodent excrement. *I'd hoped to find something to make myself a sling. That's not it.*

Riley surveyed the second room. *No back door. I'll have to figure out an escape plan.* She leaned out the open window next to the bedframe and scanned the high grass and river behind the cabin and the trees off to the right. *Not much of a drop to the ground. Good emergency exit.*

She returned to the main room. *Maybe I can use the lid on the tin can to rip enough cloth from my scrub top to make a sling.* As she opened the stove door, she froze at the sound of a distant car. Riley willed herself to rush to the small tree where her clothes were drying. She stepped into her boots and pulled down her sweatshirt and jeans and wrapped them around her neck. After she dropped her scrub top onto the ground, she scooped her holster, ammo, and pistol onto the top then picked up the corners to make a bag. As the sound of the car became louder, she scurried, as well as she could, into the woods and back into the brush. She slid down with the aid of her stick to sit on the forest floor then peered through the brush. *Good; I can't see the shack. I'm far enough away.*

She remained still and listened as the car stopped before it was near the spot where her kidnappers had tossed her into the slow-moving river; she flinched when two car doors slammed.

"Why did we have to come back here?" Smoker man asked.

"You don't need to know," the driver said. "Tell me again, was she breathing when we tossed her in?"

"I already told you, no." Smoker man's voice quivered.

"You didn't know if she was breathing or not when we were in the car." The driver's tone was accusatory.

"Yeah, but when you pulled her out, she wasn't breathing; her face was blue." Smoker man's shaky voice had shifted to resolve.

"I noticed that too," the driver said. "Her face was blue. So, we're supposed to examine the riverbank in case her body surfaced or was lodged where it could be seen. We don't have to take all day.

Just long enough to say we came here and found nothing. Do you see anything?"

"No, I don't see nothing."

"I don't either. I'll text the guy and tell him we didn't find anything. Let's get outta here. He'll text me where to meet him for the rest of our pay, then we need to disappear fast. I don't trust him."

The two car doors slammed, and Riley exhaled at the sound of the car driving away. She listened until she couldn't hear the engine noise anymore. She waited before she rose to be sure they didn't return. Riley heard a crack in the distance then a second; she remained still. She stared at the dark clouds that had gathered in the sky. *Must have been thunder.* After she picked up her sack and stick, she rose with the aid of her walking stick then clutched it to rest from the effort. When Riley stared at the thicket of blackberry bushes complete with briars in front of her, her eyes widened, and she shook her head. "How on earth did I get through that?"

She slipped her right arm into her sweatshirt as protection against the thorns on the bushes and picked all the fat, dark berries she could reach and dropped them into her shirt bag. *My arm was scratched up by the briars, but it was worth it.*

After Riley draped her sweatshirt and jeans around her neck again, she picked each step around the blackberry thicket; when she cleared it and was in the trees, she rested again.

Bob White whistled.

"Thanks for the encouragement, Bob."

Riley returned to the small tree and hung her sweatshirt and jeans then removed her boots and sat with her shirt spread out with the blackberries, holster, and hardware on it. She blew on each blackberry then popped it into her mouth. "Grandma told me to blow on a blackberry before I ate it in case there are any tiny red spiders on it."

A mockingbird sang through its tunes, and Riley rolled her eyes. "They're sweet, tart, and juicy. I feel better already. Scoff if you must."

The mockingbird flashed its white tail as it flew away while Riley finished her blackberries.

Riley exhaled then removed her still-soaked socks and coughed. "Phew. These stink."

She hung the stinky socks on a branch; after her feet dried, she slipped on her boots and limped to the shack. She removed the can from the stove and returned to her tree.

Riley sat in the grass and used the ragged edge of the can lid to rip a two-inch wide band across the bottom of her shirt in the back then cut the material free at the seams. *Not quite long enough.* She cut a second band then tied the two pieces together at both edges. After Riley draped the circle of material around her neck from the right side to her left arm, she made a loop then threaded her left arm through the loop to support her arm.

A tear slipped down her cheek. "I wish it was a better sling, but it isn't." More tears slipped down her face until Riley was sobbing. *I don't know what I'm doing. I'll never see Toby or Ben again.*

Bob White whistled.

Her sobs slowed to hiccups. "Thank you, Bob. I hurt, I'm exhausted, and I need to be home, but I appreciate your company." She swiped at her nose with her forearm. "I don't know what I would have done without you."

Riley closed her eyes and rested under her tree while her clothes dried. When she woke, she had more bites on her legs and arms. She smacked at a mosquito on her arm and rose to check her clothes. *Seams are still damp on my jeans, but they're dry enough. Guess I'll put them on the same way I took them off.*

"I need to plan better. Getting up and down is wearing me out." Riley stood on her left leg and held her jeans as low as she could without aggravating her rib pain beyond what she could tolerate. She stepped into the right leg of her jeans while beads of sweat broke out on her forehead. When her toes showed at the bottom of her jeans, she held onto the waist and tugged. After she pulled up the jeans as far as she could, she used her walking stick to ease to the ground. Riley lay on her back and held onto the waist while she fought to get her left leg inside her jeans. After her left leg slid into her jeans, she sat up and picked up her cell phone.

"Are you still there, Bob? Here goes nothing." Riley turned on her cell phone and held her breath as the screen lit up, the logo appeared, then her phone prompted for a pin number. She exhaled and quickly tapped in her pin. The screen went dark then opened to her apps. Riley tapped in a text to Ben as fast as she could: "I'm alive;" as she tapped send, the screen went dark. Riley tapped and tried to turn on her phone again, but it didn't respond.

"I don't know whether my text went through." Riley felt the panic in her stomach rise to her throat. *Stop. Wait a while then keep trying until the phone won't turn on at all.*

When the approaching dark clouds rumbled, she gathered her shirt sack and rose then removed her sweatshirt and wet socks from the tree branch. She glanced at the darkening sky as she limped to the shack. *Another stormy night.*

Riley sighed with relief when she was inside the shack. *Maybe I can block the door with the bed.* She tugged on the iron bed, but it didn't budge. *I have to secure the door somehow.*

She went outside to the forest and picked up a sturdy branch then wrapped her sling around it and dragged it to the cabin. When she reached the cabin, tears streamed down her face from the pain; she pulled the large branch inside, closed the door, and pushed the branch against the door. She wept uncontrollably as she made her way to her corner; after she put on her sling, she screamed with pain and desperation and slid to the floor.

* * *

After Ben and Toby had been on the road for three hours, Ben said, "Rest stop coming up. Let's take a break. We still have a little time before dark, but a stretch will do us good."

While Toby wandered the dog walk area to find the perfect place to relieve himself, Ben called the sheriff.

"Toby and I are at a rest stop about two hours away from the last reported location. Do you have anything?"

"Glad you called. We got a brief, faint signal from Riley's phone. Same location. The experts say it probably means her phone is damaged and unable to transmit, but that's what they've been saying all this time when there was no signal. They couldn't explain to me how they could tell me they have a transmission to a cell tower then in the same breath, tell me her phone can't transmit. I want to know what her phone transmitted."

"Absolutely. Do you think the signal wasn't strong enough to get to my phone but there may be something?"

"I don't know what I think, but I'm not satisfied with their canned answer; I've escalated the issue to their executive management. The good news is that you are headed to the right location, as far as I'm concerned."

Ben chuckled as he hung up. *The sheriff thinks Riley tried to contact me, and so do I.*

Toby trotted to Ben and yipped.

"I'm ready too."

Toby led the way to Ben's truck. While Ben merged onto the highway, he said, "Riley tried to text me. She's somewhere close to where we're going. We'll find her."

Toby whined.

Ben nodded. "Absolutely; as soon as we can."

After an hour, Ben exited the highway and pulled into a truck stop. He filled his tank, went inside the store, and bought a small bag of dog treats and a box of dark chocolate pecans from a south Georgia pecan farm before he parked at the far end of the tractor-trailer lot. He fed Toby then called the sheriff while Toby sniffed the grass.

"I have a new theory that I like much better," Sheriff Dunn said. "A technician suspects Riley's phone dropped the signal a split second before it sent the text. I'm going to text you the new coordinates that the technician sent me; she told me they are more accurate. They're within a half mile of the other coordinates we had, so it won't be a waste of your time. She said the new location is on this side of what the locals call Little River. I don't see it on the map, but it might be a landmark for you. Keep me informed."

As he and Toby climbed back into the truck, Ben said, "We're getting closer." After they were on the highway, Ben frowned at a low roll of distant thunder and the gathering clouds in the darkening northwest sky.

"Don't rain. Not yet," he whispered, and Toby whined.

After a half hour, Ben said, "We'll take the next exit." He peered at the sky. "Sun's going down and I've seen streaks of lightning. We're in a race with the weather, Toby."

Toby yipped, and Ben snorted. "I can't speed; it would be too embarrassing to be stopped, but worse than that, it would slow us down."

Ben glared at the traffic ahead. "Speaking of being slowed down, there must be either road construction or a crash in front of us. Everyone in the right lane is bailing into the left lane."

Ben eased into the left lane, and they crawled along with the rest of the traffic. When they were a mile from their exit, traffic stopped; Ben drummed his fingers on the steering wheel, and Toby whined.

"I hate it too, but we can't do anything about it," Ben fumed.

Ten minutes later, the car in front of Ben's truck inched forward and stopped then moved forward a few feet before stopping again.

Ben exhaled. "This is maddening. We're almost at our exit, though."

When they reached the exit, Ben shook his head. "There's our problem: the overturned eighteen-wheeler is blocking our exit. The good news is that the next exit isn't that far away."

When raindrops splashed on the truck's windshield, Ben moaned. "And there's our bad news."

The traffic picked up to a rolling speed, and Ben said, "Ignore the speedometer," as he accelerated past the line of slower moving traffic and sped to the next exit. After he exited, he jumped back onto the highway going south and raced to their exit.

Toby yipped.

"Don't nag," Ben said as he slowed for their exit, and the rain intensified. As he headed away from the highway, lightning flashed, and thunder boomed.

After they had traveled five miles, Ben said, "We need to watch for a small river or creek. I don't know how obvious the bridge will be, but if we go over one, we'll turn around."

Ben turned the windshield wipers to high and watched the right side of the road for a dirt road, a driveway, a creek, or a bridge. After a half hour, he said, "I think I missed it. I'll turn around as soon as..."

Ben narrowed his eyes and pointed to a dirt lane on the right. "We might have found it." As he turned into the lane, he glanced to his left. "There's our Little River."

Ben dropped his truck into four-wheel drive when it slipped and lost traction on the slick, muddy, clay road. Toby hopped into the front seat and put his paws on the dash. Ben lowered Toby's window a few inches, and Toby stuck his nose out of the window. Toby whined, barked, then scratched at his window. Ben drove a few more feet, but Toby became even more frantic as he jumped from the front to the back and pawed at the windows.

When Ben lowered the front windows more to be able to see better alongside the road, Toby howled then barked as he jumped to the front seat, leapt out of the truck, and raced down the lane. Before

Ben could react, Toby disappeared. *That's not the smartest thing I've ever done.*

The thunder and roaring wind drowned out Toby's barking; Ben crept down the lane as he watched for Toby.

CHAPTER EIGHT

Riley stirred then opened her eyes and listened. "It wasn't a dream. Toby's barking!" She grabbed her walking stick and wobbled as she rose. "I'm stiff from sleeping on the floor. Not complaining, shack. It's a dry floor."

She bit her lip when she took her first step toward the door but moved as quickly as she could as Toby's barking grew louder. She pushed away the large branch from the door enough to open the door and call out, "Toby! Here, boy."

She tried to whistle, but her mouth was too dry.

"Toby," she called again. *I can't even clap my hands. What if it really was a dream, and Toby's not there?* A tear slipped down her cheek.

Toby bounded to the shack and slammed against the door. "Come inside. You're all wet." Riley chuckled as she leaned against the wall and bent to hug Toby. Toby sniffed her stick and her arm.

"I'm better now that you're here. Where's Ben?"

Toby dashed back out into the rain and barked until headlights streamed through the cracks in the shack.

Riley attempted to open the door wider, so she could get out without bumping her arm, but her hand slipped on the wet door, and she lost her grip and screamed in frustration; the truck stopped and Ben was at the door. Ben pushed, the branch slid back, and the door opened.

His eyes were wide as he reached for her, then he froze and stared at her sling.

"My arm's broken," she said.

He gently wrapped his arms around her and held her as she leaned against him. He kissed the top of her head and her forehead and moaned. "I was so worried."

"I sent you a text. Did you get it?"

Ben smiled. "Almost. What did it say?"

"I'm alive."

Ben had a catch in his voice. "Shall I carry you to the truck?"

"It might be faster. Can we take my walking stick?"

Ben chuckled. "Whatever you want, sunshine. I'll load up your new shack if you want to take it along too."

Riley smiled. "I'm glad to see you."

Ben picked her up. "Front or back seat?" he asked.

"Front seat."

He carried her to the truck with Toby leading the way; Ben smiled when she leaned against his shoulder.

"You smell better than I do," Riley said.

"You look and smell wonderful." Ben set her on the front seat then opened the back door, and Toby leapt in.

Ben returned for her walking stick before he jumped into the driver's seat. "I have hot tea and sandwiches." He showed her the box of chocolate pecans. "And an appetizer while you wait for hot tea."

She smiled at the candy. "This is definitely heaven."

He handed her a sandwich then made her hot tea while she munched on the sandwich. After her first bite, Riley sighed. "This is so good. The survival rules claim I would have survived three weeks without food. I think the survival rules have their timing off. I'm starved."

While she devoured her sandwich, Ben set her tea on the console between them then unwrapped a sandwich for himself. When Toby whined, Ben gave him a treat. After Ben ate his second sandwich, Riley finished her first one.

He opened the box of chocolate pecans; Riley took one, and Ben took two.

"My new favorite dessert," Riley said.

After she'd eaten the first one, Ben asked, "Want another one?"

"Maybe later. My stomach's still a little queasy from the river water."

"What?" Ben's eyes narrowed.

"I can tell you on the way home if you won't get mad. You have to be able to drive safely."

Ben started the engine and turned around. "That bad?"

Riley nodded. "Pretty much. Do you want me to start at this morning, or do you want me to jump to the part where I'm alive?"

"I need to call Sheriff Dunn to let him know we found you." Ben stopped the truck and picked up his phone.

Riley leaned back and listened. *I love hearing Ben's voice.*

"It's Ben. Toby and I found Riley. She's injured, but safe. I'll call you when we get to town."

After he hung up, Ben exhaled then headed toward the road that led to the interstate. "Start with this morning, but warn me before you get to the bad parts."

"I ate breakfast because of your note, and Toby and I went to work right before the storm started. Now, I'm at the bad part."

Ben snorted. "That didn't take long to tell the good part."

"Not to jump ahead, but there was one other good part, but I'll tell you about that later."

Ben turned onto the road and accelerated. "Can you just tell me the highlights about the bad parts then the details later, so you can sleep on the way back home?"

"Sure. I fought the two kidnappers, but I broke my arm deflecting a blow to my head and twisted my knee when one of the kidnappers pulled me out from under my car. I'm not clear on all the details, but they may have cracked my ribs, and I know they punched me in the face because my eye was swollen, then they knocked me out. They thought I was unconscious when they threw me into the river to drown then left. The good part is that I didn't drown; I climbed out, dried my clothes, ate some blackberries then waited for you and Toby in the shack."

"Did you get a good look at them?"

"Not really." Riley yawned.

"We'll talk more later," Ben said. "Get some rest."

Riley leaned back in her seat and listened to the hum of the tires.

* * *

After he'd driven three hours in the torrential rain, Ben straightened his back. *I'm fighting droopy eyes. I need a break and maybe some coffee.* While Riley slept, he took the ramp at the next exit and headed toward the truck stop. After he filled his truck, he parked on the side of the building that was away from the bright lights and left the sleeping woman and dog in the locked truck with the engine running. *I don't need to worry about anyone trying to steal the truck or kidnap Riley. Toby would not let that happen.* Ben snorted. *As long as Riley doesn't jump out of the truck without him.*

After he bought a cup of coffee, he stood under the awning and within sight of his truck while he sipped his hot coffee and called Thad.

"You find her?" Thad asked as soon as he answered his phone.

"Yes, and we'll be home in about two hours. Riley and Toby are asleep; I had to stop and take a break. She's injured, so we'll go to the emergency department. Her arm is broken, and she may have cracked ribs. I'm not sure what all her other injuries might be."

"We'll bring you breakfast wherever you are. Be safe, and call if you need me. Anytime."

Ben finished his coffee then dropped the container into the trash. *It's good to have friends.*

The rain slowed to a light shower as Ben turned at the emergency entrance a little after midnight. When he stopped under the canopy and turned off the engine, Riley leaned forward and blinked. "This isn't home."

"We need to have your arm and other injuries evaluated. I'll be right back after I grab a wheelchair."

When Ben walked into the entrance, a middle-aged man in scrubs met him at the door. "Deputy Carter?" he asked. "Wheelchair or gurney? Sheriff told us you'd be bringing Riley Malloy here. I've been watching for you."

"Wheelchair is fine."

The man hurried to a hallway then returned with a wheelchair and another man with a hospital ID that had RN printed in large letters on it.

After Ben helped Riley into the wheelchair, the RN whisked her away.

"If you'll park your truck," the middle-aged man said, "I'll take you to Ms. Malloy. Toby can come inside because Sheriff told us Toby is a K-9 deputy."

Ben parked then texted the sheriff and Thad to let them know Riley was at the hospital while Toby watered a nearby bush before they went inside.

The middle-aged man was waiting at the door. "The doctor finished his exam. Right this way, Deputies."

Toby held his head high while he trotted alongside Ben to find Riley. After their guide led them down a long hallway away from the emergency department and made several turns, he pushed the button on an elevator. After they exited the elevator on the second floor, the man led them to a closed door and whispered, "Tap on the door then go right in."

When Ben tapped on the door, the man grinned and hurried away. Ben went inside and frowned as he scanned the room: a freshly-made bed, an empty pitcher and a cup on the bedside stand, and the nurse who had his back to Ben as he placed a hospital gown and a muslin sling on the bed.

"There you are." The nurse turned and smiled. "The x-ray department will be here soon, but Riley and I decided she'd have enough time for a therapeutic shower to clean her bites and wash the minnows out of her hair. She told me she smelled like a swamp, and I didn't disagree. Have a seat, Deputy. She'll call me when she's ready for her new sling and snazzy gown."

Ben exhaled in relief as he sat, and Toby lay down next to his chair. "Has the doctor seen her?"

The nurse nodded. "We've got a full evening planned for x-rays, lab work, you-name-it. You and Toby may want to go home to get some rest after you see her because she'll be away from her room tonight more than she'll be here. When all the tests are done, I'll text you while we wait for the doctors to decide on a treatment plan." The nurse pointed to a plastic bag on a shelf under Riley's bed. "Those are her clothes she was wearing when she came in. If you take them with you, I strongly advise leaving her boots outside to dry and throwing her clothes in the washer right away."

Riley opened the bathroom door just a crack. "I'm relatively dry." Toby rushed to the door and pushed it open, and Riley laughed.

"I guess you know that Toby and Ben are here," the nurse said. "Shall I have Ben step out while we put on your gown?"

Riley snickered. "Hi, Ben. Close your eyes."

Ben smiled when she added, "And no peeking."

. "I'll hold up the gown while you slip in your right arm then I'll put on the sling and tie the gown in the back over the sling," the nurse said. "Might not be the usual method to put on a gown, but I suspect it will be easier on you when they take the x-rays."

"I'm sitting on the shower chair. Do I need to stand up?" Riley asked.

"No, please don't," the nurse said. "I'll have to write a report if you fall. I can help you to your bed after your gown is tied or get a wheelchair."

"I can limp with help."

When Riley came out of the bathroom with the assistance of the nurse, Toby bounded to her, and Ben strode to help her into bed. After the nurse put up the side rails and raised the bed, he headed to the door. "I'll be back in a few minutes. Use the call button if you need any help."

Ben smiled and stroked her wet hair away from her face. "No minnows."

Riley laughed. "The nurse told you about that? The possibility of small river creatures in my hair was freaking me out, but the worst part was when I raised my arm to take off my sweatshirt. I almost fainted from the strong odor of stinky river water. The nurse decided I needed a mental health shower."

Ben bent over her and inhaled. "You smell like Riley to me."

He leaned closer and kissed her gently then lightly nibbled on her bottom lip before he gazed at her and smacked his lips. "Mmm. You taste like Riley too."

Riley giggled. "The hospital toothpaste is designed specifically to attract a good kisser. So far, it's working."

Toby whined then licked Riley's hand.

"You're a good kisser too, Toby. I'm really lucky."

Toby put his paws on her bed, and she rubbed his face. "Sweet boy."

The nurse returned to the room with a technician. "Time for your x-rays."

The technician pushed his gurney from the hallway to Riley's bedside, and the nurse helped Riley to move to the gurney and covered her with a sheet; Riley waved to Ben and Toby as the technician rolled her out of the room.

"I'll write your cell number on her chart," the nurse said. "Here's my cell phone number. Text me if you have any questions or trouble sleeping. I expect she'll finish her tests by four, but set your alarm for five, in case I get slammed by a trauma and don't text you. The doctor won't be here until seven; we won't know any results before then. I'll show you the way to the main elevator."

Ben and Toby followed the nurse as he made one turn then pointed straight ahead. "The elevator is straight down this hallway at the end. When you return in the morning, stop at the information desk and sign in."

When Ben hesitated, the nurse said, "We'll take good care of her. Get some rest."

As Ben strolled to his truck, Toby stopped for a quick break then caught up with him. On the way to the house, Ben said, "I have no idea how I'm going to rest."

Princess yowled at them when Ben opened the door, and he shook his head. "Sorry, Princess. The good news is that we found Riley."

He dropped Riley's belt and holster on the kitchen table before he refilled the water bowls then stumbled to dump her clothes into the washer to wash them immediately. After he dragged himself to the bedroom. removed his belt and holster, and put them on Riley's dresser, he kicked off his boots, set his phone alarm for five, and collapsed on the bed.

* * *

When the alarm woke him, Ben pushed himself up and moaned. *Too much driving in one day.* He started a pot of coffee and let Toby out before he undressed and showered. He chuckled as he dried off and dressed. *Wonder where I can buy some hospital toothpaste.*

He found a coffee cup with a dog on it that looked like Toby. After he filled his cup, he opened the back door, and Toby trotted inside. After Ben's first gulp of hot coffee, he removed the clothes from the washer and tossed them into the dryer as Princess weaved between his legs, and Toby yipped.

Ben smirked. "I can take a hint."

He filled their bowls, and Toby gobbled down his breakfast. Princess sniffed hers then glared at Ben while she cleaned her paws. "Suit yourself. It'll be there when you're ready."

Princess yawned before she took a dainty bite and another until her breakfast was gone.

Ben downed his coffee then asked, "Ready to go, Toby?"

Toby rushed to the door and waited while Ben gathered clean clothes for Riley and dropped them into the recycle tote that he found in the pantry.

When Ben and Toby went inside the hospital waiting area, Sheriff Dunn rose from a bench near the door and waited for them to join him. "How'd you sleep?" Sheriff asked.

"I collapsed on the bed fully dressed and woke up at five when my alarm went off. I didn't realize how exhausted I was."

The sheriff nodded. "That's the way it goes. I checked on Riley a few minutes ago, and she was sleeping. Let's grab a coffee in the coffee shop."

As they strolled to the coffee shop, the sheriff asked, "What's in the sack?"

"Clean clothes for Riley."

After they went through the line and bought large cups of coffee, they sat at a table away from the steady stream of visitors and staff who were looking for their first cup of morning coffee.

The sheriff scanned the coffee shop before he drank his coffee. "Riley is really special to me. There aren't many people around here who remember that her dad and I were best friends all through school and even after he left for college. We were so close, I knew when Frank Malloy died the second he took his last breath, and part of me died with him." The sheriff glared at Ben. "I have a vested interest in Riley's happiness."

Ben nodded as he sipped his coffee. *I'm getting the dad talk.*

"Men are more complex than some people realize; take you, for example. You have the veterinary skills that your uncle taught you, and you're a good law enforcement officer." The sheriff narrowed his eyes. "You're trained to protect and take care of others."

"Right," Ben said.

"If that's what you're looking for here with Riley, you need to move on."

Ben stiffened his back and frowned. "I don't understand what's wrong with..."

The sheriff interrupted with a wave of his hand. "Nothing wrong with it at all. It's in your core, and you'd do that if you were a fry cook, right? I'm telling you Riley deserves more."

The sheriff rose. "More coffee?"

Ben swallowed hard before he followed the sheriff to the line.

After they returned to their table, the sheriff peered at Ben. "There is no way you can keep Riley safe."

Ben shook his head and sighed. "That's the truth."

Sheriff drained his cup then nodded. "If you're going to stick around, your best bet would be to make her happy. So, why did you bring her dry clothes?"

Ben furrowed his brow. "Well, I thought she'd like to have clean clothes to go home in."

"See? You're on the right track, and I don't have to fire you and run you out of town after all. I won't keep you any longer; I know you and Toby are anxious to see her."

The sheriff rose and strode out of the coffee shop while Ben stared before he turned to Toby. "Ready to find Riley?"

While Ben and Toby waited for the elevator, Ben shook his head. *That was one intense discussion, but I got the dad message: I better not screw up.*

When they went into Riley's room, her eyes were closed. "You better be a doctor or a man with a dog."

Toby bounded to her bed and put his paws up on it, so he could kiss her face, and the nurse chuckled. "Ah ha. Toby had the secret password."

Ben smiled and strode to the smiling Riley and kissed her forehead.

She examined his face. "How did you sleep?"

"I was too exhausted to do anything else."

The nurse nodded. "One of the most effective ways to combat insomnia: exhaustion."

"Can I have breakfast now?" Riley asked.

"Make that the first question you ask the doctor," the nurse said.

"That reminds me," Ben said, "I owe Doc Thad a text."

After he sent the text he said, "Claire planned to cook your breakfast. I let Thad know we're waiting for the doctor's okay."

The nurse smiled. "I'll be leaving soon. I enjoyed taking care of you, Riley, but I hope I don't see you again, except in the grocery store or at the gun range. Be safe."

After the nurse left, Ben pulled a chair close to her bed and took her right hand in his. "How are you doing?"

"I don't stink, which is absolutely glorious. Ready to hear about the bad parts, now that you're not driving?"

Ben listened while Riley told him about the fight, waking up in the car, the conversation she heard, the men throwing her into the river, getting to the riverbank, Bob White, drying her clothes, the men returning, their conversation, finding blackberries, and pushing the branch against the door. "That's basically it." She leaned back in her bed. "Bob was a good friend."

"I have a million questions, but they can wait until later. Does the sheriff know all this?"

"Sure. After I came out of x-ray, he asked me what happened."

Ben shook his head. *Sheriff was here all night.*

A tall, middle-aged woman with an MD on her ID badge came into the room followed by a younger RN.

"Hello, Riley Malloy." The doctor smiled. "Both your ulna and radius in your left arm are fractured from the blow. We'll put a splint on your arm to stabilize the fractures before you leave, then I'd like to see you on Monday in my office, so I can assess it further after the swelling's gone down. Our most likely next step is surgery to reduce the bones and stabilize them. Your head, face, and eyes are fine, in spite of the fact that you have the blackest blackened eyes I've ever seen. Your nose isn't broken, which was a surprise. No fractured ribs but more ugly bruises. I can't tell you how happy I am that your body purged itself of the river water. I'm not fond of treating nasty diseases of the intestines caused by waterborne microbes; your stool sample was fine, and your bloodwork showed no signs of infection. We'll send you home with a cream for your ant bites, so they won't get infected. You can eat whatever you like but take it slow. You may be queasy for a few more days."

"Can I go to work tomorrow?" Riley asked.

The doctor narrowed her eyes. "You can't lift anything with your left arm for at least six weeks. You almost drowned and suffered terrible injuries from a fight with two thugs. You came into my emergency department dehydrated, exhausted, scratched, and with bug bites and a probable concussion. Let's talk on Monday."

"Thanks, Doc," Riley said as the doctor left.

"I'll take you to the cast room for a splint to stabilize your arm while we wait for the swelling to go down. Do you have clothes you'd like to change into?" the young nurse asked.

Ben smiled as he placed the sack on her bed near her feet. "Clean clothes. Toby and I picked them out."

"Perfect. I'll lower your bed, then we'll shoo Mr. Deputy out of the room while you change."

"He can stay because he'll close his eyes," Riley snickered.

"And no peeking," Ben added as he pulled the visitor's chair away from the bed.

"Turn your back," the nurse said.

Ben smirked as he turned the chair with its back to Riley. After he took his seat, Toby sat next to him and faced the same direction as Ben. Ben chuckled then closed his eyes and felt Toby's face resting on his knee. Ben scratched Toby behind the ears and listened while the nurse directed Riley as they put on the clean underpants and jeans. The nurse and Riley whispered then giggled before the nurse said, "The shirt is great. It buttons down the front."

What was so funny? I'll ask Riley later.

"Socks and slippers, then I'll brush your hair."

"Ben, are you going with me to the cast room?" Riley asked.

"I'd like to; can I open my eyes?"

When Riley chuckled, Ben smiled. "I love your laugh, Riley. Toby and I are ready."

After they neared the cast room, the nurse said, "I'm sorry, Deputy, but you'll have to wait out here; the room's too small for you and Toby." She rolled Riley down the hallway then opened a door, and they went inside.

The nurse returned to the bench where Ben waited. "I'll pull together her release papers then meet you here."

Ben texted Thad. "Still at hospital. Will be leaving after Riley gets a splint."

Thad replied: "I'll let staff know. Claire plans on cooking dinner for you tonight."

Ben: "Thanks."

The nurse returned and breezed past Ben on her way to the cast room. "Won't be much longer."

Riley smiled at Ben when she came out of the cast room, and he and Toby rushed to her side. "We're going by your room first to make sure you have all your things," the nurse said.

After they were inside the room, Riley asked, "Where are my clothes?"

"I took them home last night and threw them into the washer. Your boots are on the back porch."

Riley nodded. "My clothes might need a second washing."

The nurse placed all of Riley's hospital toiletries in a bag then handed Riley a small sack. "These are your medications. We talked about them earlier, but this sheet is your reminder of what they are and when to take them." She pointed at the next sheet. "You have an appointment on Monday at nine o'clock. This is the address. If you have any problems, call the doctor's office. She has a service that will contact her if you call after office hours. You can't go to work before Monday. I've already talked to Doctor Faraday."

Riley's eyes widened. "I thought you were the nice nurse."

The nurse smirked. "I'm the devious nurse. Your nurse last night was the nice nurse."

Ben snorted, and Riley glared at him while the nurse laughed.

As the nurse rolled Riley to the waiting room exit, she said, "Actually, I knew you saw a loophole when the doctor listed your injuries and said she'd see you Monday. When you thanked the doctor, it was because she didn't say no, wasn't it?"

"You're right," Riley said, "you're devious."

The nurse beamed as she tossed her hair. "I take that as a compliment coming from you, Riley."

As they headed toward the exit, the nurse said, "Deputy, if you want to go ahead and pull up your car under the canopy, we'll meet you there."

Ben and Toby strode to the truck. When Ben drove to the visitor's entrance, Riley and the nurse were outside. He parked then helped Riley into the truck.

Riley leaned back and closed her eyes. "I'm looking forward to being home."

"I'll make a pot of coffee, or would you rather have hot tea?"

"I would really love a cup of coffee and something to eat like ice cream."

"If you don't have any, I'll get some later. Would toast and a scrambled egg be a good substitute?" Ben parked in her driveway.

"Coffee, toast, and an egg sounds normal. I think I'd like to have a normal morning."

Ben helped her out of the truck and into the house while Toby yipped in excitement.

"I'm excited too, Toby," Riley said.

When Riley sat at the kitchen table and sipped her coffee, Ben scrambled an egg, Toby lay under the table on her feet, and Princess curled up on her lap.

Ben set the plate with the egg and buttered toast in front of Riley. "Are the three of us hovering enough for you?"

Riley giggled, and Ben smiled.

While she ate, he stripped the bed and remade it with clean sheets then returned to the kitchen and placed the sheets in the washer. *I hope sleeping on clean sheets in her own bedroom will make her happy.*

After she ate, Ben cleared her dishes. "The sheets on your bed are fresh and waiting for you."

"That sounds wonderful."

Ben helped her to the bedroom then returned to the kitchen. After he loaded the dishwasher and washed and dried his frying pan, he tiptoed to her bedroom. Riley's pants were in a heap on the floor, and she was asleep under her sheet.

Her walking stick is still in the back of my truck.

After Ben retrieved her branch, he removed his boots before he quietly carried her stick to her bedroom and placed it in the corner near her bed.

Ben picked up the pillow Riley had used when she slept on the sofa and removed his belt before he sat and texted the sheriff. "At Riley's. She's asleep."

Sheriff: "Get some rest. Come to work tomorrow."

Ben: "Thanks."

Ben texted Thad to let him know Riley was home.

Thad replied: "Claire asked ok for supper at six thirty?"

Ben: "Yes. Thanks."

Ben stretched out on the sofa with his feet dangling off the other end and smiled as he closed his eyes. *Clean sheets made her happy.*

* * *

Riley woke with a start then relaxed. *I'm not in the shed; I'm at home in my own bed.*

She peeked at the floor next to her bed and smiled at the sleeping Toby. She frowned as she tried to move her feet. *I must have twisted my feet in my sheet while I slept.*

When Riley wiggled her feet to be free of the sheet, Princess meowed in protest then marched to Riley and flopped down next to her. Riley stroked Princess under her chin, then when Princess rolled, Riley stroked her tummy, and Princess purred.

As Riley petted Princess, she asked, "How long were you and Marcy together?"

Princess sat up and hissed.

"What? You were in a cage then the food lady put you into a carrier before the car ride? Seriously?"

Princess headbutted Riley's right arm, and Riley resumed smoothing down her fur.

"So, you didn't know the lady who drove the car."

Princess hissed again as she rolled for another tummy rub, and Riley nodded. "Got it."

Princess leapt off the bed and stalked the sleeping Toby. When she crouched to pounce on him, he lifted his head and softly growled a warning; Princess flicked her tail and marched to the hallway. Riley snickered as Toby closed his eyes and went back to sleep.

"Marcy didn't leave me a cat. What was she leaving me?" Riley mused as she slowly rose to sit on the edge of her bed.

"I need lunch."

Toby's eyes opened, and he trotted to the bedroom door to wait for her.

"Give me a few minutes; I'm not sure how I'm going to do this." Riley scanned her room then smiled. *Ben put my walking stick in here.*

She made her way to the living room. *Ben's sleeping on the sofa. Kind of.* She snickered then headed toward the back door. When Riley opened it, Toby dashed outside, and she followed him. After she sat in the rocking chair, she leaned back and listened to the calls of the cardinals, sparrows, crows, and mockingbirds. *I miss Bob White.*

Toby trotted to her and leaned against her chair, and she stroked his back with her fingertips. "I guess ole Bob isn't much for cities. I don't blame him. We need to go to Grandma's cabin, Toby." She frowned. "I wonder where my car is? I'll have to ask Ben when he wakes up. I need a new cell phone."

She picked up a boot and sniffed then coughed. "I need to do something about my boots; I'm not sure it's appropriate to go to the store in my slippers."

Ben came outside and joined her on the porch. "How do you feel?" he asked.

"I'm cranky," she said. "Are you ready for lunch?"

Ben nodded. "Thanks for the warning; lunch sounds good. What shall I..."

Riley interrupted. "I'm cranky, not an invalid. I'll help with lunch. I'll smear mayonnaise on the bread, then you can put together the sandwiches."

Ben helped her to the table, then after she sat, he handed her the mayonnaise, a knife, the bread, and plates. Riley frowned at the mayonnaise.

"Would you open it for me?" she asked.

After she spread mayonnaise on one piece of bread, she said, "This is harder than I thought."

Ben nodded then made their sandwiches.

While they ate lunch, Ben asked, "What's got you cranky?"

"Mostly my cell phone." She sipped her sweet tea then picked up her second half of her sandwich. "My cheese sandwich is perfect. Thanks."

After she ate most of her sandwich, Riley said, "My boots stink."

"We'll sprinkle in some baking soda. If it works, you'll have a pair of work boots; if it doesn't, you can toss them. We can order a phone online from your cell phone company, and they'll get it to you by Monday."

Riley snickered. "It sounds a little funny for me to worry about fashion, doesn't it? I'm officially over being cranky. Let's try the baking soda then shop online for the cell phone because I want one exactly like I had."

Ben helped her to her computer, then Riley pulled up her cell provider on her laptop, found an updated version of her cellphone, and completed the transaction. "It might be here on Saturday; that would be awesome. I'd like to go to the cabin, but I can't go in these slippers. I want to get new boots."

"Sure. I'll meet you at the door." Ben picked up his backpack and strode to the door while Riley pulled herself to her feet with the assistance of her walking stick. After she had made it halfway to the front door, she stopped to catch her breath. "I think I've worn myself out."

Ben helped her to the sofa, and tears slipped down her face. "I thought I could push through the pain, but it was too much."

"Sorry." Ben sat next to her and put his arm around her, and she leaned against him.

"Thanks. You know, we can go to the cabin and spend a few days there when I'm a little stronger. When I was a kid and stayed with Grandma, I slept in Grandma's room on what she called a 'rollaway bed.' It was the most comfortable bed in the world; I think she kept it in the attic when I wasn't there." Riley smiled. "I'd forgotten all about it."

"We'll see if we can find it."

"That would be nice. I thought it was a big bed when I was eleven; it's probably still fine for me."

They relaxed together on the sofa until Ben's phone buzzed a text from their landlord, Helen.

"Call at your convenience."

Ben showed his phone to Riley, and she sat up while he called Helen. While he waited for Helen to answer, he glanced at Riley. "We'll be okay," he whispered.

When Helen answered, Ben said, "Hi, Helen, I'm with Riley; I've put you on speakerphone."

"Hello, you two. I've got bad news and great news."

CHAPTER NINE

Riley reached for Ben's hand; after he squeezed hers, she relaxed.

Helen continued, "First, the bad news: the sewer pipe from the house you were going to rent to the street collapsed, and the neighbors hate me. I have no idea how long it will take for the line to be replaced."

"That's terrible, Helen," Riley said.

"I agree, but I'm happy Ben hadn't moved into the house. Now, for the great news, I have a two-bedroom house that will be vacant on Monday. I'll need a couple of days to clean it and have the few pieces of furniture that I already ordered delivered to the larger house. This house is in fine shape. If you'd like to see it this afternoon, we can meet there after five. The renters agreed I could show it to you. They have three months before their lease is up, but I'm returning their deposit because they are moving back to Atlanta, so she can take care of her father who is in declining health. Nice folks, I'm sorry to see them leaving town. I'll text you the address, Ben."

After they disconnected, Ben received the text and showed Riley, and she smiled. "The street is only three blocks away. I'll wait in the truck."

Ben exhaled in relief. "I'd appreciate it."

I knew he was worried.

When it was close to five o'clock, Toby loped to the truck while Ben helped Riley. On the way to meet Helen, Riley said, "After you've looked at the house, we could go by the grocery store and pick up fried chicken and a salad from the deli."

"I forgot to tell you that Claire is cooking tonight, and Thad will deliver our food at six thirty. Can you think of anything that we might need from the grocery store on our way home?"

"While you're checking out the house, I'll work on a list."

When Ben reached the end of their street, he turned right and counted as he passed the streets. "One, two, three, and we turn here."

After Ben turned right then passed two houses, he parked in the driveway of the next house. "I won't be long, but I'll leave the engine running and lock the door."

When Toby put his chin on Riley's shoulder, she smiled and lowered her window. "If you lower Toby's window and turn off the engine, we'll enjoy the fresh air."

Helen waved from the porch, and Ben strode to join her, then Helen tapped on the door before they went inside.

Riley pulled out her notepad and pen from her backpack and stared at the page. "The quickest way to make my mind blank is to have a clean sheet of paper in front of me."

Toby moved to his lowered window and sniffed the neighborhood. Riley closed her notebook and scanned the nearby yards. "There's a tricycle on the porch next door." Riley pointed to the house on her left. As she tried to peer at the corner house's yard, her eyes widened as a car drove past the intersection. "That's strange, Toby. The driver looked like Eli Reeves. Wonder what he'd be doing here?" She blinked her blurry eyes then rubbed them. "Maybe it wasn't. My eyes are still blurry and burn sometimes, but at least they aren't as bad as they were."

She leaned back and closed her eyes to rest them. When Ben and Helen came out of the house, Helen said, "It does give you options."

Riley sat up as Ben nodded then hurried to the truck. When he slid into the driver's seat and started the engine, she showed him her notebook and grinned. "Here's my list."

Ben chuckled then headed to the grocery store. "We still need ice cream; we can work on a list for next week's meals on Sunday when I'm off work. You'll like the house; it's much nicer than the other one. Two bedrooms, a master bath with a shower, a regular bathroom, large eat-in kitchen, living room with a fireplace, and a utility room with a washer and dryer and lots of shelves. It has wooden floors, and the walls are painted a neutral tan color."

"Sounds really nice."

"The tenants did a great job of decorating. I took pictures, so I could steal some ideas. Helen thinks I can move on Wednesday. Would you be okay with that?"

Toby whined, and Riley smiled. "That would be great."

When Ben parked at the grocery store, he asked, "What did Toby say?"

Riley glanced back at Toby. "He agreed."

Toby grinned as Ben strode to the store.

"Thanks for not busting me, Toby," Riley said. "I think both of us are getting used to Ben being around all the time already, but I have a feeling that three blocks won't make that much difference."

When a car parked next to them, Toby barked, and Riley peered at the passenger in the back seat. "She's a cute poodle, isn't she? I like her pink collar with the rhinestones. Very fancy."

The poodle held her head high then side-glanced at Toby and yipped. Toby sat on the back seat and pushed out his chest.

"Nice," Riley whispered. "She's looking at you."

Ben opened the driver's door and placed a sack of groceries on the console. As he made his way to the road, he asked, "What's wrong with Toby?"

Riley shook her head. "Nothing's wrong. He's looking manly for the poodle in the car next to us."

"I need to take lessons, Toby," Ben said.

After Ben helped Riley to the dining table, he put the ice cream in the freezer before he reached into the sack and pulled out a cheesecake from the bakery. "This jumped into the cart on my way to the checkout."

Riley smiled. "Claire may send dessert too."

Ben joined her at the table and chuckled. "That's okay because there's no such thing as too many desserts."

Ben's phone buzzed a text, and he grinned as he read it. "Thad's out front. I'll be right back."

When Ben returned with a large, fancy picnic basket, he said, "Thad told me if he didn't come inside, then Claire couldn't grill him on how you were doing while he ate his supper. She wants you to call her as soon as you get your new phone."

Ben emptied the basket contents onto the table: two generous portions of lasagna, a tossed salad, a sliced baguette wrapped in foil, and tiramisu. "Ah." Ben put his index finger and thumb together and made a smacking noise as he flicked his wrist to move them away from his mouth. "Siamo italiani stasera."

Riley giggled. "What?"

Ben grinned. "We are Italian tonight. I had a good friend in college who was third generation Italian. He said he didn't speak any English until he was five. He taught me a few phrases." He shook his head. "We had big dreams of traveling in Italy and working in vineyards."

After they ate their Italian supper and tiramisu, Riley tried to scoot back her chair but grimaced.

"You've had a long day. Are you ready to take it easy? It's time for your pain medication."

"I guess it's all catching up with me. I'm even too tired to argue with you. Maybe tomorrow I'll be strong enough to take a bath. That's number one on my wish list."

"I'll close my eyes and help you get ready for bed."

"Thanks, but I think I can manage if you'll help me to the bathroom and bring my pajamas to me. I'd like to wash my face and brush my teeth before bed."

After Riley washed and put on her pajama bottom, she stared at the top. "This won't work."

Riley cracked open the door. "Ben, I need a shirt that opens in front."

She listened while Ben rummaged through her closet then returned.

"I couldn't find anything in your closet." He stuck his arm inside the door and handed her one of his shirts. "Wear this."

"Okay, but I'll need my sling off to take off my shirt," Riley said.

"Turn around, and I'll untie it." After he untied her sling, Riley unwound it from around her splint then Ben pulled on one end of the sling and removed it.

She pulled up her shirt on the right side then pulled her right arm back through the sleeve until it was under her shirt. After she pulled her shirt over her head, it was easy to slide the shirt off her left arm. "Getting my shirt off was not easy, but it would have been impossible with the sling on."

"You're right," Ben said from the other side of the door.

Riley put her left arm then her right arm through their sleeves then pulled on the shirt and giggled. *It goes down to my knees.*

She opened the door. "Ben, would you button it for me?"

Ben furrowed his brow in a vain attempt to maintain a serious demeanor but burst out laughing. "Sorry, but it was the best I could do."

He buttoned the shirt before he repositioned the sling and retied it. "If you call the pawn shop tomorrow before I get off work, I can stop and pick up shirts for you."

Ben helped Riley to bed; after he returned to put her walking stick in the corner, he kissed her forehead then stroked her hair away from her face before he turned off the light. "Good night."

* * *

When Riley woke the next morning, Princess jumped up on the bed and purred, and the sunlight brightened her room. "This is different. It's not cloudy." Princess jumped off the bed and paraded out of the room with her tail high.

Riley swung her feet to the floor. After she stood on her left leg, she grabbed her stick then tested her right leg by shifting some of her weight to it. "Not bad, but not quite good enough."

Toby trotted to the bedroom to greet her, and she hugged him before she limped to the kitchen and smiled at the spoon Ben had left on the table then read the note. "Yogurt for breakfast and a sandwich for lunch are in the fridge. Coffee is set up. Already fed Toby and Princess."

Riley turned on the burner then opened the back door for Toby to go out before she grabbed her yogurt and set it on the table. When Princess meowed her cry of hunger, Riley said, "I know Ben fed you before he left."

Princess hissed and marched to pout behind the sofa.

"You have no reason to be huffy; you should be embarrassed." Riley sat and ate her yogurt while Princess sneaked back to the kitchen and lay across Riley's feet.

When the coffee was ready, Riley stared at the sofa and sighed as she poured half a cup then stood at the counter to drink it. *I need a tray that goes around my neck so I can carry my coffee out of the kitchen.*

After she drank her second half-cup, she let Toby back into the house then limped to the bedroom to change clothes. She stepped out of her pajama bottoms, put on a pair of soft lounging pants, and rolled her eyes. *I almost don't even need pants with Ben's shirt on.*

When she opened her closet door, she frowned at her shirts. *I don't have any shirts I can wear and no way to call or get to the pawn shop for any shirts.* She sniffed back her tears and hung her head as she made her way to the sofa to read. She picked up her book then closed her eyes. *I'll just rest for a minute.*

Riley woke with a giggle when Toby nudged her. She yawned as she sat up. "I didn't last very long with reading, did I?"

Toby whined, and she rose with the assistance of her stick then walked with halting steps to the back door and went outside with Toby. "It's warmer today than it's been all week, and the humidity is so thick, it's smothering." She leaned back in her rocking chair and listened to a mockingbird. After Toby checked the backyard, he flopped down on the porch next to her and panted.

"Let's go inside and get you a drink. I just remembered I haven't checked my mail since Tuesday."

While Toby drank his fill, Riley picked up a plastic sack to carry the mail and stepped out front to check the mailbox. After she dropped the mail into her sack, she went inside and dumped the contents onto the table.

She sorted through it and placed all the advertisements in a pile. "Here we go, Toby. Two thick letters from the University of

Georgia: one is addressed to Ben, and the other one is addressed to me. I'll bet these are the applications."

Riley opened her letter. "I'm too tired to process all of this. I'll wait for Ben."

She glanced at the clock on the stove. "Lunch then nap. All this relaxation better help me heal faster, Toby."

Riley put her lunch sack on the table then sighed as she sat on her chair. "Everything tires me out."

When she opened the sack, she grinned. "Ben's awesome. I have a sandwich and a slice of cheesecake, and he even included a fork for my dessert."

After she ate lunch, she made her way to the sofa and lay down. She closed her eyes. *I'll take a short nap.*

Riley woke when Toby whined. "I think I forgot to take my medicine this morning."

As Riley sat up, Princess jumped onto the sofa and leaned against Riley's right arm and purred.

"Everything does hurt. Thank you for your sympathy, Princess."

Toby trotted to the front door and whined.

"Ben? Already?"

When Ben opened the door and came inside, Toby greeted him at the door, and Princess rushed to join in. Ben chuckled. "Let me put away the groceries, then I'll feed you."

As he put the small vase of yellow flowers on the table and the groceries into the refrigerator, he said, "Glad to see that you ate your lunch."

"I see you ran into Mrs. Smythe." Riley smiled.

Ben grinned. "She helped me pick out our meals for this week from the selection of fresh meal kits. Her rescue of a potentially disastrous dinner party with peanut butter and jelly hors d'oeuvres is a legend, isn't it? I'll bet half the town has yellow flowers at their parties to commemorate Mrs. Smythe's brilliant recovery. How was your day?"

"I slept most of the day, and our applications from UGA arrived. I tried to look at mine, but I was too tired." She frowned. "I forgot to take my medicine."

"I'm glad you slept." Ben strode to the table and read the medication sheets from the hospital. "You can take some now." He poured a glass of water and brought her the bottle of medicine. "I'll open it for you, but I wanted you to see it's your pain medication."

After she took her medicine, she continued, "Thanks. I was really bummed because I wanted to go to the pawn shop and get some shirts, but what was worse was that I didn't have a cell phone to call to see if I could…" Riley pursed her lips and sniffed to keep from crying.

"Call the pawn shop while I feed Toby and Princess." Ben handed his phone to Riley.

Riley smiled as she made her call. "Hi, this is Riley Malloy. I have a broken arm and need some shirts that button or snap in front. I really love cotton."

"Hey there, Riley. This is Mary Ruth. I heard about your injuries. You'll need a short-sleeved shirt with a good wide sleeve, so you can slip the sleeve over your splint then your cast. Do you care about color? Solid or plaid?"

"Not really. I'd like to have four or five shirts, so I don't have to do laundry every day."

Mary Ruth laughed. "I hear ya, girl. You probably wear a medium, am I right?"

"Not in a few years," Riley giggled. "I need size large."

"Gotcha. I don't like my shirts to bind my bosom either. What else do you need?"

"Ben and I put some baking soda in my boots that got soaked in river water, but they still smell a little funky. I need a pair of size seven boots."

"What style?"

Riley smiled. *Mary Ruth would make a great personal shopper.* "I like a rounded toe and a short shaft."

"I've got a pair that might be perfect."

"Ben Carter can pick them up. I'll try to come along for the ride. I've been a little weak since I got out of the hospital," Riley said.

"I understand completely. Don't push yourself for at least a day or two. I'll get right on it and have everything ready for the deputy when he shows up. Anything else?"

Riley smiled. "No, the shirts will make a huge difference for my mental health. Thank you."

After she hung up, Ben said, "That sounded promising."

"Very. Mary Ruth will find shirts and a pair of boots for me, and you can pick them up, but I'd like to go along. One minor point: I love your shirt, Ben, but I can't go into the store wearing it."

Ben shrugged.

Riley squinted at his shoulders then laughed. "That's it!"

Ben stared at her.

"I'll pick out a T-shirt that you can cut along the left shoulder seam from the neck to the sleeve then continue down the sleeve, so that the shirt is open, then you can help me put my right arm into the right sleeve then pull the shirt over my head."

Ben narrowed his eyes. "I can see that, but what about that left shoulder, won't it flop down?"

Riley raised an eyebrow. "Not if you secure it with duct tape."

Ben furrowed his brow. "What about the duct tape showing? Although, I'm sure you have an answer."

"Of course. I'll put on my sweatshirt, and you can adjust the left side to cover the tape. We'll zip it up part way, so it won't slip."

Ben laughed. "It's crazy, but even crazier, I'm sure it'll work."

After Ben cut the T-shirt, Riley took it to her bedroom and slipped off his shirt then put on the T-shirt under Toby's supervision. She whispered, "Do you suppose he didn't bring me a bra at the hospital because he forgot or because he knew I couldn't manage it?"

Toby grinned.

When Riley and Toby went to the living room, Ben had the duct tape ready and taped her shirt then helped her with the sweatshirt before they left.

When Ben turned at the pawn shop parking lot, he asked, "Do you want to wait for me, or shall I drop you in front and park then be right in?"

"I'd like to go in."

When he stopped, he said, "I'll bring in your backpack, but give me a second, and I'll help you out of the truck."

"Good idea. I'm not sure I'm quite up to leaping out of the truck."

When Riley limped into the store with Toby by her side, Mary Ruth met her at the door. "I knew you'd want to come in. I've got your things in the back. Give me a few minutes to gather everything, and by the way, you are amazing."

Riley smiled. "Thanks."

She stopped and placed her stick into a cart then held onto the cart for balance while she browsed the sale items. She stopped and examined a set of metric wrenches then dropped it into her cart, and Toby whined.

She pushed her cart away from the sale bin and whispered, "It's a quality set at a good price; I might need them at the cabin."

While she admired the different Western hats for women, a man came up behind her. Toby stepped between the man and Riley while she casually lifted her walking stick out of the cart then turned, ready to strike with her stick. She stared at the man with dark blond hair who smiled at her. *Eli Reeves, Georgia Bureau of Investigations.*

"I thought it was you." Eli's dimples deepened as he smiled even more broadly. "I stopped by the clinic, but I didn't see anyone I knew. Did you have a bad fall?"

"A minor accident, but I'm fine." She shifted her stick to her side but maintained her grip. "Are you here to wrap up the Truman case?"

"No, that's closed, and I work only active cases."

Riley narrowed her eyes at his condescending tone.

Eli continued, "I'm supervising a double murder not too far from here, and thought I'd drop by."

Riley waved her hand at an imaginary gnat in front of her face to hide her disgust at his self-importance.

"Maybe you heard about it? Two guys found dead near Little River?"

Riley shook her head. "Is that something recent?"

"Looks like they were shot Wednesday, but enough about business. Are you well enough to go out to dinner?"

Toby's hackles raised, and Riley furrowed her brow after she glanced at his tobacco-stained fingers on his right hand. "I already have plans."

She glanced behind Eli and smiled as Ben came inside the store, and the cashier called out, "Welcome, Deputy. She's looking at cowgirl hats."

"Would you care to join us?" Riley asked Eli as Ben strode to her side.

"No, thanks for the invitation, but I have to get back to the scene to be sure nobody's slacking off. Maybe another time."

Riley smiled and nodded. *That was a clumsy about face, Eli. Are you allergic to Ben?*

"I doubt it," Ben mumbled as he crossed his arms until Eli strode out the door; Ben continued to glare at Eli until he was out of sight.

"What was that all about? What was Eli Reeves doing here?" Ben asked.

"Good questions. We can talk in the truck."

Ben wandered the aisles while Riley waited for Mary Ruth at the front of the shop.

Mary Ruth wheeled a cart with two sacks and a large boot box to the front. "We've already scanned everything in, and I'll check you out. If there's anything that doesn't fit or you don't like, Deputy Carter can bring it back for a refund."

When Ben joined them, he had an electric drill and spare battery set in his hand.

After they checked out, Riley waited at the shop door with the cart while Ben hurried to his truck. Riley scanned the parking lot and narrowed her eyes as Eli pulled out of a spot not far from Ben's truck then drove to the exit and turned toward the highway.

On the way home, Riley said, "I have no idea why Eli Reeves was in the pawn shop. He came up behind me, which is a dangerous thing to do right now. He told me he was working a double murder at Little River, but that's five hours away. Is there another Little River that's closer to us? Do you know anything about a double murder?"

Ben frowned. "I haven't heard anything about a double murder. I'll ask around tomorrow at work if anyone knows of a nearby Little River. There are two tributaries around Atlanta named Little River, but none near us on the map."

"He told me two guys were shot on Wednesday," Riley said.

"That explains why I didn't hear anything about it." Ben grinned as he parked. "We've been busy."

As Ben helped Riley out of the truck, she said, "When he asked me if I was well enough to go out for dinner, Toby's hackles raised."

"Good, boy, Toby; mine did too," Ben said, and Toby grinned then loped to the front door.

Riley stared at Ben and Toby. "Anyway, that's when I asked him if he wanted to join us; I knew he'd decline."

After Ben helped Riley inside to the sofa, he asked, "What would you have done if he'd accepted?"

"Probably fainted." Riley smiled.

Princess jumped onto the sofa and stretched out next to Riley.

"Ah. A little dramatic but probably effective," Ben said. "Care for some cold tea while I prepare your gourmet dinner?"

"Tea really sounds good." Riley moaned as she shifted her weight to rub Princess's ears. "I wore myself out, but it was worth it."

Ben put the recipe card on the counter then pulled out a frying pan and a pot. "We're having spicy shrimp and rice. All the prep work is done at the grocery store, and the kit includes all the ingredients, even the spices; all I have to do is follow the instructions. Mrs. Smythe told me this shrimp recipe was one of the easiest to prepare."

"I don't remember seeing meal kits in the grocery stores in Pomeroy," Riley said.

"That's because us country folk in Barton are more upscale." Ben chuckled as he removed the ingredients from the meal kit and filled the pot with water.

Riley stretched out on the sofa and closed her eyes to ignore her throbbing knee pain.

"Riley," Ben said softly. "Our dinner is ready. Do you want to eat now or later?"

She opened her eyes. "Now."

After she sat up, Ben helped her to her feet then he assisted her to the table.

She leaned over her plate and inhaled. "Mmm. Smells wonderful."

"Good." Ben refilled their glasses with tea then joined her at the table. While they ate, he asked, "Did you have any problems today?"

"Not really. The only problem I had other than just being generally whiny was carrying my drinks to the table or to the sofa."

Ben frowned. "We should have thought of that. We could have a cooler next to the sofa with cold bottles of water in it, and I could fill a thermos with coffee and put it on the table before I leave in the morning. I don't have an easy answer for tea, though."

Riley gazed at Ben. "You are really smart. I can have iced tea in the evening."

Ben met her gaze and beamed. "After we eat, I'll get the laundry going."

Riley's pace slowed as she ate; she paused and frowned at her plate before she ate the shrimp then drank her iced tea.

"I can tell when you're getting close to being full," Ben smiled. "You slow down then pick out the food you like best. That's really smart."

After Ben cleared the dishes and loaded the dishwasher, he gathered their laundry and started the washer.

"Let's work on those applications. If we can finish them up tonight, I'll drop them off at the post office on my way to work in the morning."

Riley read the first page and rolled her eyes. "The first page is simple; I have no idea what confused me earlier except I got stumped because I didn't know your parents' address."

"It's hard to push past pain and exhaustion." Ben filled in the address for Riley before he read and completed his first page then continued.

"Done," Riley said.

Ben signed his last page. "So am I. Let's swap and proofread."

After Riley finished reading Ben's application, she leaned back and waited. When he finished he said, "You read faster than I do."

"I probably have more practice reviewing records than you do." She smiled.

Ben picked up his envelope and hefted it on his palm to test its weight. "I may have to wait until the post office opens for the postage, but we're done. Want to celebrate with a bath bomb? Do you know what that is? I don't."

When Riley chuckled, Ben grinned as he pulled out a small box from the grocery sack he'd left on the counter. "Mrs. Smythe said the Epsom salts and the scent of lemongrass green tea would be soothing and relaxing."

"Sounds wonderful." Ben helped Riley to the bathroom then handed her the box of bath bombs.

After Riley washed her face and neck at the sink, she ran a few inches of water in the tub before she dropped in the bath bomb and inhaled the relaxing scent of lemongrass. She pulled off the duct tape from the left shoulder and removed her shirt before she eased herself into the shallow water with the assistance of her walking stick. *This is heavenly.* When the water cooled, she climbed out of the tub, dried, and put on her pajama bottoms and one of Ben's shirts over her sling. *I didn't even notice when Ben put clean clothes on the counter.*

When she opened the bathroom door, Ben came to help, and she said, "I need you to help me take off the sling, so I can put my left arm through the sleeve."

"I'm going to make it simpler for you to slip off the sling and put it back on by leaving it around your neck like a scarf," Ben said. "Your arm won't be as secure, so you'll have to be careful."

After he was satisfied with the position of the sling, he asked, "Bed or sofa?"

"I'm ready to call it a night."

Ben helped her to her bedroom. "Your new shirts are hanging in your closet. I'll be right back." He returned with a small glass of water and her evening medications. After she took her medicine, Ben kissed her lightly and placed her walking stick close to her nightstand before he turned off the light.

CHAPTER TEN

Millie sipped her glass of house wine and lingered at her table after her evening meal as she gazed at the waitstaff and the other customers. *A few solo women like me.* She smiled as she eavesdropped on the couple sitting behind her while they argued about their apartment décor in rapid Parisian French. *It's a decided advantage and certainly entertaining to be fluent in other languages.*

A young server with her hair in a tight bun on top of her head approached Millie. "Did you enjoy your dinner, Madame?" She spoke in Marseillais, the soft French dialect from the Marseille region in the south of France.

"It was excellent, as usual." Millie responded in Parisian French. Her phone buzzed in her purse, but she ignored it. *If it's important, they'll leave a voice mail.*

After she finished her wine, she strolled three blocks to her hotel. The streets were well-lit, and even though it was after ten, there were other solo women, small groups, and couples enjoying the night air.

When she returned to her hotel room, she kicked off her shoes and listened to the voice mail message from an old friend. "Your niece was abducted and badly injured earlier this week. I didn't know if you'd heard. She was admitted to the hospital but is at home recuperating. I thought you might like to give her a call."

"That snake," she fumed. "I distinctly told him that Riley was not to be harmed." She drummed her fingers on the table then called Riley. When Riley's phone immediately routed to the message that the phone was not available, she called her brother's old friend the sheriff.

When he answered, she said, "It's Millie. I just heard about Riley and tried to call her but couldn't get through."

"Riley's fine. She has a broken arm and is angry about not being able to go to work until next week. We had a bad storm, and her phone got wet. I think she'll have a new one soon. Do you want me to tell her to call you? She can fill you in on all the boring details."

"As long as she's fine, she doesn't need to call me; I might be hard to reach the next few days."

After Millie hung up, she stared at the night sky. *Sam didn't seem too excited about her broken arm, but he's always been a master of understatement.*

"Okay, Mister. I'll give you the weekend to call and fill me in on your status, and it better be good; otherwise, I'm calling in some favors on Monday, and you'll be history."

* * *

When Riley woke early Saturday morning, she heard the back door open. Ben said, "I'll go out with you, Toby."

She found her slippers and her walking stick and made her way to the kitchen. *Not as rough as yesterday.*

When she neared the back door, Toby yipped, and Ben said, "Really?"

Ben opened the door, and Toby rushed to her side. "Toby told me you were up. Were we too loud?"

"No, I think I've caught up on my sleep deficit," she said as Ben poured her a cup of coffee.

"I was ready to cook breakfast. Care for an egg and toast?" Ben asked.

"If it won't slow you down." Riley sipped her coffee. "I feel a lot better."

"That is really good news."

While they ate, Ben said, "I put a cooler with a couple of ice packs and six bottles of water at the end of the sofa. I'll fill the thermos before I leave. Anything else you can think of?"

"I can't think of anything. I'm planning on dragging a chair to the front porch, so I can watch for my new cell phone."

"Please don't. The sheriff will get calls from the neighbors who will think you've been locked out or something. Better yet, go ahead. Maybe the sheriff will send me to investigate." Ben wiggled his eyebrows, and Riley laughed.

"What about you?" Riley asked. "What can I do for you today?"

"Just take it easy." Ben cleared the table and refilled her coffee then leaned to kiss her cheek, but she turned and pulled him close before she kissed his mouth that he had opened in surprise.

After she released him, she stroked his cheek and smiled. "It was my turn. Good friends kiss."

He sat down and held her hand and pushed back her unruly hair from her face. "I needed that. Thank you."

Riley beamed, and he kissed her forehead.

"Be safe." Ben grabbed his lunch sack from the counter and hurried out the door.

Riley finished her coffee. "We really like Ben, don't we?"

Toby lifted his head and grinned, and Princess purred.

Riley rose from the table without using her walking stick for support. "That was a major milestone. For my next trick, I'm going to put on one of my new shirts."

Riley walked slowly to her bedroom, and Princess followed her while Toby napped.

"That wasn't bad at all, but I'm not going to push it," Riley said. "I certainly don't want to have a setback." Princess jumped up onto the bed while Riley examined her new shirts in the closet.

"Shall I wear solid or plaid? Snaps or buttons?" Riley scratched her head, and Princess purred.

"Plaid with snaps it is. Thanks, Princess."

Riley sat on the bed and carefully slipped off the sling from her left arm the way Ben had showed her, so she could take off his shirt. After she put on her new shirt, she slid the sling back into place.

"Success." She peered at her open shirt then snapped each white pearl, metal button closed. "That was really easy, Princess."

After she put on her soft pants, Riley returned to the kitchen and poured half of a cup of coffee then slowly carried it to her computer. While she drank her coffee, she checked on her new phone. "My phone is supposed to be here later this morning. Ready for some fresh air, Toby?"

Toby growled.

Riley rolled her eyes. "I meant out back. We won't sit on the front porch and scare the neighbors."

Princess slipped out the back door between Toby's legs. After Riley sat on her chair, Princess hopped up on her lap, and Toby flopped on the porch next to Riley.

"Did Ben tell you to stay close?"

Princess purred, and Toby grinned.

Thought so.

Riley closed her eyes and listened to the birds. "I'm getting around pretty well without my walking stick and officially bored. Let's go inside, and I'll find a book to read."

As Riley rose, Toby huffed a soft "boof."

"Maybe it's the delivery truck." Riley carried Princess inside and set her on the floor while Toby trotted to the front door and whined.

The delivery truck pulled away from her house as she opened the front door, and Riley picked up the package that the driver had leaned against the door jamb. She sat at the dining table, opened the package, and pulled out the instructions. Princess jumped up on the table and investigated the box.

"This looks easy. Turn on the phone, call the 800 number, and follow the prompts."

Riley set the empty box on the floor, and Princess leapt from the table into the box while Riley activated her phone.

After she walked through all the steps, she sent a text to Ben to let him know she had her phone then called Claire.

"I'm so excited to hear from you," Claire said. "Everyone else is with patients right now, but I'll let them know when they come to my desk. So, how are you?"

"I've been mostly cranky. Who can sit around all day and be puny without being cranky? My twisted knee was giving me the most problems, but it's a lot better today. My arm is still broken and in a splint; I see the doctor on Monday, and she'd better release me to go to work, or I'll unleash my full cranky on her."

Claire giggled. "We knew you had a doctor appointment scheduled for Monday, and we've made plans for me to take you, so Ben won't have to take any more time off. Doc Julie Rae and her family are returning home today. Amanda's downright cranky too and wants to work remotely, so Zach is looking into it. Everything else is just our usual animal hospital drama. Pia said that somebody must have handed out free samples of clueless water because we've had some real doozies."

Riley chuckled. "Thank you for dinner. Our cooking skills are improving, so we aren't starving. I always made my lunch every day, so I had basic sandwich skills, but I never did much cooking when it was just me, and I think Ben was the same." Riley sighed. "I really miss being at work. Isn't that pitiful?"

"Definitely pitiful, but don't tell the doctor that on Monday. You don't want to sound desperate, even though you are, and I totally understand about cooking. When Thad and I were first married, neither one of us could cook, and we were basically broke. It's a wonder we didn't die of malnutrition our first year of marriage. We ate a lot of plain pasta, processed cheese, and crackers. Now, the thought of processed cheese makes me ill. What are your plans for tonight?"

"I think Ben is off tomorrow. If he is, I'd like to go to the cabin for an overnight and have cabin food: hot dogs or hamburgers. I made a new friend on Wednesday, a quail, Bob White. I'm hoping maybe he, or one of his relatives, might be at the cabin. I really miss him."

"Bob White kept you company?" Claire asked.

"He sure did, and my spirits up. I felt like I wasn't alone," Riley said.

"When's your doctor appointment on Monday?" Claire asked.

"Nine o'clock."

"Good. I'll be at your house at eight thirty. See you then."

After Riley hung up, Toby nudged her arm and whined.

"You're right; it's time for lunch."

Her phone buzzed a text from Ben: "Cool."

"I've heard from Ben; I feel better now," Riley said.

She pulled out her lunch sack. "Sandwich and carrot sticks. I guess we finished off the cheesecake." She refilled her empty cup from the thermos and ate lunch.

Later in the afternoon while Riley was deep into one of the classic Western books, her phone buzzed a text from Ben.

"Off tomorrow but on call until Monday morning. Take a chance on the cabin?"

Riley squealed then replied, "Absolutely."

"We're going to spend the night at the cabin." Riley waved her arms and grinned. "Arm dancing won't hurt my knee."

Toby howled, and Princess meowed, raced to the carrier, and disappeared inside.

Riley chuckled while she made her way to her bedroom. "We have a little while before we leave, Princess. I'll give you plenty of warning."

Princess purred but remained in her carrier.

Riley stood in front of her closet and stared at the four new shirts. "I can't decide which one to take. What if we decide to stay until Monday morning?" Riley carefully rolled each shirt and placed it into her backpack, and Toby yipped.

"I've been wearing soft pants, but I might want jeans if we go for a walk tomorrow, and if we stay until Monday, I'd like to wear jeans to the doctor's office." When she filled her backpack but still had more clothes to add, she said, "I'll pack all my clothes into a little larger bag and put my hairbrush and stuff in my backpack."

After she finished packing, she smiled. "I've always packed everything I owned, so I'm kind of proud that I didn't pack any work clothes or my old shoes that I don't like."

After Riley and Toby returned to the living room, she headed for the sofa. "I need to rest a bit."

Toby yipped, and Riley narrowed her eyes. "I'm not tired; I'm conserving my energy and taking a break to read or think about a grocery list."

Toby flopped down on the floor next to Riley, and she picked up her book. When Toby yipped, she said, "Only two more pages to go, Toby."

Toby put his paws on the sofa and barked at her.

Riley put her book down. "Oh, Ben's here. Why didn't you say so?"

Ben rushed into the house. "What's wrong? Why is Toby barking?"

Riley laughed. "Toby was scolding me for not paying attention when he told me you were home. I've already packed my things, and Princess is in her carrier. We still need to pack food and stop by the grocery store."

Ben leaned down and kissed her. "My clothes are still packed in my duffel bag and ready to go. I'll just grab my bag after I change. I'll need to wash my uniform, so we might as well do laundry at the cabin, then I can iron my shirt and pants when we return to town tomorrow."

Riley said, "I was thinking about what we'd take from here: eggs, milk, bacon, sweet tea, butter, bread, condiments from the refrigerator, and coffee."

"Right, and I'll get hamburger, sandwich meat, cheese, buns, and ice cream at the grocery store," Ben said as he placed the bread and coffee into a sack and the rest of the items into the cooler. "Can you think of anything else?"

Riley shook her head. "If we decide to eat supper at the cabin tomorrow night, we could have burgers again and pretend we're roughing it."

Ben hurried to the bedroom to change before he returned with his duffel bag and the laundry basket. "I dumped all our laundry into the basket." He frowned. "I should have asked earlier: you don't mind commingled laundry, do you?"

Riley rolled her eyes as Ben dropped her large bag of clothes and her backpack on top of the laundry.

"Did you want to take your laptop?" he asked.

"I hadn't thought about it, but if you end up going into town on a call, it might be nice to have. I could research the fall schedule of UGA classes."

While Ben packed her laptop in its case, he said, "The sheriff knows we'll be at the cabin and told me if it was necessary that he'd meet me on the scene if I have a call."

"That was really nice," Riley said.

"It was, wasn't it?" Ben added the laptop to the laundry basket and carried out the basket and his duffel bag then returned and carried the cooler to the truck.

When he came back inside, he said, "If there isn't anything else, we're ready to go."

"I think I'd like to take my warm coat, just in case. I'm kind of not interested in being cold again for a while."

Ben picked up Princess's carrier, and Riley handed him the warm coat. Toby dashed to the door while Riley grabbed her sweatshirt and her walking stick.

After Ben locked the house, and everyone was in the truck, he asked, "What about your bath bomb?"

Riley smiled. "I'm roughing it."

After Ben bought groceries, they headed toward the cabin. When they passed the city limits, Riley said, "I am so excited about the cabin. Do you suppose it will be cold enough for a fire tonight?"

Ben chuckled. "If not, we'll open the doors, turn on the fans, and build our fire."

While Ben carried the laundry basket and his duffel bag inside, Toby wandered away to explore, and Riley sat on the porch with Princess in her carrier.

Princess yowled and complained.

"Are you sure you want out?" Riley asked.

Princess meowed.

"Seriously? I didn't guess because you weren't afraid of us, and you like Toby."

"Seriously, what?" Ben asked as he carried in the cooler.

"Princess is feral. She wasn't afraid of us because I understood her like the food lady did. She likes Toby because he isn't a stupid dog: her words, not mine. She wants out of her carrier, so she can stay here. I think we should let her out."

"You are a very complex cat, Princess," Ben said, and Princess meowed.

Ben sat in the rocker next to Riley and took her hand. "Dad always had at least one barn cat."

Princess purred.

"Okay, Princess, but you're always welcome in the cabin, and you can go home with us anytime." Riley opened the carrier, and Princess marched out and meowed before she darted into the tall weeds.

"Will she stick around?" Ben asked.

"I think so. She liked the idea of being our barn cat."

"Does she know there isn't a barn here?"

Riley shrugged. "Shed cat; same thing."

While Ben put away the food Riley rocked and listened to a mockingbird run through its repertoire before it flitted to the next tree then flew away. Ben joined her on the porch, and Toby returned, nudged Riley's hand with his nose, and whined. A mourning dove called its sad cry.

"If Princess wants her supper, she knows where we are and wouldn't be shy about letting us know that she's hungry," Riley said. Toby laid his head on her knee, and she stroked his face.

"I thought we could grill our hamburgers but forgot to pick up charcoal," Ben said. "I checked the pantry and found an unopened bag of charcoal. I thought we were going to have to have plain, pan-fried burgers."

"Grandma tried to always be prepared." Riley furrowed her brow. "We talked about doing laundry, but now, I can't remember whether I left any detergent here when I moved to town."

Ben smiled. "There was a full bottle of detergent in the pantry. I checked before I started the laundry."

"I forgot my pillow," Riley said, "but Grandma has spares in the bedroom closets."

"Show me where the access to the attic is, and I'll check for your rollaway bed. After I bring it down, I'll make the bed if you'll find sheets for me. We'll be ready for supper by then, don't you think?"

"I think we'll be starving," Riley said.

"I agree. I'll light the charcoal and make the burgers, if you'll sit at the table and supervise."

"I can slice the onion and tomato." Riley narrowed her eyes, and Ben looked away.

Before Riley reached the door, a Bob White quail called.

"Hi, Bob." Riley grinned.

Ben smiled. "You're home."

"The access is in the hallway." Riley pointed. "Give me a second, and I'll grab a flashlight for you. I think there's a light switch up there somewhere, but I'm not sure."

After Ben climbed into the attic, he said, "Your grandmother may have planned on finishing this for a loft. It's insulated, and she finished the walls with drywall. There isn't a lot up here, but I found your rollaway bed. It must have been cumbersome for one person to manage. I wonder how she did it? Oh, I see, now. She has a strap around it; she must have lowered it. Well, I'll be."

"What?" Riley asked.

"She has a pulley system rigged up here. I'm sorry I didn't know her; she must have been awesome."

A tear escaped down Riley's cheek. "She was."

"Stand back. I don't want to drop the bed on you if my hands or the straps slip."

Ben lowered the bed then climbed down and raised the attic ladder.

"The bedroom or living room?" he asked.

"Living room is perfect. There's lots of room there in the corner opposite the fireplace," Riley said. "Grandma used to have a large dining table there for overflow. I guess Aunt Millie has it."

Ben rolled the bed into place on its wheels then pushed the release to open it before Riley brought two sheets.

"There's a spare blanket and quilt in the top of Grandma's closet," she said.

Ben lay down on the bed, and his legs went off the end. "You're right; this is a comfortable bed except not quite long enough for me."

Riley snickered. "Still perfect for me."

After Ben put on the sheets, he brought out the blanket, quilt, and a pillow.

"I'll start the charcoal and wash the tomato," he said.

Before Ben formed the burgers, he placed the onion, tomato, knife, and a cutting board on the table.

Riley picked up the knife and stared at the onion and tomato while a tear slid down her cheek. "I'm not used to this invalid stuff. Do you know how I planned to slice the onion and tomato?"

Ben shrugged as he formed the burgers, and more tears welled up in Riley's eyes "I guess I'm feeling a little sorry for myself." She sniffed back her tears. "Sure is a waste of good tears."

"You could declare them happy tears because Bob White is here," Ben said.

"True." Riley wiped her cheeks with her shirt.

While they ate, they talked about the weather and Princess, then Riley said, "I'd like to pick up my car when we go back to town tomorrow and take it to the house."

"Makes sense to me." After Ben cleared the table, he loaded the dishwasher. "Do you want dessert on the front porch?"

"Sure, unless the mosquitos are out," Riley said.

"That's a given," Ben said. "I love your grandma's rule that a fire has to be laid in the fireplace before anyone leaves, so it will be ready for the next occupant, especially if we decided to come to the cabin after dark."

Toby stood at the back door, and Ben opened the door to let him out. "We might want to have our ice cream in front of the fireplace. The mosquitos are bad."

Ben started the fire while Riley let Toby back inside before she stretched out on the old, blue sofa. After Ben added two logs to the fire, he dished up their ice cream and leaned against the sofa when he sat on the floor next to Riley.

"I picked up more bath bombs at the grocery store, so you'd have some here," he said.

"That was really nice, thank you." Riley leaned over and kissed his cheek.

"I also sneaked all the classic Western books into the cooler and brought them too." Ben grinned.

Riley laughed. "Was that for me or for you?"

Ben smirked. "For you, of course, even though I am two books ahead of you."

"Ha," Riley said. "I read them all the summer that I was twelve, so I'm already ahead of you."

"Do you want book two?" Ben rose to take their dishes to the kitchen.

"If you're planning on reading, yes, please."

"After we finish the Western series, you'll have to decide what we're reading next."

After Ben carried their dishes to the dishwasher, he picked up books two and four.

"Here's your book." Ben placed another log on the fire before he sat on the soft rocking chair to read.

While Ben read, Riley gazed at the crackling fire and smiled. *I was bored in town. This is relaxing.*

Ben let the fire die down while they read late into the night.

Riley yawned and closed her book. "I'm ready for bed. Do you want to go outside, Toby?"

Toby lumbered to the door, and Ben joined Riley as she let Toby outside then stepped out on the porch. "It's chilly tonight; I should have put on my sweatshirt." Riley shivered.

"Go back inside. I'll wait for Toby; I'm sure he won't be long."

After Ben came inside, he carried Riley's backpack and a dining chair to her sleeping corner. "Anything else I can do for you?" he asked.

"This is wonderful. Thank you very much." She stood on her tiptoes and kissed his cheek, and he wrapped his arms around her before he kissed the top of her head.

"Good night. Do you want me to turn off the lights?" Ben continued to hold her as he gazed into her eyes.

"Yes, please. There's enough moonlight for me to see."

He checked the doors and turned off the lights.

After Riley painstakingly undressed then put on her pajamas, she snuggled down in her bed, and Toby flopped down on the floor next to the low bed. She watched the few glowing embers behind the fireplace glass then closed her eyes.

Toby snuffled, and she woke. He must be dreaming. He growled low and padded to the front door then whined.

"Shh. Don't wake Ben," Riley whispered. "Princess is at the door?"

While she made her way to the door, Ben came racing from the bedroom with his pistol. "What is it?" he whispered.

"Toby said Princess is at the door."

Ben opened the door, and Princess meowed then marched inside with her head high. After she was inside, she hissed.

"You don't have to be a feral cat, Princess. You can be a wild, terrifying housecat."

Princess meowed as she strolled to her food bowl that Riley had filled earlier.

"Of course, we shall never speak of this again."

Ben hugged Riley and whispered, "Everyone here is crazy. I love it."

He kissed her then returned to the bedroom, and Riley lay down on her bed and giggled as she pulled up her covers and closed her eyes. *Ben included himself in the crazy crowd.*

CHAPTER ELEVEN

Riley woke and inhaled. *Coffee. Nice dream.* When she opened her eyes, Toby was staring at her face, and she hugged him then laughed when he licked her ear.

"Good morning, sunshine," Ben said from the kitchen. "How did you sleep?"

Riley sat up then pushed her hair out of her face. "Great. How about you?"

"Better than I have in a long time. It's very calming in the trees at the cabin, isn't it?"

Riley smiled as she pulled out clean clothes from her bag then padded to the bathroom. After she dressed and brushed her hair, she made her bed.

"Your coffee's ready. Put on your sweatshirt, and we can rough it outside with our coffee then warm up by the fire before breakfast."

"Sounds wonderful." Riley picked up her sweatshirt and moaned as she struggled to get her right arm inserted and the sleeve pulled up. Ben gently pulled the sweatshirt around her left shoulder then kissed her cheek and grinned as he carried their coffee outside.

While they sat on the front porch, Ben said, "I fed Toby and Princess. She really surprised me. Have you ever heard of an adult feral cat who decided to be a housecat? Sorry, wild, fierce, farm cat. That shows a level of intelligence and self-understanding that I wish some people had."

Riley smiled, sipped her coffee, and rocked.

Ben finished his coffee. "More?" he asked.

Riley drained her cup and handed it to him. "Yes, please."

Riley frowned when his sheriff's department radio tones sounded. Ben carried the two cups of coffee as he came outside.

"Did you hear the alert on my radio? It wasn't for me." Ben handed Riley her coffee. "I had turned up the volume last night, so I wouldn't miss anything, but after I heard Toby's low growl and your whisper, I should have realized that I don't have to worry about sleeping through a call."

"Where are Toby and Princess?" Riley asked.

"They went out back after I fed them. I suspect Princess is honing her hunting skills, and Toby's investigating the tree farm to see if anything has changed since the last time he was here."

"It makes me nervous to think of Princess running free in town, but I'm comfortable with her running wild on the farm. Is that strange?"

"Not really, but I'm not sure I could explain it; maybe there's more room here for her to escape any danger and there are fewer threats?"

A quail called, "Bob White."

"Hi, Bob," Riley and Ben said; Riley chuckled.

"Ready for breakfast?" Ben asked. "Bacon, eggs, and toast. One of us needs to learn how to make buttermilk biscuits. I looked at the premade biscuits in the grocery store, but I don't think they are for us."

"We are breakfast snobs; however, I make great cinnamon rolls. Could that be a substitute?"

"Definitely. Could you talk me through it until your arm heals? We can plan for cinnamon rolls next weekend if I'm off again."

"Good plan. How can I help with breakfast?"

"Set the table and tell me if I'm about to burn the bacon."

Riley smiled. "Deal."

While they ate, Ben's phone buzzed a text.

"I gotta go." Ben scowled at his phone then hurried to the bedroom and changed to the extra uniform he brought in case he was called to work.

On his way out the door, he said, "Leave the dishes. I'll take care of everything after I'm back."

* * *

As Ben started his truck, he glanced again at the text from the sheriff: "Meet me at the office in 30 min."

Just a drill?

Ben parked next to the empty deputy's cruiser then hurried into the building.

The sheriff stood with his arms crossed outside his office. "Follow me in your cruiser to Riley's house. We'll talk there."

Ben hurried to the cruiser to wait for the sheriff then followed him to Riley's. When they arrived, a neighbor stood in the front yard, and the sheriff climbed out of his car and shook hands with the man. When Ben joined them, the sheriff said, "Mr. Alvarez lives behind Riley's house. He heard something about five this morning and thought it was a trash truck."

"Thanks again for your help," the sheriff said, and Mr. Alvarez nodded before he headed down the sidewalk then turned at the end of the block to go home.

As the sheriff and Ben walked around the house to the back, the sheriff said, "Mr. Alvarez kept an eye on the house for me, so I could wait for you at the office. He found the back door broken in about forty-five minutes ago and called me on my cell."

When they reached the back, Ben glowered at the door. "Somebody used an ax to break in before they broke the hinges."

"That was exactly my thought too. Who would have known that you and Riley were going to the Malloy cabin?"

"The vet hospital office staff and any nearby neighbors who saw me loading my truck yesterday evening after I got off work. I'm sure it was obvious by what I loaded that we'd be gone at least overnight."

"I haven't been inside." The sheriff put on his leather gloves and nodded when Ben put on his gloves too.

Ben lifted the door out of the way, and the sheriff reached to flip the kitchen light switch.

"Electricity's off," Sheriff Dunn said as he entered the kitchen. "It's not dark in the house but watch your step. The kitchen's in shambles."

Ben stepped in next to the sheriff and scanned the damage: the empty refrigerator was on its side, and its contents were spilled on the floor; one cabinet door dangled by a hinge, and the rest of the splintered doors were strewn about the room. All the drawers were pulled out and their contents dumped onto the floor.

"Is this vandalism, or was someone searching for something?" Ben asked.

"Good question. If someone was searching for something, they either were in a rage or made it look like vandalism."

Ben's stomach tightened into knots as he went from room to room. The sofa, its cushions, and the soft rocker were slashed, the shower curtain was ripped; when he stopped at the bedroom, he immediately hurried outside for fresh air.

A few minutes later, the sheriff joined him on the porch. "It's rough, but her bedroom…" Sheriff Dunn's face was grim as he shook his head. "It was calculated to shock. This was a deliberate violation of Riley's sense of security and privacy."

Ben glowered. "Everything is violently slashed, ripped, or torn except her bed. How long did it take for him to slice the mattress into so many tiny pieces? It reminded me of a cruel decapitation. I need to check her closet." Ben shuddered.

"It's completely empty." Sheriff spoke in a quiet voice and put up his hand to stop Ben.

"He took all her clothes? What about…"

"Her chest of drawers is empty. He wanted to leave the message that she no longer exists."

"What do we do?" Ben asked.

"We turn this over to the GBI, and they'll secure the scene, then the forensic team will scour for clues. I'm more worried about Riley. This has all the earmarks of a warning of more to come."

"What do I do? Do I send Riley to Mom and Dad's?"

"Sounds good, but that would be worse, wouldn't it?"

Ben exhaled. "You're right; her support system is here, and Mom and Dad would be in danger too."

The sheriff pulled out his phone then paused. "Is there any reason your fingerprints would be in her room?"

Ben's eyes widened. "She insisted on sleeping on the sofa before she was abducted when I couldn't move into Mr. Richard's house; I slept in the bed until she was out of the hospital."

Ben frowned. "I kept my clothes in the bedroom in my duffel bag and took my duffel bag with all my clothes to the cabin." *Sounds suspicious even to me.*

The sheriff nodded. "You'll have to stay at the office until the GBI shows up. I'll go to the cabin to talk to Riley."

Ben's shoulders slumped as he headed to his cruiser.

* * *

As soon as Ben left, Riley cleared the table before she loaded the dishwasher and washed the frying pan by hand. Toby scratched at the back door, and she let him inside. After he drank his fill of water, he trotted to the back door.

"Give me a minute, and I'll go out with you. I wouldn't mind taking a short walk." Riley slipped on her boots and sweatshirt and grabbed her walking stick.

"I may not be able to go very far, but I need fresh air and some outside time."

The wind blew Riley's hair in her face as she picked her way along the lane while Toby raced through the trees then across the lane to the other side. Before she reached the driveway, a sudden gust of cold wind from the northwest blew her sweatshirt off her left shoulder, and she shivered.

"That's enough fresh air for me. It's cold out here. I need a poncho to stay warm until I'm not in a cast if I'm going to be outside very long." She turned back, and Toby trotted along beside her.

When they were inside, she said, "It's time for a fire and another pot of coffee." After she lit a small fire, she started the coffee before she set up her phone with internet for her computer, so she could search for a poncho.

When she found a poncho that she liked, she saved it. "I'll call Mary Ruth later to see if she has anything at the pawn shop."

Riley poked at the fire to help it burn out before she stretched out on the sofa with a book. She'd read only two chapters when Toby yipped.

"A car? I don't hear...yes, I do. Ben will complain that I did the dishes, won't he?" Riley giggled.

She hurried to the back door and raised her eyebrows at the sheriff's cruiser as it crept down the lane. After the sheriff parked, he climbed out of his car. "A doe was in the middle of the lane; she watched me until I was close to her then bounded into the trees. I was slowed down even more to watch for any young ones. Your new neighborhood watch?"

Riley smiled. "Something like that. Come on in; the wind is getting colder."

When the sheriff came inside, he scanned the room. "When I was younger, we'd come inside to warm up from a day of hunting before we went home. I've had a lot of hot chocolate sitting in front of that fireplace."

"How about some coffee? I just made a fresh pot."

"Sounds good; I'll pour." The sheriff strode to the stove while Riley set her cup and one for the sheriff on the table.

"Fireplace or table?" he asked after he poured the two cups full.

"Toby and I took a short walk, and I'm still chilled. The fire's almost out, but it's still warm; let's sit in the living room," Riley said.

Sheriff Dunn carried the two cups then handed Riley hers after she sat on the sofa. He shifted the soft chair closer to her before he sat.

"Riley, Ben's waiting at my office for the GBI. Somebody broke into your house early this morning and wrecked everything. I don't think it was vandalism because nothing is spray-pointed on the wall like we normally see. I think the intent was to intimidate you."

"Should I be intimidated?" she asked.

The sheriff shrugged. "You? Not hardly. Of course, anyone else would be." He frowned. "There's more: all of your clothes are gone."

Riley's eyes narrowed and her nostrils flared. "He stole all my work clothes? Who would do that?"

"Is that all that was at your house?" Sheriff gazed at her.

Riley sighed. "I tried to pack light, but I thought we might be here two nights, then I couldn't decide what to wear, so I brought everything that fit me. I didn't pack my uniforms, T-shirts, shorts, or worn-out shoes."

Sheriff glanced around the room as he drank his coffee then chuckled. "I assume Ben's not sleeping on that rollaway."

Riley snickered. "He lay down on it to see how comfortable it was."

The sheriff laughed. "I can just imagine. More coffee?" When Riley nodded, he refilled their cups.

"Is Ben going to be long?" Riley asked. "We were going to pick up my car this morning."

"He may be quite a while. Do you feel okay to drive? Are you taking any pain medication?"

"No pain medication since Friday morning, and I'll be fine to drive. If I get a little help straightening up, will I be able to stay at my house?"

"None of the furniture is salvageable, and I don't know how long the GBI will need to process the scene. You'll have to stay with friends in town."

"I can stay here. Claire Faraday will go to the doctor with me tomorrow, so Ben can go to work. I'll meet her there."

"I can't leave you here alone," the sheriff growled.

"Ben will be back tonight, won't he? I'll be fine."

When the sheriff frowned but didn't say anything, Riley glared at him. "Okay, if you don't want to tell me anything about Ben then let me know if he won't be back tonight, and I'll stay with Claire. I need my car because Toby and I have some shopping to do."

"Do you have enough food?"

Riley raised her eyebrows. "I have enough sandwich meat, bread, ice cream, bacon, and eggs to last for at least a week. Ben shops as efficiently as I pack."

The sheriff laughed. "You win; I'm ready when you are."

"Will Ben be home for lunch, or should I take him a sandwich?"

The sheriff looked away, then he met her gaze with pain in his eyes. "I don't think he'll be able to make it for lunch, but if you make him a sandwich, I'll take it to him. I'm going to the office after I drop you off. Do you have your car keys?"

"I'm not sure where they are; Ben might have them, but I keep a spare set in my backpack."

While Riley packed the lunch for Ben, she asked, "Do you know what time Mary Ruth opens the pawn shop on Sunday? I need a poncho."

"It is getting right nippy out there. Mary Ruth is usually there right after church lets out."

"That's great. Will I be able to go see the damage in the house?"

"Not until GBI has completed their investigation. Might be a few days. I'd plan on at least a week until we know more."

"Do you think this is related to the two men who were shot near Little River earlier this week? Eli Reeves told me he was in charge of the murder investigation."

The sheriff narrowed his eyes. "When was that?"

"I saw Eli on Friday evening. I was at the pawn shop getting some shirts and new boots, and we spoke briefly."

"Ben know about this?" Sheriff asked.

"Ben was in the shop but didn't hear the conversation. I told him about it later."

"Good. Ben and I will check on that because I hadn't heard anything. I didn't know Agent Reeves was in town, but if he's supposed to be working the Little River investigation, he was pretty far afield."

Riley shrugged and finished packing the lunch. "He said the two men were shot on Wednesday, but he was pretty vague about what he was doing here."

The sheriff nodded. "Eli's always been tight-mouthed about his business. I'm surprised he told you he was in charge of the investigation."

"I'm ready." Riley picked up her backpack and sweatshirt.

Toby trotted to the back door and yipped, and the sheriff picked up Ben's lunch and smiled. "You're welcome to ride along. I'd feel better if you were with Riley too."

When they reached the outskirts of town, Riley said, "There's something you aren't telling me."

"You're probably right," the sheriff said. "Am I forgiven?"

Riley narrowed her eyes. "It depends on how mad I am when I find out what it is."

Sheriff Dunn nodded. "That's a fair statement."

"It has to do with Ben, doesn't it?"

The sheriff side-glanced at her as he parked at the animal hospital next to her car. "You're just like your grandmother. We could never get away with anything around her. I'll wait to make sure your car starts before I leave."

Riley glared as the sheriff opened the back door for Toby; she seethed and climbed out of the cruiser with her backpack and walking stick then slammed the door as hard as she could.

She unlocked her car and opened the door for Toby. When Riley turned the key, the engine immediately started, and the sheriff drove away.

"I was going to call Claire, but I'm too angry at the sheriff. I certainly don't want to dump anything on her. Let's see if we can cruise by my house, then we'll go to the pawn shop."

Toby growled, and Riley exhaled a long sigh. "Fine. We'll skip the house and go to the pawn shop."

She put her car into reverse then lightly pressed the accelerator while she backed up before she changed gears then drove to the road. "So far, so good, Toby."

When Riley reached the pawn shop, other customers were already parked near the door. "Just as well," she said. "I'd rather park where it won't be so tight getting out."

Before she turned off the engine, her phone rang, but she didn't recognize the number. She shrugged and answered.

"Oh, good. You answered. I was afraid you might not. This is Luanne, Marcy's cousin. Did you hear about Marcy? I'm sure you did. We're all devastated. So, I've called all of Marcy's friends, and no one has my cat. Marcy was taking care of him for me while I was out of town, and I rushed back as soon as I heard, but I can't find him or his carrier anywhere. Somebody said Marcy probably asked you to take care of him for her. Could you bring him to Pomeroy? I know you understand how important cats are to their owners, or do you want me to come get him? You do have his carrier, don't you? He doesn't like to travel in anything else. I thought you might want to see some of your old friends from work. Everybody asked about you."

Him?

"The white cat, right?" Riley asked.

"Yes, exactly. You have him, don't you?"

"No, but Marcy mentioned him one time. What was his name, again?"

Luanne giggled. "I called him 'Cat,' not very original was it?"

Riley rolled her eyes. "That's so cute. Well, I'm sure somebody has him."

"Well, it must be you because nobody else does."

"Sorry, I don't. Did you check with the shelter or that agency that rescues cats? Marcy might have been a volunteer there. She had a big heart."

"I want my cat," Luanne hissed.

"I'm so sorry for your loss. Please convey my condolences to all the family; I'm sure everyone is as shocked as you must be. Marcy was a wonderful, caring person."

Luanne hung up on her.

"That was a bizarre call, but Princess is definitely not the cat that Marcy's cousin is looking for," Riley said.

She and Toby strolled inside, and Mary Ruth waved while she waited on a customer at the gun counter. Riley dropped her backpack and slid her walking stick into a cart then pushed it to the women's clothing section; Toby stayed close to her.

"What on earth are you doing here?" Pia stopped her cart with two fifty-pound bags of dog food next to Riley.

"Mary Ruth has dog food?" Riley's eyes widened.

Pia laughed. "She always bought Jordy's dogfood for Doc Witmer because he couldn't find it anywhere in town. She heard Jordy was with us, so she ordered his special dogfood and called me."

Riley giggled. "That sounds like Mary Ruth. I'm here because I need a warm poncho."

Pia peered at Riley's face. "You are really rocking that tough, 'I got the last beer' look. Are you sure your arm is all that's broken? Don't tell Doc Julie Rae I said that about the beer. We're supposed to be supportive. If you decide to go after those guys, take me with you."

Riley giggled. "I've missed your personal touch of caring and backup."

"When are they going to replace that splint with a cast?"

"Maybe tomorrow. I can't even maneuver my sweatshirt, and I'm not so fond of being cold lately."

"I guess not. When are you coming back to work? Tuesday?"

"That's my plan, but I'm not telling the doctor. She's a wet blanket."

"Oh, maybe surgery, right? Plates and screws?"

"That's what I'm afraid of." Riley furrowed her brow, and the corners of her mouth drooped.

"It's normally outpatient. Claire's going to the doctor with you tomorrow, right? One of us will take off for your surgery or whenever you need us. Doc Julie Rae's already approved it, and Zach can handle the load. We should have known he'd be good; Amanda wouldn't have recommended him if he was a dud. So, let's find you that poncho."

Pia held up a poncho. "What about this red and gray plaid one? It looks like a horse blanket. Try it on." Pia dropped it over Riley's head, and the poncho covered her knees.

Pia laughed. "It'll keep your legs warm."

"You're right about the horse blanket. I love it."

"You just don't want to shop, do you? Here's one that might fit better. The tan and cream plaid will look good on you too." Pia helped Riley remove the first poncho and held the tan one while Riley slipped it on.

"This is much better," Pia said. "You have a hood to keep the wind from chilling the back of your neck. The poncho comes to your knees but not past them like the other one." Pia pulled the hood up over Riley's head. "Oh, look. There are flaps with snaps on the hood." Pia snapped the hood.

"The snaps will keep the wind from blowing off my hood. Nice," Riley said.

"I think so too. I'm going to see if they have any more like this in a little bigger size for me. Ms. Mary Ruth has an awesome eye for what people need, doesn't she?"

"She certainly does," Riley said as Pia helped her take off the poncho. "Thank you. Running into you made my day. I've missed you."

"You too, chica."

Riley and Toby headed toward the checkout while Pia searched for a poncho for herself.

Mary Ruth met Riley and led her to the gun counter. "I'll check you out here. I should have thought about a warm poncho for you when you were in here on Friday. I got them in early last week, and I'm very pleased with the quality. Your poncho will really make a difference with the cold and the wicked wind, won't it?"

"Sure will. Will you take the tag off for me? I'd like to wear it."

After Riley and Toby stepped outside, Riley pulled up her hood. "This is awesome."

She checked her phone and sighed. *Nothing from Ben.* She pushed back the hood and cleared her arm from the poncho to drive.

Her phone rang, and she furrowed her brow. *Why is the sheriff calling me?*

"Are you still in town?" he asked.

"Yes, I'm at the pawn shop, but I'm ready to go to the cabin now. Why?"

"Stop by my office, so we can chat."

Riley bit her lip after she hung up. "The sheriff wants to talk to us at his office."

Toby whined, and Riley nodded. "I agree. Not a social call at all."

When Riley and Toby reached the county building parking lot, the sheriff was waiting for them near a side door. He motioned toward the side parking lot, and she drove around the main lot to park near the side door.

After they were inside, Riley and Toby followed the sheriff down a long hallway of dark offices to his office. He unlocked the door, and Riley's eyes widened at the homey fragrance of sandalwood as she scanned the bright room. Framed awards, the sheriff's college diploma, and law enforcement certificates adorned the walls. A large, framed picture of an old west sheriff with a gray moustache and a scruffy beard, who wore a beat-up cowboy hat and a tarnished silver star on his dusty vest, was the most impressive of all the wall hangings. The weather-beaten sheriff sat on an old paint horse with his back straight and his head high as he gazed at the sunset on a desert horizon. Riley placed her fingers across her mouth to hide her smile. *I'll bet that's how the sheriff sees himself.*

The sheriff pointed to a small, round table. "Let's sit there."

Toby trotted to the table then waited for Riley to sit.

The table was next to the tinted glass window that overlooked grass, trees, and a creek. The sheriff smiled. "The sun gets a little intense in the afternoon, but it's worth it for the relaxing view. The

GBI needs your statement of your abduction, what you recall before and after Ben and Toby found you, and the most recent events at your house. It's best for GBI to talk to you now, while the details are fresh in your mind. Marc's here at my request."

Riley selected a seat that would give her a view of the creek and the sheriff's door. While Toby flopped close to her on the floor under the window, she glared at the sheriff. "And Ben?"

"We'll talk more after Marc's asked his questions." The sheriff met her gaze. "You'll have to trust me."

Riley nodded. *It's about Ben.*

"I'll get Marc then be right back." The sheriff rose then paused before he opened the door. "I'm going to sit in. Is that okay with you?"

Riley peered at him. "I'd rather you did."

Sheriff Dunn nodded. "If you're too tired to continue, just tell me, and Marc will leave."

When Marc came alone into the room, he closed the door behind him and smiled. "Hey, Riley. I'm glad to see you are okay. I have a few questions, and the sheriff will sit in. Is that okay with you?"

She nodded. "I'd like for the sheriff to be here."

Marc nodded then opened the door. "Okay, Sheriff."

The sheriff sat on Riley's right, and Marc sat across from her.

"Let's start with the abduction. Tell me what you remember; I might interrupt with questions." Marc smiled. "Consider this my apology in advance."

Riley returned his smile. *This is still an official investigation even though it feels like friends sitting around the table and chatting. Marc's good.*

She told him what she had told the sheriff about her abduction.

"Can you describe either one?"

"Not all that well. One was really big and beefy, and he had a bulbous nose. The other man was tall, but not as bulky. He was the driver. The beefy guy smoked and was a complainer."

"That's interesting. What did he complain about?"

"His nose, his knees, and the driver wouldn't let him smoke in the car."

"What was wrong with his nose and knees?"

"It sounded like I broke it when I punched him, and he was the one who pulled me out from under the car. As soon as I could, I bent my knees then kicked him as hard as I could. I must have connected with his knees."

"I thought your left knee was injured," Marc said.

"The beefy guy twisted it when he pulled, and I guess I added to it when I kicked him. I was almost up when the other man kicked me in the stomach then hit me again, but I don't remember anything else until I woke up later in the car."

"Who broke your arm?" Marc asked.

"The tall guy. He had a club. I instinctively raised my arm to protect my head."

Marc shook his head. "What was your impression? Was this a random attack?"

"Not at all." She told him what she heard on the drive and before they flung her into the river.

Marc interrupted before she continued. "Just for clarification, the driver said the boss told him you wouldn't be breathing long. What was your interpretation of that?"

"The goal was for me to be dead, but there was no explanation why. I don't think the driver knew or cared, and smoker man wouldn't have asked."

Riley explained how she made it to the bank and into the shack then collapsed.

"Can we take a break?" the sheriff asked. "Would you like to visit the women's restroom, Riley?"

Riley opened her mouth to decline then nodded when the sheriff raised an eyebrow.

"I'll show you the way, then I'll take Toby outside for his break," he said.

After they turned a corner, the sheriff asked quietly, "What are we missing?"

"Marcy. Everything happened after Marcy left Princess," she said.

Sheriff slowly nodded. "That was on Monday; Marcy Nichols died later that night. You were attacked early Wednesday morning."

"Eli Reeves told me two men were shot on Wednesday near Little River, and I got a strange call earlier this morning." Riley told him about cousin Luanne's call.

"Dang. Toby and I will be back in a few minutes. You can decide what you want to tell Agent Marc, but you and I will talk more later. First, we want to make sure any investigation of Ben Carter is completed."

Thought so. Riley went into the ladies' room and stared at her face in the mirror then laughed. *I got the last beer.*

When they returned to the sheriff's office, Marc smiled. "I found a vending machine. Three waters and six different kinds of candy. You pick first, Riley."

Good technique, Marc, but no way am I going to confess.

She picked the chocolate and peanut butter candy, and Marc grinned. "I bought two of those. Good guess on my part. It's my favorite too."

He picked up the second bar, unwrapped it, and took a bite; the sheriff rolled his eyes as he unwrapped Riley's candy then opened her water.

I sure hope Marc doesn't have a peanut allergy.

"Where were we?" Marc asked after he took a long drink of his water.

You've got the notes, Marc.

"You were plying me with chocolate and peanut butter, so I'd confess." Riley grinned, and the sheriff chuckled.

Marc laughed. "I should have known you were too wily to fall for such an obvious trick."

"Back to the boring part," Riley said. "I collapsed in the shed. When I woke up it was light outside, and the rain had stopped." She told him about the men returning to look for her body.

"They didn't stay long or look very well. I got the impression they were in a hurry and even afraid of their boss. They must have been certain I was dead or close to death because they didn't bother to search me. They tossed me into the water with my cell phone in my pocket and my pistol in its holster."

Marc's eyes widened. "You had your phone and your pistol?"

Riley's face reddened, and she stared at her hands on the table. "I didn't realize it until after I took off my jeans to try to dry them."

"I'm so sorry. I didn't mean to sound judgmental at all," Marc said. "I'm just as surprised as you must have been when you found them."

"I tried to send Ben a text, and at first I thought it might go through, but it didn't."

Marc nodded. "Sheriff, I've reviewed the records from the cell phone company and added them to my notes. Riley, it appeared that your message hit the tower then failed to retain the connection long enough for it to be sent. The technical folks found that one signal to the tower."

"Sure gave us a lot of hope." The sheriff smiled.

"After my clothes dried, I started making plans for a little security for the night," Riley said. "I was asleep, then when Toby barked, I woke and saw headlights. Toby and Ben found me."

Marc shook his head. "According to the technical reports, they found you so quickly because you tried to send a text. Not for my report, but for me, if you don't mind. What did the text say?"

"I'm alive."

"That's exactly the text I would have hoped to receive too, if I were Ben or you, Sheriff." Marc exhaled. "Let's move to yesterday. Tell me why you weren't home."

"The doctor said I couldn't go to work until I saw her on Monday. I was tired of being an invalid and wanted to go to my grandma's cabin where it was more relaxing. Ben was off today, except for being on call, so we packed yesterday after he got off work and stopped at the grocery store before we went to the cabin."

"What did you pack?" Marc asked.

"Only what I thought I might need," Riley said.

Marc frowned. "I might have asked the wrong question. What did you leave at home?"

"My work clothes, old T-shirts, and maybe some worn-out shoes in the back of my closet somewhere that I should really throw away. I packed everything else that I could wear with my sling, so I'd have choices."

"Right question, Marc," the sheriff said.

Marc rolled his eyes. "What did you do at the cabin?"

"We took a short walk, had hamburgers, and read before we went to bed. Ben slept in the bedroom because he's tall, and I slept on a rollaway bed in the living room."

"Did you take any pain medicine or sleeping pills before bed?" Marc asked.

"No, I don't have any reason to take either type of medication. I don't have any pain with my arm because it's splinted, and my knee has improved with rest."

"Could Ben have left while you were sleeping?"

"No, because I'm a fairly light sleeper, but if I didn't wake up when he left, either Toby or Princess would have told me."

"Who's Princess?" Marc asked.

"My cat."

"What do you think, Sheriff?" Marc asked.

"You were thorough."

"Thanks." Marc looked over his notes. "Thank you, Riley. I appreciate your help."

"I'll walk you to the door and lock it behind you. Riley and I are parked in back."

Marc rose, and the two men left.

"Do you think Princess will be irritated that we left her alone for so long, Toby?"

Toby yipped, and Riley laughed.

The office door opened, and Ben asked. "What's so funny?"

Riley squealed, "Ben!" While she pushed back from the table, he strode to her and grabbed her into his arms.

CHAPTER TWELVE

The sheriff walked into his office and cleared his throat. "Riley, tell us about your Marcy theory and Marcy's cousin, then y'all can finish your weekend vacation."

Ben sat next to Riley with his arm around her as she spoke.

"Everything happened after Marcy left Princess at my house on Monday," she said. "Marcy was murdered in Pomeroy Monday night, then I was attacked early Wednesday morning. After my attackers came to the shack on their assignment to see if they could find any sign of my body, they drove away, and I thought I heard two cracks. I couldn't tell if the cracks were gunfire because I was exhausted, wet, and cold. It could have been a hallucination, but on Friday, Eli Reeves told me two men were shot on Wednesday near Little River, and I got a strange call earlier this morning." Riley told them about cousin Luanne's call.

"So, Luanne didn't know anything about this cat that was supposedly hers, but she was definitely interested in the carrier," Ben said.

"Thank you; you two can go on. I'll meet you at the cabin later. I want to ask Marc about the shooting at Little River," the sheriff said.

Riley and Ben headed to the door.

"I'll follow you, Riley," Ben said.

After Riley and Ben parked at the cabin, Toby bounded into the tall grass and flushed a quail who pretended to be in distress. Toby ran to the shed then raced around the yard before he dashed to the front door and yipped.

"We actually were not gone all that long, Toby, but I'm glad everything is okay," Riley said.

"Where's Princess?" Ben asked.

Princess pranced from behind the shed, head-bumped Ben's leg, and purred.

"I missed you too, Princess," Ben said.

When they were inside, Ben picked up the carrier, and Princess hissed.

"We need to check it," Riley said. "You can pick one out yourself at the farm store if Ben tears it up."

Princess flicked her tail and leapt onto the sofa while Ben placed the carrier on the dining table.

Riley joined Ben at the table. "Okay. You have permission to dismantle the carrier."

Ben pulled out his pocket knife to remove the cover from the bottom cushion, but after he examined the seam, he said, "Well, I'll be dogged. The cover has a hidden zipper, which actually makes sense." He pulled his exam gloves out of the small case on his utility belt.

When he peered inside, he said, "There seem to be two parts: a sealed bag with beads or something in it like a beanbag-type cushion and a foam one. I think the cushioning comes out, so we can get a better look."

After he carefully removed the beanbag cushion, he said, "This may have been added later. I would have expected more room inside the cover."

Princess hissed, and Toby barked when Ben pulled out the sealed bag.

"What's wrong with you?" Ben asked over the din.

Riley raised her eyebrows. "They want you to put the cushion back."

Ben shrugged, but after he shoved it back inside the cover, Toby and Princess settled down.

"The beanbag must have been added for additional comfort, but the spongy, open cell foam would have been more than enough. If the carrier is as new as it looks, Marcy would have added it, but only if she was the type to be worried about the comfort of the occupant."

Ben glanced at the glowering Princess. "Do you disagree?"

Princess meowed.

"Princess said you need to leave the cushion alone," Riley said, and Princess closed her eyes and relaxed.

Ben removed his gloves and threw them into the trash. "Somebody is b-o-s-s-i-e-r than you are."

Princess opened her eyes and hissed, and Riley said, "I am not."

When Ben snorted, Riley grabbed her poncho and stormed to the back door with Toby and Princess on her heels. Riley slammed the door then shivered when a gust of cold wind blasted her from the northwest; she slipped on her poncho and pulled up the hood.

Riley headed down the lane, and Toby dashed past her to lead the way.

"What are we missing?" she asked; Princess diverted away from the lane and crouched before she crept into the trees and disappeared.

"So, Princess doesn't have any idea at all, does she?" Riley and Toby continued down the lane before they turned back half-way to the driveway.

As they neared the cabin, she stopped and gazed at the blue sky and the high, wispy clouds. "We're looking at it all wrong."

Riley quickened her pace. "My knee likes the bit of stretch." She slowed as she neared the cabin. "And that's enough for now."

When Riley and Toby went into the cabin, she bit her lip to hold back the tears. *Ben started a fire. He knew I'd be cold.*

Ben glanced at her. "Am I in trouble?"

"Not at all; thank you for the fire. I guess I needed to walk off some stress and clear my head. It seems to me that we've been overthinking. We need to think like Marcy: impulsive and more self-centered."

Ben nodded. "Tell me more about Marcy."

When Riley sat on the sofa to be closer to the fire, Ben joined her.

"Marcy was social. She talked about going back to school, and we were going to take classes together, but evening and online classes interfered with her social life. She liked to be the center of attention and the first to know anything, no matter how trivial, so she could tell her friends and impress them. She didn't like to spend her own money; she brought her lunch to work and ate lunch with me nearly every day for three years. She had no qualms about gossiping if it increased her social standing."

Ben frowned. "So whatever she had or knew would have somehow increased her social standing?"

"Maybe," Riley said. "Or maybe her motive was money, so that she could impress her friends." Riley frowned. "This is a long shot, but we had access to the inventory records and invoices at Truman Clinic, so we could check the inventory. I wonder if she found something."

"Wouldn't GBI have seized all those records?"

Riley shrugged. "Marcy and I had access to the scanned, electronic invoices, but is that getting too complex for Marcy to have downloaded a copy of the invoices?"

"Maybe not if her motive was money, but to follow the Marcy path, wouldn't she have told her friends?" Ben asked.

"Yes, absolutely, but I never knew any of their names." Riley frowned.

"What about her cousin?" Ben asked.

"Marcy mentioned her only once, maybe twice, in the entire time I knew her. I got the impression there wasn't much that Luanne could bring to the table, as far as Marcy was concerned."

When Toby yipped, Riley heard the car on the lane. "The sheriff's here," she said.

"Do we drag him down the Marcy rabbit hole?" Ben asked.

Riley giggled. "Up to you, but it is kind of entertaining even though we don't have much, except there are no notes or hints in the carrier. Do you think he should take the carrier, so the GBI can examine it?"

Before the sheriff reached the door, Riley's eyes widened, and she palm-smacked her forehead "I totally forgot."

"What's that?" Ben asked.

"The last time I talked to Marcy, she was moving to Atlanta because her mother found her a fancy job at a pet boutique clinic. Her new job that she had in Pomeroy replaced her immediately. What was she doing in Pomeroy?"

"Now, that's sheriff-worthy," Ben said as the sheriff tapped on the back door.

The sheriff strode into the cabin when Ben opened the door and asked, "So what did you find in the carrier?"

Ben sighed, and Riley said, "We hoped there would be a note or papers, but we didn't find any. Ben even unzipped the cushion cover and examined the inside, and other than a beanbag-type cushion and a foam cushion, there wasn't anything."

"I guess that would have been too easy. Do you have any coffee? I think the wind picked up."

"I'll make a fresh pot," Ben said. "Should I make a small pot or large, Riley?"

"Make a full pot. I'm cold."

The sheriff nodded. "Sometimes it takes a while to feel warm again after being wet and cold for an extended time."

Riley bit her lip. "It may take me a while to get over being terrified that I might be that cold again, but I wasn't afraid about being alone because Bob White kept me company."

Sheriff smiled. "You do make friends wherever you go."

Riley's smile was weak. "He kept me going."

After the coffee was ready, Ben poured three cups, and Sheriff carried a cup to Riley then sat next to her.

"I have seniority," he whispered. "I get to sit wherever I like."

Riley giggled. "Dad always told me what a good friend you were."

Sheriff sipped his coffee. "He was a good man. The best I knew."

The sheriff shifted to the soft chair and winked at Riley when Ben carried his cup from the kitchen to sit next to Riley.

Riley breathed in the hot vapor while she sipped her coffee. "Sheriff, I just remembered that the last time I talked to Marcy, she told me that her mother, who lives in Atlanta, found her a job at a boutique-type of clinic. Marcy had just started a new job in Pomeroy, but they replaced her immediately, so what was she doing in Pomeroy when she was killed?"

"When did she leave for Atlanta?"

Riley furrowed her brow. "When I moved from the cabin to town."

"It's not like she was in the middle of moving." Sheriff tapped his finger on his coffee mug then grinned. "Marc told me the news media reported yesterday that two men were shot at Little River on Wednesday. Marc claimed that was all he knew, but when I told him Eli Reeves was in Barton on Friday, and Reeves told you that he was in charge of the Little River investigation, he was surprised. I need to ask Marc about the investigation into Marcy Nichols' murder. All the media reports assume she was a Pomeroy resident. If that's the focus the investigation has, this will blow his mind."

The sheriff rose and carried his cup to the sink. "Thanks for the coffee. Keep me posted. Ben, you've maxed out your on-call hours. See you in the morning."

When the sheriff opened the back door, Princess dashed inside and raced to the soft chair and hissed.

Riley stared at her. "Sheriff, maybe it would be a good idea for you to take the carrier and give it to Marc, so the GBI team can examine it."

Ben handed the carrier to the sheriff then closed the door after the sheriff left.

"There must be something about the carrier that we couldn't find. Did Princess tell you to give it to the sheriff?" Ben asked.

"I'm not sure if there's something there or if she just didn't want the reminder of Marcy," Riley said.

Ben peered at Princess while she licked her paws and smoothed her fur. "What do you think about sitting on the front porch for a bit? It's okay if you want to stay by the fire."

"I wouldn't mind the fresh air at all."

Riley slipped on her poncho, and Ben asked as they headed to the front door, "Anybody else?"

Toby trotted to join them, and Princess closed her eyes.

While they rocked, Ben asked, "How many people know how to get to the cabin? Does Eli Reeves know where it is?"

"There's a sign near the gate that says Malloy Tree Farm, but it's faded so badly that it's almost impossible to make out the letters. I don't think there are a lot of people still around who know how to get here. Aunt Millie talked about it being a vacation rental, but I don't know how often she rented it out. Eli Reeves knew I was staying at my grandmother's cabin, but as far as I know, he doesn't know where it is unless he's checked the assessor's records."

Ben frowned. "Even with the assessor's information, it would still be a little difficult to find. There's no mailbox, and there are a hundred gates on country roads around here that look just like the one at your driveway; most of them access hunting property. I might be able to take the sign down. I'll put it in the shed."

"That's fine. It's a wonderful sign; maybe I could clean it up and put it on the front of the cabin or even over the fireplace."

"I'll see what I can do about the sign after you're ready to go inside," Ben said. "Speaking of hunting, I took your pistol to a gunsmith to clean and make sure it's safe to use; I'll pick it up tomorrow."

"That's awesome. I'll feel a lot better with my pistol. Do you suppose we could find me some waterproof matches?"

Ben smiled. "I'll make it a priority."

"I'm ready to go inside before it gets any colder."

"I'll bring some wood from the shed to the porch before I hunt for the tree farm sign."

While Ben and Toby went to get firewood, Riley went inside and stoked the fire then put on the last log.

When Ben opened the front door, he wore the leather tool belt that he'd found in the shed. "I've stacked some wood on the porch; I'll bring it in later. I've got my cell phone if you need me."

Riley pointed to her phone, and he closed the door.

* * *

Ben and Toby trotted down the lane then turned onto the long driveway toward the road. "Feels good to get in a run, but I feel like I'm back in rookie school with all this extra weight on my second belt."

Ben tromped through the brush and weeds to the faded wooden sign near the driveway; two sturdy four-by-four posts supported the heavy weight of the four-foot-wide, three-foot-tall sign. "It would be a shame to take this down, Toby. Let's do something else."

Ben walked to the road and stared at the sign. "All it needs is something in front of it, like a small tree. Let's go back and get the chain saw."

As they trotted back to the cabin, Ben said, "I didn't realize how sturdy and big that sign is. I would have had to put it in the back of the truck to take it to the cabin."

Ben carried an armload of firewood into the cabin. "I didn't realize how big the sign is, so Toby and I decided to leave it where it is and cut down a large branch to lean against it. It won't take much to hide it from the road. I'm taking my truck down."

"I think I'd like to go along. If I get cold, I'll wait in the truck."

"I'd like that," Ben said. "Are you going, Toby?"

Toby flopped down near the fireplace, and Princess leapt off the soft chair and landed next to him as Ben and Riley left by the back door.

Ben helped Riley into his truck then hurried to the shed and picked up the chainsaw. After he jumped into the driver's seat, he said, "You might want to just sit in the truck. The wind's picking up."

"I'll be brave for a few minutes." Riley smiled.

* * *

Ben parked his truck in a stand of trees off to one side of the driveway. "You'll have shelter here if you decide to stay outside but be out of the wind."

"Thanks," Riley said as Ben helped her out of the truck.

While Ben traipsed through the trees to look for a low branch, Riley stood with her back to the wind. *Love my poncho.* A nearby mourning dove called its sad song of longing.

"You need Bob White to cheer you up," Riley said. "It worked for me."

Riley tried to whistle Bob White's call, but the air was cold, and her whistle was too breathy. When Ben started up the chainsaw, she raised her eyebrows. "He hiked all the way up to the lane to find the branch he wanted."

She furrowed her brow at the distant sound of a car on the road. She stepped behind the truck and peered at the road. When the slow-moving car that was headed toward town continued past the driveway, she frowned. "What is Doc Preston doing out here?"

Riley waited, listened, and watched the road, but no cars passed the driveway in either direction. She walked to the middle of the driveway for a better view of the road as she continued to watch and listen.

"Found it," Ben called out; when she turned her head, he waved, and she returned his wave as he dragged a large, leafy branch down the driveway.

"That's huge," she said when Ben was close, and he beamed.

He stopped when he reached Riley. "I need a short break."

Ben put his arm around her, and they stood behind the truck and out of the wind.

"The gusts are getting fierce," Ben said. "Do you want to wait in the truck while I lean the branch against the sign?"

"I'll be okay. I want to see what it looks like."

Ben hurried to the branch then dragged it to the sign. Before he began lifting, Riley said, "Wait a minute. Come look."

Ben joined her at the driveway. "Well, I'll be darned. The branches reach up to the top of the sign, and the leaves obscure the sign."

Riley smiled. "I think that's what they call good enough for now."

"Let's get warm," Ben said.

On their short drive back to the cabin, Riley said, "I saw Doc Preston Ansell drive by. He was headed toward town and drove very slowly. I'll ask Claire tomorrow if he has a meeting or something with Doc Julie Rae."

"That could be, but what is he doing way out here? Did he see you?"

"No, when I heard a car coming, I stepped behind the truck."

When he parked, Ben said, "I need to think, but first, let's get you in front of a fire while I grill our hamburgers."

Riley sat on the sofa with Princess snuggled next to her, and Toby at her feet while Ben added a log to the fire. Riley watched the log smolder until a tiny flame appeared.

"I need to call Claire to let her know the change in plans," she said.

Riley smiled at the cheerful sound of Claire's voice.

"Pia told me about seeing you at the pawn shop," she said. "A warm poncho sounds perfect for our weather. So, what's up?"

"Ben and I picked up my car, so you don't have to give me a ride to the doctor's office tomorrow, after all."

"Up to you, but we've got it all arranged at the office, and Doc Julie Rae approved it. She and her family are home. Doc and Charlie are exhausted, the boys and Chuck are excited to be together, Amanda's still doing fine, Zach might have a new girlfriend, Pia and Jackson have started running, and I'm bored. Oh, Doc Julie Rae said Doc Preston's going to come to the office tomorrow, so they can talk. How are you feeling?"

"I think I'm right there with you on the bored thing. At least it's relaxing at the cabin, and Ben brought up more firewood, so I won't starve or freeze."

"I heard the vandal stole your clothes. What are you going to do?"

"The thief got mostly my work clothes. Maybe I can find a couple of scrub tops after my doctor appointment."

"See? That's a reason for me to meet you at the doctor's office. I'll research to see who might have scrubs that would work for you, so you won't be worn out by going from store to store. How are Toby and Princess?"

"They love the cabin. I think Ben, Toby, and Princess would prefer to stay here if it ever came up for a vote."

After they hung up, Ben asked, "How's everything?"

Riley caught him up on the animal hospital news.

"I'll talk to the sheriff tomorrow morning about Preston Ansell," Ben said. "Supper will be ready after I grill the burgers. Would you like cheese and jalapenos on yours?"

"Sounds good."

Ben started the grill then came back inside to feed Toby and Princess.

When Riley sat at the table, Ben set her plate in front of her. "Thank you for cutting my cheeseburger into quarters. It'll be easier for me to eat it one-handed."

Ben smiled. "I thought it might."

After they ate, Ben asked. "Dessert now or later?"

"Now, so I won't miss it if I fall asleep."

While Ben started the dishwasher after dessert, Riley moved to the sofa; Ben picked up their books then joined her.

Riley woke when Ben brushed back her hair and kissed her cheek. "I hate to wake you up to tell you to go to bed, but Toby and I have been out, and I'm ready for bed."

Riley rose and went to the bathroom to change then dropped onto her bed. "Goodnight, Ben."

* * *

Riley woke when the aroma of coffee tickled her nose. She opened her eyes, and Ben smiled. "I debated about waking you for breakfast. I'm glad you woke up. Toby and Princess have been fed, and I was about to cook some eggs."

She padded to the bathroom and dressed then made her bed before she hurried to the table as Ben poured her coffee.

"How did you sleep?" Riley asked before she sipped her coffee. "Mmm. You make the best coffee in the world."

"Best sleep I've had in a while, and thank you," he said. "What about you?"

"Same." After she drained her cup, Ben refilled it.

"Text me when you leave, when you get to town, and after you see the doctor." Ben placed her breakfast in front of her.

Riley smirked. "Who's b-o-s-s-y now?"

Ben chuckled. "You're awfully sharp for someone who just woke up."

After they ate, Ben quickly loaded the dishwasher then hurried to change to his uniform shirt. He kissed her then rushed to the back door.

"Text me every fifteen minutes." He laughed as he left.

"Dang," Riley said. "He caught me off guard and got the last word."

Toby grinned, and Princess yawned.

"Let's go for a short walk, Toby. I have a little nervous energy I need to burn off."

When they returned, Riley poured a cup of coffee and carried it to the sofa then relaxed with her book. After she read the last page, she checked her phone.

"Perfect. I finished my book, and it isn't too early to leave to meet Claire."

She sent Ben a text: "Leaving cabin."

When she and Toby headed out the back door, Princess sauntered out with them.

"We'll be gone until this afternoon sometime, Princess. Is that okay with you?" Riley asked.

Princess strolled to the shed then disappeared.

"Let's go, Toby."

As she drove to town, Riley raised her eyebrows when they passed the white house with the red barn near the tree farm. "Did you see the For Sale sign, Toby? I didn't notice it before, but it's not placed to be seen easily by drivers coming from the other direction. Maybe I missed it. That's interesting. Now, I wonder if that's what Doc Preston was doing."

When she turned at the doctor's parking lot, she smiled. "Claire's already here, Toby."

Claire waited on the sidewalk while Riley parked then approached the driver's side, and Riley lowered her window.

"We're half an hour early. Do you want to go in or wait a few minutes?" Claire asked.

"Climb in with us. We can wait in the car for twenty minutes. It's better than sitting in a waiting room."

"If they're stuffy about Toby, we'll go to the park around the corner." Claire opened the passenger's door and climbed in.

"That's a great idea, and a lot more interesting for Toby. I don't plan to come here often enough to be all chummy anyway," Riley said.

Claire snickered. "I can't imagine you not being chummy. That would almost be worth going in to watch. Toby, what do you want to do?"

Toby yipped, and Riley said, "He likes the idea of the park."

Claire nodded. "I'd take the park over sitting in a doctor's waiting room anytime too. I have more Doctor Ansell news. Thad ran into a brick wall in his search to find anyone at UGA who remembers Preston Ansell. In fact, Thad got a call from someone at GBI telling him that he needed to stop asking questions. Thad was suspicious, so he called the regional office, and they were very terse but confirmed the call he received was legitimate. Tell me that's not bizarre."

"What do you and Thad think? Witness Protection or something like that?"

"Could be, but there's more. Thad checked, and Preston Ansell is licensed to practice as a veterinarian in Georgia," Claire said.

"That's a total disconnect, isn't it?" Riley frowned.

"I couldn't let Thad outdo me, so I researched Evy Ansell but found nothing. I tried Evelyn and initials, but still couldn't find any historical fiction or any other published novels. So, maybe she's unpublished, published in magazines or journals, writes under a pen name, or is a phantom just like her husband."

"She probably uses a pen name, but I really like your phantom idea," Riley giggled.

"Thank you." Claire pushed her hair behind her ear. "It would be a real bonus if she came with him today."

Riley sighed. "I should probably go inside."

"We'll head to the park. After you've seen the doctor, wait for us inside the office, so we can be here when you come out. We don't want you to disappear on our watch."

"Will do."

Riley went into the building, found the doctor's office, checked in, and sat in the empty waiting room. *I forgot to text Ben.*

She sent her text: "At doc's office."

A young medical assistant opened a door. "Ms. Malloy?"

Riley rose, and the assistant said, "This way."

After Riley sat next to the small counter in the exam room, the medical assistant took her blood pressure then left.

Riley glanced at the lone, mass-produced print of an empty, brown field on the wall. *Not a lot of warmth here. They need local art on the walls like Doc Julie Rae.*

The medical assistant returned. "The doctor wants more x-rays. I'll take you to x-ray and wait for you." After the x-rays, the medical assistant walked with Riley back to the exam room.

"I hope it's okay to tell you that I really admire you, Ms. Malloy. I hear you applied for veterinary medicine at UGA. I just learned on Friday that I've been accepted by the Medical College in Augusta. Are you scared? I am."

Riley gazed at the young woman and nodded. "The only advice I'd have for both of us is to remember everyone else is scared too. Be the brave one."

The medical assistant smiled. "Thanks, I can do that."

The doctor breezed into the room. "Let's check that arm, Riley."

After the doctor removed the splint and the bandaging, she said. "Excellent. The abrasions are looking good, and the swelling is down. Because both bones are broken, I'd like to insert plates and screws to ensure the bones heal correctly. It's outpatient surgery and only takes about an hour. There isn't a good alternative to the surgery, but we can do it this week or next week. That's your choice. You won't require a cast, but you will need a splint to make sure nothing shifts and a sling for comfort. I would think the sooner, the better, as far as you're concerned, so you can return to work with the understanding that your arm has to heal before you can use it."

"When could I go back to work?"

"If we schedule your surgery for tomorrow morning, you can return to work on limited duty on Thursday."

"There are no alternatives to surgery?"

"Not really. Not with both the ulna and the radial bones fractured."

"Then you're right, the sooner, the better," Riley said.

"Good. My medical assistant will go over the instructions with you while our scheduler arranges a time. See you in the morning."

The doctor left, and Riley sent a text to Ben. "Surgery tomorrow am. No time yet."

Ben replied, "Thanks."

Ben's been really busy this morning.

A few minutes later, the medical assistant brought in the information and consent papers and reviewed each sheet with Riley. As they reviewed the last page, another young woman tapped on the door and handed a sheet of paper to the medical assistant then left.

"Eight am tomorrow; be here by six," the medical assistant said. "You will probably be out of here before noon."

Riley frowned. "The doctor told me it would only take an hour."

The assistant nodded. "That's how long it takes her. There are a few things to be done after surgery like dressing the incisions, making sure your vitals are stable, and applying the splint and sling."

"You're right. What else do we have?" Riley asked.

"The usual. Nothing to eat or drink after midnight. Wear comfortable clothes, but no jewelry, and your driver has to stay here with you the entire time." She smiled. "You'll have a good team."

Riley returned her smile. "Thanks, and I'll remember to be brave."

When Riley was in the waiting area, she texted Ben the arrival time for her surgery before she texted Claire that she was ready.

Claire: "Two minutes."

Riley met Claire and Toby outside the building; Claire's face was red, and Toby was panting. Claire grinned. "We raced. Let's go by the office, so we can cool down and get water. I'll drive."

When they went inside the back door, Riley inhaled. "Ahh. Dogs and cats. I love this place."

Claire grabbed a dog bowl before they continued to the breakroom; Zach met them in the hallway. "I thought I heard you, Riley. Are you back at work now?"

"Not quite yet. I'm planning on Wednesday, but it might be Thursday."

Zach smiled. "That would be great. You could pick an exam room and sit while you supervise."

"Not a bad idea, Zach. I was afraid I'd be stuck at the front desk. No offense, Claire."

Claire set the dog bowl of water on the floor for Toby. "Too late; I'm offended."

Doc Julie Rae hurried into the breakroom. "Riley, it's great to see you. Sit down."

Claire poured three cups of coffee and joined Riley at the table while Riley told Doc Julie Rae about her doctor's visit before Zach left.

"Don't let us wear you out," Doc Julie Rae said as she carried her cup to the door, "but it's great to see you. Come to work when you feel like it."

"Before you leave, Doc, have you talked to Doctor Ansell? Wasn't he coming in today?" Claire asked.

"He'll probably be here later this morning. He's looking at some homes, so he can report back to Evy. Preston said she had some very definite ideas of what she wants. I'm glad I could get back in time to interview him. Thad shared his concerns with me, so I intend to grill the good doctor."

After Doc left, Claire asked, "Was it just me, or did you get the shivers when Doc Julie Rae talked about grilling Doctor Ansell?"

"He might be surprised how tough our sweet boss is." Riley nodded.

"I'm going to give Pia a quick break," Claire said. "Is that okay with you, or are you too tired?"

"That's fine." Riley sat at the table, then after Claire left, she wandered down the hall until Zach came out of an exam room.

"How are you doing, Zach?"

He smiled. "I'm really glad to see you. I'm learning a lot about being more efficient but still giving our patients the attention they need. I love it here. When are you coming back?"

"Not as quick as I would like. Maybe next week. My surgeon is a stodgy killjoy for someone in her thirties."

Zach shook his head. "Take care of yourself. Let me know if you need a short Asian to come to your rescue. My little sister's fierce."

Riley laughed as Zach grinned and went into the next exam room. Riley returned to the breakroom and sat at the table. *I love this place.*

After twenty minutes, Claire returned. "Pia needed to make a couple of personal calls. I'd promised her I'd try to give her a little time this morning. Ready to go shopping?"

After they were in Claire's car, Claire said, "Pia will be your surgery driver tomorrow. I don't know all the details, but I think Ben's taking you there, then after Pia drops off Jackson at school, she'll be your alternate driver, so Ben can leave if he has a call. It's not exactly in accordance with the surgical center's rules, but they're willing to accommodate the sheriff's department."

"I love living in a small town," Riley said.

"I am so glad I was at the desk. This is totally bizarre. You won't believe this, but Evy called."

"Evy Ansell? That's a surprise," Riley said. "I thought we decided she was a phantom."

"Turns out we were closer to the truth than we thought. She said she was in Sacramento for a writers' conference. When I told her I tried to look up her books, she apologized and said she was very embarrassed, but she's not used to much attention because she's the ghost writer for a very famous author."

"Really? She said that?" Riley's eyes narrowed. *Sounds like baloney to me.*

"That's what she claimed, and she apologized because she couldn't say who the author was because of her contract. According to her, she goes to all the writers' conferences with the author to help field any questions about the books. She implied the author hasn't even read them. Evy said she's written several of her own historical fiction novels, but they aren't published. Then, guess what?"

"She's also an alien from a far galaxy?"

Claire giggled. "That's about as believable as the rest of it, isn't it? She asked me if I'd ever thought about being a development editor. She said she needs one to check her novels."

"I'll bite. What's a development editor?" Riley asked. *This is definitely bizarre.*

"Kind of like a collaborator. Anyway, she's going to send me a few chapters to see if that's something I might like to do."

"Well, then, congratulations," Riley said.

Claire giggled. "I don't plan to hold my breath. I was a teacher for too many years. I can definitely smell a coverup story a mile away."

"So what do you think is going on?" Riley asked.

"Who knows? Maybe she and Preston are having problems. She didn't mention him, the clinic, or moving to Barton once."

"Interesting."

"Anyway, my short career as a development editor is probably over."

"I'm so sorry. Do we need to plan a party?"

Riley and Claire giggled.

When Claire parked at the card shop, Riley asked, "Weren't we looking for scrub tops?"

"I found something better. The card shop carries an excellent selection of artist supplies, and they have artist smocks."

"That's interesting." Riley climbed out of the car, and Claire opened the door for Toby.

When they were inside, Riley inhaled the soft vanilla fragrance, and Claire led the way to the back of the shop to the art supplies and the artists' smocks that hung on two clothing racks.

"The artist smocks have snaps and open in the front. We need to focus on finding a size that will work for you and ignore the colors."

Riley's eyes widened. "I'm not sure I can ignore the polka dots, tie-dyed, or neon colors. Is it okay if I hope for a plain one?"

"I'm with you on that," Claire mumbled as she flipped through each smock. "I think a larger smock would be easiest for you to manage. I've found a large, an extra-large, and a 2XX. Let's start with the large."

Riley slipped her left arm out of her sling and supported it with her right hand. After they slipped the smock sleeve over her arm,

Riley looped her sling back around her neck then slipped in her right arm and fastened the top three snaps.

"It's easy to put on, but it's quite roomy, isn't it?" Riley asked as she pulled the material an arms-length away from her.

Claire giggled as she helped Riley remove the top. "I didn't realize how generous an artist's smock might be; so much for my brilliant idea to go with one of the larger sizes. I'll look for a medium."

Claire hung the large at the end of the rack then searched the rack again. "There are quite a few mediums. Here's one to try on."

After Claire helped her with the size medium smock, Riley said, "It wasn't hard to put on, and it's roomy enough that I could wear one of my shirts under it. I don't think I could put on one any smaller. Medium is perfect."

While Riley removed the smock, Claire pulled out all the medium ones. "Here are five. I'm actually surprised there were that many. You'll need four? Or all five?"

"Not the tie-dyed. It makes me dizzy, but the others look like the artists were in a paintball fight, and I kind of like that."

"Paintball fight, it is," Claire said.

After Riley purchased her tops, Claire asked, "What about lunch? We could pick up sandwiches and take them to the office or to the park."

"I'd like to pick up my car first then lunch in the breakroom sounds perfect. I wouldn't mind being around when Preston Ansell shows up."

"I'll drop you off then meet you at the office. Light lunch or are you hungry? It's my treat."

"Light."

When Riley reached the back parking lot, she frowned at her usual parking spot. "Let's park away from the shade of the building, Toby. Maybe the car will be a little warmer if I park in the sun."

After Riley parked at the far end of the lot, she strolled into the breakroom with Toby by her side; Doc Thad followed them and handed Riley her keys. "I've had these and forgot to tell Ben. I'm glad to see you. Claire told me about the last beer, but you're actually looking more like the last sweet tea." He chuckled as he left to examine his next patient.

Riley set her backpack and car keys on the table before she sauntered to the receptionist's desk. Toby trotted ahead of her, and Pia smiled and rubbed Toby's ears.

"Where's Claire?" she asked.

"Getting lunch," Riley said.

"Perfect. Zach can take over the desk, and we'll can eat together, just like old times the week before last. We need to talk about Doctor Ansell, but not because I know anything; I just want to talk about him."

Riley's eyes widened as she stared at the front parking lot.

"What is it?" Pia turned to look then frowned. "Eli Reeves? What's he doing here?"

"I have no idea, but I'm sure he'll have some farfetched excuse."

Pia raised an eyebrow. "Want me to show him out?"

"No, I'm interested in what he's got up his sleeve."

Claire joined them. "What are we staring at?"

"Eli Reeves, and Riley has a plan or a trap. I'm not sure which." Pia rose and motioned for Claire to take the receptionist's seat then frowned. "It's not normal for the three of us to be hanging around the desk like it was a trap or something, even though it is. I'm going to be out of sight."

"Perfect," Riley said.

"I'll follow your lead, Riley," Claire said.

"Just be your receptionist-self," she said.

When Eli strode inside, he smiled at Claire and Riley. "I've missed my lunch companions." He lifted up a sack.

You've never even met Claire before. Riley smiled. "Oh, you should have called this morning to warn us. We already ate. Doc Julie Rae's with a patient. Did you want to talk to Doc Thad?"

"Not really. He's not quite as easy on the eyes as you two."

Riley touched her cheek and chuckled. "That's funny. So, just a social call?"

"I have a meeting with Sheriff Dunn this afternoon. He needs my help with a small case that is giving him trouble. He asked for thirty minutes of my time, although I'm sure I won't need that long to solve the case."

"That's nice," Riley said.

Claire nodded. "It was nice to see you, Eli, but I need to get back to my inventory. Thanks for dropping by."

Riley smiled again before she turned to leave. *Way to go with the flow, Claire. My face is getting tired.*

"Before you go, I've had something in the back of my mind that's been bothering me. Did the two men who kidnapped you ever mention any names?"

"You haven't had time to read the GBI report, have you?" Riley raised her eyebrows. "They didn't mention any names. I'm really sorry I can't be of any more help."

"They were wanted in a county near Atlanta. I thought they might have mentioned one of the detectives looking for them."

"I didn't hear them talk much at all," she said.

"They didn't say anything about their boss or what their orders were?"

"No." Riley raised her eyebrows. "You know who their boss is, don't you? I'm so sorry I can't confirm a name for you."

Eli chuckled. "Thought I'd try."

Claire cleared her throat. "Riley, do you want to sit here?"

"Thanks, Claire. I do need to get back to the inventory." Riley smiled at Eli. "I was allowed to help out today only if I stayed off my feet."

Riley left for the hallway then joined Pia to listen.

"Is she okay?" Eli asked.

Claire said, "She's doing great. Please excuse me, but I have several appointments to reschedule. It was nice to see you."

Pia's phone buzzed a call, and she showed her phone to Riley. *Claire.* They stifled their giggles.

"He's cleared the parking lot," Claire called out.

"I'll tell Zach he's got the desk," Pia said. "I'm starving, and I want to hear what that was all about."

After they were in the breakroom, Claire said, "He certainly sounded like he was trying to impress you, Riley."

"I agree," Pia said. "I almost gagged."

Riley raised one eyebrow. "Impress me or lull me into letting down my guard? Don't you like how casually he asked if the bad guys told me the name of their boss? In the first place, I don't think they knew, and in the second place, I wasn't exactly on buddy-buddy terms with those two thugs."

"I liked how you turned it around," Claire said. "So, if his goal was to impress you, he thought he succeeded."

"And you were appropriately clueless. Well done," Pia said. "So, why was he here, really?"

"I have no idea; he might have been fishing to find out what I knew, but the most revealing tidbit is that he doesn't have access to the GBI file."

Claire's eyes widened. "You're right."

"Are you going to tell Ben?" Pia asked.

"Of course." Riley smiled.

Claire and Pia side-glanced each other, then Pia said, "We know you, Riley. You will right after you ask the sheriff about his meeting with Eli."

Claire chuckled. "Let me have your keys, Riley. I want to show Pia the cool work smocks we found."

"Sure. Here you go." Riley tossed her keys to Claire, and Toby followed Claire to the back door.

After Claire and Toby went outside, Riley smacked her forehead. "I forgot. Claire's going to think I lost the smocks or my mind."

"Forgot what?" Pia asked.

Riley sighed. "I stuck my smocks into my backpack, so we could show you. I guess she'll figure it out."

"It's Claire; she won't be mad. If it were me, I'd be furious at you for letting me go out in the cold for nothing. Although, maybe

I wouldn't be all that angry because Toby's getting some outside time," Pia said.

CHAPTER THIRTEEN

After Claire and Toby were outside, Claire strolled to the back of the parking lot to Riley's car then raised the fob to unlock the door. When she was close to the car, Toby growled as he leapt, snatched the keys out of her hand, and raced across the road with them.

Claire shouted, "Toby! What are you doing?" as she chased him across the road to the other side of the empty lot.

When she caught up to him, she put her hands on her knees to catch her breath as she glared at him. "Drop it."

Toby opened his mouth, and the keys fell to the ground. He stared at her with his mournful eyes.

"Oh, you silly goof." Claire knelt next to him and hugged him while she picked up the keys and pointed the fob at Riley's car then pressed the remote button to unlock the door.

The blast of the explosion rocked the building and knocked Claire to the ground; she lost her hold on Toby.

Claire coughed from the smoke that encircled her as she pushed herself to a sitting position. "Toby, where are you? Are you okay?"

Toby limped to her then licked her face. She buried her face in his thick coat. "I'm so glad you're okay. Thank you for saving me."

The entire staff of the animal hospital rushed out of the building.

Thad shouted, "Claire," then raced across the road and knelt next to her; he clutched her and brushed the hair out of her face. "Sweetheart, are you okay?"

"Thanks to Toby, I'm fine, but Toby might be hurt; he was limping." She opened her mouth to pop her ears. "My ears are ringing."

Her body shook, and Thad held her tighter and spoke in a soothing voice. "It's okay. I'm here with you."

Claire continued, "If Toby hadn't taken the keys from me and run away from the parking lot, I would have been standing next to Riley's car when it exploded."

Claire covered her ears. "Those sirens are loud."

She leaned against Thad while she sobbed, "Toby saved me."

* * *

The sheriff and Ben were the first to arrive; they parked near the vacant lot. Ben raced across the barren lot and wrapped his arms around Riley who stared at Claire in shock.

"Are you okay?" he whispered.

"I was inside. Claire was going to get my new work smocks out of my car, but I'd forgotten I have them in my backpack." Riley bit her lip. "Claire was hurt because of me."

While Thad held onto Claire, Riley and Ben stepped closer while Claire kept her tight hold on Toby. "Toby snatched the keys out of my hand when I got close to the car and ran here," she said between sobs. "I chased him and pressed the fob to unlock the door then… the loud noise, and I was knocked to the ground." Tears streamed down her face. "I didn't know where Toby was, and when I called him, he limped to me."

The ambulance parked behind the sheriff's and Ben's cruisers, and the fire engine and the fire chief pulled into the clinic staff parking lot. Doc Julie Rae sent Zach back to the office for an exam table sheet then directed Zach and Pia to take Toby inside with the makeshift stretcher, so she could evaluate his injuries.

The sheriff motioned for Ben to join him near their cruisers, and the two men spoke quietly.

After Claire and Thad left in the ambulance, Zach came out of the clinic and hurried to Riley. "I x-rayed Toby's leg, and it's not broken. Do you want to come inside to see if we missed anything? We think he might have a sprain."

Riley nodded, and Zach put his arm around her to walk her into the clinic.

"Riley's going to check Toby," Zach said as they passed Ben and the sheriff.

"Good, I'll be there in a few minutes," Ben said.

Toby was relaxing on the exam table when Riley stepped into the exam room. "How are you, Toby?"

Toby yipped.

"Sorry about that, but I'm glad it's okay now. Zach, Toby was scrambling to get to Claire when he twisted his foot. He says he can walk just fine now."

"I thought that was what he telling me, but I wanted you to give us the go ahead."

"Your instincts are great, and with a little more experience, you'll learn to trust them."

"Okay, Toby, we'll help you off the table, then you're good to go." Zach called Pia to help, and they lowered Toby to the floor. When Pia opened the exam room door to the back hallway to leave, Toby followed her.

Zach frowned. "He's still favoring that foot. I'd be second-guessing myself if I'd turned him loose."

"He'll be fine, and so will you." Riley smiled.

Ben came into the exam room. "Toby looks like he shook it off. The sheriff and Doc Julie Rae are waiting for us in her office."

After they went into Doc Julie Rae's office, Ben closed the door after Toby came inside too.

Doc motioned to her conference table. "We can all sit there."

After the four of them were seated at the table, Toby flopped down across the door.

"Riley, you've become a target; we don't know why, but as long as the attacker knows how to find you, you're an easy target," the sheriff said. "Ben and I believe the only way to ensure your safety is to remove the easy access. We believe the best way to do that is to send you away, so no one knows where you are."

"I hate saying this, but the sheriff and I talked, and no one includes all the office staff," Doc Julie Rae said. "We believe it would be for your protection and ours if we have no idea where you are."

"After you leave, we'll tell your close friends that you are at the cabin with Ben, but that's not where you'll be," the sheriff said.

Ben stared at the sheriff, and Doc Julie Rae said, "You do realize her close friends include the entire staff at the animal hospital, don't you, Sheriff?"

The sheriff sighed. "Fine, you can tell your staff Riley will be at the cabin."

"After I leave? I can't tell anyone good-bye?" Riley's voice cracked.

"It's as much for their safety as yours. Remember that," Ben said.

As Riley's anxiety increased, her breathing became more rapid and shallow. "When do I leave? Where am I going?"

Ben took her hand and gazed into her eyes. "Slow breaths."

Riley met his gaze as she inhaled then pursed her lips and exhaled slowly. She sighed. "Thanks, Ben. Panic over. What else?"

"Your surgeon is an old friend of mine, and she and I had a little chat. After reviewing your records, she is postponing your surgery for at least a week," Doc Julie Rae said.

Riley smiled. "I hadn't even thought that far ahead. So, I have a question. Can I talk to any of my close friends on the phone?"

The sheriff glowered, and Ben said, "No, we can't afford any slips."

Doc Julie Rae raised her eyebrows. "How long do you think it would take for you and Claire to come up with a secret code?"

Riley rolled her eyes. "Two minutes."

Doc Julie Rae nodded, and the sheriff chuckled.

"I have a million questions," Riley said.

"Save them, and for the record, we all hate this," the sheriff said.

"Let's go, Riley. Come on, Toby," Ben said.

"Can I pick up my backpack in the breakroom?" she asked on the way to the door.

Ben nodded, and they left the building in silence, then the three of them climbed into Ben's truck.

"We're going to the cabin first. Turn off your phone and set it in the glove compartment for now," Ben said as he headed out of town. "You won't be alone because I'm going with you, and Toby and Princess, of course."

"This seems so extreme, almost surreal." Riley frowned at the familiar surroundings as Ben sped to the cabin.

"How long do you think it will take you to pack?" Ben asked.

"For our adventure to the unknown? Ten minutes."

He smiled. "You have the most remarkably resilient attitude."

"What about my computer?" she asked.

"Bring it along; it might come in handy, but leave it turned off."

"While I'm packing, could you grab some books?" Riley asked as Ben turned at the driveway.

"Good idea."

Ben loaded a backpack with books then packed their ammunition into a carrying case. He carried their rifles inside their cases to the truck then returned for the books and ammo. He loaded a box with water and their few snacks and fruit then added the bags of dog food and cat food, boxes of treats, and food and water bowls.

Riley carried her duffel bag to the kitchen and grabbed her pillow.

"Good idea." Ben hurried to the bedroom and brought out his pillow and stuffed it into his duffel bag before he carried their bags to the truck.

Princess meowed at Riley. "We're all going on an adventure together. We don't have a carrier for you. Do you want Ben to stop somewhere and pick one up? We can ask him to put a box with a quilt in it for you on the backseat. It would give you a place to relax."

Princess hissed.

"Okay, I'll ask Ben to put in a quilt for Toby too."

As Ben came inside, he said, "I heard, but we're out of boxes. I'll spread out a quilt on the seat then fold one for Princess."

After Ben carried out the quilts, he and Toby returned. "Time to leave. Do we have everything?"

"If we don't, we did our best," Riley said. Toby and Princess followed Riley to the truck while Ben locked the cabin.

Ben helped Riley inside then opened the back door. Toby jumped in, and Princess leapt in behind him.

As Ben drove down the driveway, he said, "My phone is in the console. What time is it?"

Riley peered at the screen. "Two forty-eight."

"Perfect. Do I have any texts?"

"Yes. One from the sheriff. Shall I read it?"

Ben nodded, and Riley read the text. "He said Claire's been treated and released. That's a relief."

Ben smiled. "He knew you'd be worried. We won't reply."

Ben turned the truck away from town when he reached the road.

"We're not going to the highway?" Riley asked.

"Nope. I fueled up the truck earlier, and there's no other reason to go into town."

"Can you tell me where we're going now?" she asked.

"I'm waiting to hear from the sheriff. You'll know when I do because you're reading me my texts." Ben grinned.

"Eli Reeves was in town right before we ate lunch. He said he was in Barton for a meeting with the sheriff this afternoon. Do you know if that's true?"

"Not that I know of. Why didn't you say anything earlier?"

"Oh, I don't know. Explosion?" Riley smirked, and Ben laughed.

"Who else knows what Eli Reeves said?"

"Claire, Pia, and me."

Ben nodded. "Send a text to the sheriff for me. Don't say it's from you; he'll know. Tell him to ask Pia about Eli Reeves."

Riley glanced at him as she picked up his phone. "That's smart."

"Thanks," he said, "but don't sound so surprised next time."

Riley laughed then sent the text.

"How are our passengers doing?" Ben asked.

Riley checked the backseat. "Both of them are asleep."

"Good. You're welcome to nap if you can. You're supposed to be convalescing."

"I think I'm too wound up to nap."

Ben's phone buzzed a text.

Riley looked at his phone. "It's from the sheriff. It says, 'Plan A, but wait.'"

"Thanks."

"What are we waiting for? Do I get to know what Plan A is?"

"Not yet," Ben said.

Riley pulled her pillow from behind her back and rested her head on it. "Fine." She closed her eyes. "I'll just rest a minute."

When Ben stopped the truck, Riley woke and yawned.

. "Are we there?"

"Toby whined, and I promised him we'd stop at the next rest stop. Do you want to get out too?"

"Yes, I'm stiff from sitting in one position."

Ben nodded. "I need to stretch my legs too."

When Riley stepped out of the truck, she admired the neatly trimmed grass and bushes around the information building. "This is nice. Where are we?"

"At a well-kept rest area with a dog walk."

"You are not funny," she grumbled and turned her head to peer at the line of parked eighteen-wheelers before she smiled.

"Then why did you smile?" Ben chuckled.

"Because seeing trucks makes me happy."

Ben nodded "Ah. Another fascinating glimpse of your complexity."

Riley giggled. "Okay, you're funny."

After they were back on the road, Ben's phone buzzed a text from the sheriff. "Change to Plan B."

After Riley read him the message, Ben frowned. "My guess is that Sheriff talked to Pia. What time is it?"

"Four-seventeen."

"Plan A was for us to stay at my parents' house. Plan B is for you to stay at my parents', and I'll return tomorrow morning for work and stay at the cabin, at least until I can move into Helen's two-bedroom house. Plan C would be for us to leave the state and not tell anyone, including my parents or the sheriff, where we've gone."

Riley's eyes widened. "Plan C sounds drastic."

Ben's face was tight. "Yes. After the sheriff said to wait, I was worried about what he'd found. Not going to Plan C means that he cleared Marc and everyone at the clinic."

"That's good, but I'm confused. We've been on the road for two hours, and Carson's only an hour away from Barton. How could the plan be for us to go to your parents' in Carson if we're going the wrong way?"

"Sheriff Dunn wanted us out of town immediately for your protection while he sorted everything out; we've stayed within thirty miles of Carson, so we're not that far away."

"Won't your folks be surprised by a sudden houseguest?" Riley asked

"Not at all. Dad and I have been discussing it for a while, and Mom was excited. The sheriff talked to Dad after Claire was hurt to be sure my folks knew how deadly serious our problems are."

"Don't I have any say at all?" Riley pouted.

Ben sighed. "Yes, you do. The final decision is yours. The sheriff and I kept it quiet until he had everything in place."

"So, how is any decision mine?" Riley turned to face Ben.

"You're the one with the instincts. Anytime something doesn't feel right to you, Toby, or Princess, tell me; we'll do whatever is necessary, including disappearing."

"Thanks. So, when will we be there?"

"Twenty minutes, and I'm sure the sheriff let Dad know we're on our way."

When Ben pulled into the long driveway of the old, white farmhouse with a red barn, Riley smiled. "No wonder you laughed about the white house with the red barn."

"I did, didn't I? I always told people to turn at the white house with a red barn when I was a kid. I didn't know how many houses there are just like it around here."

Toby whined.

"Do you have a dog?" Riley asked.

"Our old collie passed away last year; Dad says he wants another dog, but Mom says it has to be the right one."

When the driveway curved to the front of the house, Princess put her paws on the window and meowed.

"Ben, Princess would like to be the barn cat."

"Mom will want to feed you, Princess. Is that okay?"

Princess purred, and Ben smiled. "Even I understood that."

Riley peered at the house when Ben parked. "I'm nervous; I'm not that comfortable with new people."

"I think you're awesome, and Mom will put you at ease with all her stories."

"I hope so." Riley exhaled.

When Ben opened the back door, Toby bounded out of the truck, and Riley snickered when Princess crouched before she jumped out and landed next to him.

"Did you notice Princess's mountain lion leap?" Riley asked.

"Dad will be glad to have a barn cat again," Ben said. "Mom refuses to go into the barn because of the mice. We haven't told her about the rat snakes we relocate from the chicken coop to the barn."

When Ben's dad strode out of the barn to the truck, Riley smiled. *Ben even has his dad's walk.*

"Dad, this is Riley."

"Call me Jake, Riley. It's nice to meet you." Jake's smile was as infectious as Ben's.

Toby nudged Jake's hand, and Jake scratched his ears. "What's your name?"

Toby grinned.

"This is Toby. Princess ran to the barn," Riley returned his smile.

"You've brought a barn cat? Ben told us you were brilliant."

A woman came out the front door. "Riley, it's wonderful to meet you: I'm Melissa, but Jake and my friends call me Mick."

"This is Toby," Jake said as Toby trotted to greet her. "Princess disappeared to take over the barn cat duties."

Melissa stroked Toby's neck. "What a sweet boy. I knew about Toby but didn't know we were getting a bonus barn cat. That's great.

Come inside, and I'll show you your room then ply you with cookies and sweet tea for all kinds of information that is none of my business while I cook supper."

Riley giggled. "Would it be okay if I called you Ms. Melissa?"

"Of course. It's hard to forget one's upbringing, isn't it? Your mother must be proud of you."

"My grandmother was my biggest influence when I was growing up. She's gone now, but she certainly made sure I knew my manners."

"Sounds like my grandmother. The rest of my family was afraid of her, but I always thought she was terrific, and she told the best stories in the world about dragons. One of my older cousins had the audacity to tell me that dragons weren't real, but I'll save my misadventures as a child for later."

As Melissa and Riley strolled together to the house, Toby followed them.

"I can't leave you with a cliffhanger, though," Melissa said. "I was grounded for a week over the black eye I gave my cousin. He's a lawyer, now, and claims he still intends to sue me over his egregious injury."

"According to my uncle, Mom's story about him isn't true, but the rest of the family still loves to hear her stories, even though we're never sure what's true and what isn't." Ben carried their bags to the house. "Where do you want Riley's things, Mom?"

"First floor bedroom, and your uncle has grown stuffy in his old age." Melissa winked at Riley, who giggled.

Ben placed Riley's bags in her room then carried his bags upstairs.

"Ben's right; I do love to tell stories," Melissa said. "Do you want to stretch out and rest until supper's ready or have some iced tea and talk to me while I cook?"

"Tea sounds good," Riley said.

Ben stopped in the kitchen. "Mom, we brought books. Okay if I put them in the living room?"

"Go right ahead," she said as she poured Riley a glass of tea. "Would you like some sweet tea?"

"Not quite yet. I'd like to unload the truck first."

After Ben carried in his last load and downed his tea, he and Toby left, while Melissa pulled a pan of chocolate chip cookies out of the oven then peeled potatoes. "I can't ask you about current events, so tell me how you and Ben met."

Riley told her about the crash and the two Yorkies, Bella and Carlie, and the cranky cat named Mr. P that Ben called 'Psycho.'

"Poor Mr. P: misunderstood and maligned," Melissa said.

Riley smiled. "He was a cranky but tender-hearted cat. He worried about Carlie and her injuries."

Melissa finished peeling and cutting the potatoes. "Ben told me that you're an animal-talker. Just a second."

She slid the still-warm cookies onto a plate in the middle of the table. "Watch this."

Ben, Toby, and Jake hurried to the kitchen. Jake, put one cookie in his mouth before he grabbed two more cookies. Ben followed his dad's example then gave Toby a dog treat on their way out.

"They have cookie radar." Melissa grinned. "Help yourself before they come back then tell me about how you understand animals so well."

"You did warn me." Riley smiled as she selected a cookie. She took a bite. "Mmm."

After she'd eaten it, she said, "I have a theory that most kids communicate with animals. I know I did but just never grew out of it. I think because I didn't want to."

"That makes total sense. I'll bet you were a shy, quiet child. Maybe a little lonely?" Melissa pointed to the plate and raised her eyebrows.

Riley grinned as she picked up another cookie. "I was shy, but I was never lonely because I was never alone."

"Of course not. You had animals. Is that why you became a vet tech?"

"Partially. Dad and his mother encouraged me to become a veterinarian, but after Dad died, I lost interest. Grandma told me to go to vet tech school because I needed to stay busy during my healing time. After she died, I finished vet tech training, signed up for online classes to complete my bachelor's degree in biology, and found a job at a clinic in Pomeroy."

Melissa nodded.

"So, how did you and Mr. Jake meet?" Riley asked before she took a big bite of her cookie.

"Well played, sweet girl," Melissa chuckled before she spun a tale about a sailing ship with a young sailor who fell overboard, but a beautiful mermaid saved him from being dragged to the deep by a lecherous octopus.

"That's my favorite story," Melissa said. "The boring story is that when I was in third grade, and he was in fifth grade, I thought he was rudest boy I'd ever met. He confirmed it when he was a senior in high school and completely ignored me because he was so gaga over that hussy that I dubbed Octavia. When I came home from college right after I graduated, he was home on leave from the Army, and there was something about his gorgeous eyes and that uniform: such a cutie. The biggest scandal in town for quite a while was that we were married before his leave was over. No one can convince me that I didn't save him from that octopus hussy."

"I like both of those stories," Riley said.

Melissa smiled. "We have about forty-five minutes until I have our supper on the table. Why don't you stretch out on your bed? I'll give you a ten-minute warning."

"Thank you. I'm suddenly exhausted."

"Good. That means you're finally allowing yourself to relax." Melissa turned to the stove and checked the chicken that was roasting in the oven.

Riley slowly walked to the guest bedroom and closed the blinds. After she kicked off her boots, she dropped her jeans on the floor before she climbed under the covers and closed her eyes. She felt the heavy pull of sleep as she drifted away on a sailing ship with a handsome young man in a deputy's uniform under a white lab coat that flapped in the breeze.

* * *

"Where's Riley?" Ben asked when he returned to the kitchen for another cookie.

"She's asleep in her room. I closed her door, so the kitchen noises wouldn't disturb her. I like Riley, Ben," Melissa said.

"I knew you would; I like her too. Dad sent me to ask how much time we have before supper and to get more cookies."

Melissa chuckled. "He's just interested in the cookies. You two have thirty minutes before you'll need to come in and wash for supper. Make it twenty, and you can wake up Riley for me."

Ben grinned as he snatched up the remaining cookies and sauntered to the back door. When he reached the barn, Ben handed his dad half of the cookies. "Mom said we have thirty minutes."

"Princess already caught a mouse and brought it to me." Jake ate two cookies. "My neighbor down the road called me earlier; he found two Labrador Retriever puppies yesterday that someone had dumped on the side of the road. He took them to the vet to be checked; they're twelve to fourteen weeks old."

Ben narrowed his eyes. "That's just barely old enough to survive without their mother."

Jake nodded. "The good news is that both of them are healthy. He's looking for someone to take them. Do you think I could convince your mom it's time for us to have dogs again?"

"Now's the ideal time for new puppies because Riley and Toby would train them, and Princess would teach them to respect cats," Ben said. "It would be hard for Mom to say no because puppies will give Riley something to do here."

"I like how you think." Jake smiled. "I'll bring up the topic at supper. I've got a few tools to put away, then I'll go inside."

"If you don't need me, I'll wake Riley from her nap."

"Go ahead. I won't be far behind you."

Before Ben left, Jake asked, "Are you and Riley getting serious?"

Ben met his dad's gaze. "I don't know, Dad; I know I am."

Toby and Princess followed Ben into the house and to the kitchen

"How's my timing?" Ben asked.

"Perfect," Melissa said. "Where's your dad?"

"He's picking up tools."

Ben fed Toby and Princess before he headed to the guest bedroom and cracked open the door. After he tiptoed inside, he smiled at Riley's jeans on the floor. *She feels safe here.*

He brushed her hair away from her face. "Riley?" he whispered.

Riley blinked then gazed at him while she reached up and stroked his cheek. "We went sailing."

Ben's eyes widened. *Mom told her the octopus story.*

"I'm glad you're okay," she whispered.

He sat on the bed and slipped his arm under her and gently hugged her then released her. His eyes twinkled as he leaned down to pick up her jeans and dangled them in front of her. As he rose, he dropped them on the bed and grinned. "Unfortunately, supper's almost ready."

Riley's cheeks reddened, then she giggled. "I was tired, and you're a terrible tease."

Ben swaggered to the door and closed it behind him.

When Ben entered the kitchen, Melissa turned and pointed at the four tall glasses with ice. "Would you pour the tea, Ben? Is Riley awake?"

"Yep. She'll be here in a minute." Ben sighed while he poured tea then glanced at his dad, and Jake smiled.

When Riley came into the kitchen, Melissa asked, "Did you sleep well?"

Riley nodded. "The best I've slept in ages."

"Good," Melissa said. "We're having chicken, and I cut yours into bite-sized pieces. I hope you aren't insulted."

Riley's eyes overflowed, and she brushed away the escaping tears.

"Oh no, was that wrong of me?" Melissa furrowed her brow as she snatched Riley's plate off the table.

Riley rushed to Melissa and gave her a one-armed hug. "Nothing's wrong. It was just so sweet, and I guess I'm still a little shell-shocked or something."

Melissa sniffled as she gently hugged Riley. "I'm so sorry, sweet girl."

"My food's getting cold." Jake winked at Ben.

"No one can break a tender moment like you, Jake." Melissa shook her wooden spoon at him. "Sit down, everyone, so we can enjoy our lukewarm supper."

While they were eating, Jake said, "Somebody dumped two Labrador Retriever puppies near Mr. Rowan's farm; he discovered them yesterday. Mr. Rowan said they were hungry and thirsty when he found them. He took them to the vet for a checkup; they're twelve weeks old."

"What? That's terrible. Are they okay?" Riley asked.

Jake nodded. "The vet checked them out, and they're healthy. A few fleas and ticks, but a bath and a good brushing took care of that. Mr. Rowan's looking for someone to take them because he already has three dogs."

Melissa said, "Well, if they were collies..."

Toby whined then yipped, and Princess meowed.

Riley stared at Ben and Jake then cleared her throat. "Toby said he could help train them, and Princess offered to teach them to be nice to barn cats."

Melissa's eyes widened. "You and Ben told me you understood animals, Riley, but I guess I didn't really understand how well. Is that what you said, Toby?"

Toby grinned, and Princess meowed again.

"Well, for goodness sake. What do you think, Riley? Should we give the puppies a home?"

"You might be stuck with me, for at least a while, and I wouldn't mind helping. Training puppies doesn't take long, and Labrador Retrievers are good family dogs. Toby is most likely a mix of German Shepherd and Lab."

"What do you think, Jake?"

Jake raised his hands. "Far be it from me to go against three experts."

Princess purred, and Ben chuckled.

"Do you understand animals too? What did Princess say?" Melissa asked.

"I think I might be learning. Princess is pleased that Dad recognized she's an expert," Ben said, and Riley smiled.

"After we eat, I'll help you with the dishes, honey, then we can go to the Rowans' farm to meet the puppies," Jake said.

Toby yipped, and Princess hissed.

"Yes, you should probably go too, Toby, and you can stay here, Princess." Riley rolled her eyes.

"I can take care of the dishes under Riley's supervision, then we'll meet you there," Ben said.

When Toby whined, Ben added, "Toby will go with us."

"I understood you, Toby. It's all a matter of paying attention, isn't it, Riley?" Melissa said. "Far be it from me to turn down an offer to do the dishes."

Jake smiled his lopsided smile.

CHAPTER FOURTEEN

After Melissa and Jake left, Riley helped Ben clear the table. While Ben washed and rinsed the dishes, Riley sat at the table and sipped a cup of hot tea.

"Thanks for not busting us. What did Toby really say?" Ben asked while he scrubbed the roasting pan.

"He told me Jake wanted the puppies, and you suggested Toby could help train them, and Princess could teach them to respect barn cats."

"So, what did Princess say after Dad conceded to the experts? Was I even close?"

Riley giggled. "She told your dad 'well played, sir.'"

Ben laughed. "That's priceless, Princess."

Princess purred then strolled out of the kitchen.

"She wants to go to the barn," Riley said.

Ben hurried to the living room to open the front door for Princess. When he returned to the kitchen, he said, "I'll grab our backpacks. Anything else?"

"I'll put on my poncho," Riley said.

While they drove to the Rowans' farm, Riley asked, "When are you leaving for Barton?"

"I'd thought about leaving in the afternoon, but I think I'll leave right after breakfast."

Riley frowned. "That's a change. Any special reason?"

"Not really. I just have a feeling." Ben turned then drove slowly down the rutted driveway.

When they reached the farmhouse, Jake waited for them at the driveway, and Melissa sat on the porch in a rocking chair while the puppies climbed over her legs and tried to jump up on her lap.

"That's so funny," Riley said. "One is golden and the other one is black. No way will your mom leave either one of them."

Toby yipped, and Ben climbed out and opened Toby's door for him before he helped Riley out of the truck. On their way to the porch, Jake said, "They're both boys. The vet told Mr. Rowan to wait to neuter them."

Riley nodded. "Some vets prefer to neuter early, but I agree with Mr. Rowan's vet."

"What do you think, Riley?" Melissa's eyes shone.

Riley knelt next to Melissa. "They're as cute as can be."

"Their personalities are so different," Melissa said. "The golden one wants to be up on my lap, and the little black one is more adventurous. He's fallen off the porch twice."

Toby yipped, and the two puppies lay down on the porch.

"What on earth did Toby say?" Melissa asked.

"He told them to relax." Riley chuckled.

Toby yipped again, and the puppies explored the porch.

"They're so sweet," Melissa said, and the puppies scrambled to her.

"They know a mama's voice," Mr. Rowan said. "If you want to take them home tonight, they share a crate. I'll send you home with their crate and their puppy food and bowls. We had an old baby blanket that my wife put in their crate, and they snuggled with it and slept through the night. I'm not sure I'd call them housebroken, but their crate was dry this morning, and they didn't have any accidents in the house, but we've been outside most of the day."

"What do you think, honey?" Jake asked.

"I think they passed the Toby test, and they are such sweet, cuddly puppies." Melissa smiled. "It will be livelier at our house than it's been in a long time."

"Not all bad," Jake said.

"Come with me, Ben, and we'll gather up what I have," Mr. Rowan said.

After the two men went into the house, Melissa asked, "How do we get them to our house?"

"Put the crate on your back seat then put the puppies inside the crate. You might want to ride with them, so they won't be frightened," Riley said.

Toby yipped, and Melissa smiled. "I take it Toby agrees?"

Riley met her smile and nodded.

While Ben carried the crate to his dad's truck, Mr. Rowan handed a large bag of puppy food to Jake then gave Melissa a large tote with bowls, the baby blanket, and puppy toys and treats in it.

"My wife asked me to tell you she doesn't mean to be inhospitable, but if she sees the puppies again, she's afraid she'll change her mind."

"I understand completely." Melissa rose. "Thanks to both of you."

Jake strode ahead of them, and Riley and Toby walked alongside Melissa.

"Don't tell Jake, but I know he engineered all this," Melissa said quietly. "That man has been wanting another dog for ages. Two is like warm peach pie with two scoops of ice cream to him."

Riley giggled. "I thought so. As Princess would say, 'Well played, Mom.'"

"Oh, you have to call me Mom; it just sounds right," Melissa said then glanced at Riley. "Too early?"

"Yes, for now. Ben and I are really close friends, and I don't want to push anything and ruin a wonderful friendship."

"Then I'll behave." Melissa smiled. "Good friends are hard to find, and now that I've mentioned it, let's make a peach pie tomorrow."

After the puppies and all their gear were loaded, Jake and Melissa headed home while Ben helped Riley into his truck after Toby jumped into the backseat.

"Dad thinks Mom knows what he pulled off," Ben said on the way to the farmhouse.

"He might be right. The two of them are very close, aren't they?"

Ben nodded. "Mom told me one time that she married her best friend; I think I was thirteen. I was concerned, so I asked her when she married Dad, and she laughed so hard that she cried. When I apologized for hurting her feelings, she laughed even harder, but all I saw were her tears, and I felt awful."

Riley laughed. "That's hilarious. You must be terribly scarred."

"Exactly." Ben chuckled. "I'm glad you understand."

Riley frowned and bit her lip.

"Did I stir up a bad memory?" Ben glanced at Riley with concern on his face.

"Not really. My mother had issues. For a long time, I thought it was my fault, but Grandma explained to me that people have problems sometimes that are hard for others, especially kids, to understand. I don't know what my mother's problems were, but she left Dad when I was in high school, and we never heard from her again. She was very critical of me, especially my weight and my red hair. When I was six, Grandma told me my weight was perfect, and red hair was a sign that I was a favorite of the fairies." Riley smiled.

"Sounds like your grandmother was a wise woman," Ben said.

Riley nodded. "She knew exactly what to say, and her stories were awesome."

When they reached the farmhouse, Jake, Melissa, and the puppies were in the barn.

"I'm so glad you're here to see this," Melissa said. "Princess taught the puppies how to stalk mice. Go ahead, Princess. Show them."

Princess meowed, then she and the puppies stalked to the nearest stall. When she stopped, the puppies froze and each one lifted a front paw while Princess pounced into a small pile of straw and pulled out a mouse. Princess raced out of the barn with the rodent while the puppies romped in the barn.

"Very impressive," Ben said.

"It's almost unbelievable; I've never seen anything like it." Jake shook his head. "Ready to go inside? Mr. Rowan told me the puppies have already had their supper."

"Riley, I'm not sure where we should put their crate," Melissa said as she and Jake each picked up a puppy while Ben carried the crate.

"Kind of close to the kitchen, so they won't feel isolated, but not in a main traffic walkway because that would be overstimulating. Toby and I will scope it out."

On their way to the house, Ben's phone buzzed, and he set down the carrier. He checked his phone. "I may be a few minutes," Ben said as he walked toward the driveway to answer it, and Riley followed him.

"Yes, sir. A little over an hour," Ben said before he glanced at Riley. "Yes, sir. I understand."

After he hung up, he exhaled. "Change in plans. I need to leave for Barton in the next fifteen minutes."

"How can I help?" Riley asked as they hurried back.

Ben stopped and hugged her. "You're amazing. Only you would ask that. Get the puppies situated for Mom."

Riley nodded. When they reached his parents, Ben said, "I have to return to Barton immediately. I'm not sure when I'll be back."

"Okay," Jake said. "Riley, are you staying?"

"Of course," Riley said.

Jake nodded. "Show Mick where to set up the puppies while I talk to Ben a minute."

Ben hurried to the house while Jake carried in the crate, and Melissa and Riley each carried in a puppy.

Jake set the crate in the kitchen then hurried to Ben's room.

Riley scanned the kitchen to find the best place to put the crate. "Do you ever use the back door?" she asked.

"Not really. It doesn't go to the driveway. It leads out to the old chicken coop and the garden area."

"It would be perfect to take the puppies outside, and we could put their crate near the door. They'd still be able to watch you cook and won't be too close to the kitchen table."

"It's a little overrun, and Jake will need to mow, but he can do that early tomorrow," Melissa said.

"What can I do tomorrow?" Jake asked as he strolled into the kitchen.

"We'll talk," Melissa said. "Go help Ben, Riley. We'll take it from here."

Riley hurried upstairs to Ben's room, and Ben sighed when he saw her. "I wasn't expecting to leave right away, but I hadn't unpacked much, so this didn't take long. The sheriff will contact Dad when I arrive. I can't talk to you or text you, of course. I hate this."

Riley sat on his bed. "We'll be fine. I wanted to ask you what was going on, but you would have already told me if you could."

Ben nodded. "Somebody's trying to trace you through me, and that's probably telling you too much, but I know you'll keep it to yourself. I need to be back in town tonight. I'll stop at the grocery store, so I'll have witnesses that I'm around."

"I'll walk with you to your truck."

Before he left, Ben kissed his mom then hugged his dad.

"Be safe," Jake said.

Melissa nodded then brushed the tears off her cheeks.

As Riley and Ben walked to the truck, he said, "I'm glad you're downstairs. You've got your pistol, and you might want to move your rifle to your room. Toby will alert you if anyone comes around."

Riley nodded. "Your parents might want me to move upstairs."

"It's up to you. I trust your judgement, but you can always consider your knee that's healing." Ben cleared this throat. "You might find that I took the books from our Western series that I haven't read yet."

Riley snorted. "I might?"

"One more thing." Ben reached into his glove compartment then handed Riley her phone and charger. "I need to know if you need me. Emergencies only, okay?"

Ben hugged her tight before he sighed and kissed her cheek. Riley stared at him then wrapped her arm around his neck to pull him closer, so she could reach his mouth with hers for a soul-searing kiss.

After they broke away, Ben said, "Dang. I need to leave more often. Show me that again, so I don't forget."

Riley giggled and kissed him one more time.

"I'll miss you." Ben gazed at her.

"I'll miss you more." Riley's eyes twinkled as she smiled.

"Will not." Ben climbed into the truck and drove toward the road.

Riley stood in the driveway until she couldn't hear his truck anymore. "Let's go inside, Toby. I just realized that I'm freezing."

Riley placed her phone and charger in the top drawer of her bedside nightstand before she and Toby went into the kitchen; the puppies scrambled from Melissa to greet Toby.

"It's time for the puppies to settle down in their crate. Have you named them yet?" Riley asked.

Melissa pointed to each puppy. "The black puppy is Duffy. It's from an old Irish name that meant black, and the golden puppy is Finn; Irish for fair-haired. I thought we'd celebrate a little Irish heritage, Riley."

"That's really sweet. How do you know so much about Irish names?" Riley asked.

Jake snorted. "Mick's maiden name is O'Sullivan. Don't get her started on Irish history or genealogy. Where do you think all her stories come from?"

Riley giggled. "I should have guessed. Did you catch the puppies' names, Toby?"

Toby yipped.

"Good." Riley knelt down with a puppy treat hidden in her hand. "Here, Duffy."

Toby yipped and nudged Duffy to Riley. "Good boy, Duffy." She rubbed his face and gave him the puppy treat and repeated, "Good boy, Duffy." She rubbed his belly.

"Ms. Melissa, hide a treat in your hand and kneel close to the crate and call Duffy," Riley said.

After Melissa was in place, she called, "Here, Duffy."

Toby yipped and nudged Duffy, and the puppy trotted to Melissa who cooed and rubbed his belly then gave him his puppy treat.

Finn bounded to Melissa, and Riley said, "Come, Finn. Good boy. Here, Finn." Toby yipped and Finn trotted to Riley who scratched his ears and gave him a treat.

After Melissa called Finn, he scrambled to her and put his paw on her knee. She rubbed his face, gave him a treat, and said, "Good boy, Finn. You watched your brother, didn't you?"

Toby grinned.

"Crate," Riley said after she moved to the crate, and Toby nudged the puppies to the crate. Riley scratched their ears then placed their treats inside the crate while she repeated, "Crate."

The puppies trotted inside, ate their treats, and turned circles before they flopped down on their soft baby blanket.

"Awesome," Jake said.

"Toby makes it easy, but the secret is to reward them with ear, face, and belly rubs with lots of praise. The first thing we want them to learn is to respond to their names, and the second is to go to the crate."

"Would you care for some hot tea, Riley?" Melissa asked.

"I really would. It's getting cold out there."

While Melissa brewed the tea, Jake and Toby went out to the truck to bring in the rest of the puppies' things. When they came back inside, Princess was with them.

"I'm glad to see that you decided to come inside, Princess," Riley said. "It's going to be cold tonight."

"I'll put an extra wool blanket in your room, Riley," Melissa said. "There's also a quilt in the top of your closet. I'll ask Jake to get it down for you."

Melissa joined Riley at the table with a cup of hot tea. "You were exposed to the cold for a long time, weren't you? That's why the cold worries you."

Riley nodded. "I'm not quite over it yet. It was cold, and my clothes were wet. I didn't have any way to start a fire or get warm and was positive I was going to die alone and cold. I'm still terrified of being cold like that again, but I wasn't alone after all because Bob White kept calling to me and kept me company."

Melissa shook her head. "I am so sorry. That's horrible. I can promise you warm food and a warm place to sleep."

After Melissa refilled her cup with hot water and dropped in a fresh tea bag, she asked, "Do you think you could read? I looked over the books and found a thriller series I'd like to start reading."

Riley smiled. "I'll need to find a new series to read. Ben and I were reading a series of books, and he took the ones he hadn't read yet with him."

Melissa and Riley strolled to the living room together, and Toby and Princess followed them.

"Ben and Toby found you, didn't they?" Melissa asked.

Riley nodded. "They saved me."

"It sounds to me like you saved yourself, so they could find you. I'll ask Jake to start a fire in the fireplace."

"Now, what am I doing?" Jake asked as he came in from the front door with a load of firewood in his arms.

"To me, it looks like you're a mind reader who is about to start a fire in the fireplace." Melissa stacked the books on the coffee table and organized them by series then pulled out the book she wanted to read.

Jake chuckled and set the kindling on fire before he added a small log and sat on the hearth until his fire met his satisfaction.

After Riley and Melissa had read for an hour, Melissa asked, "What's our plan for tomorrow for the puppies?"

"You can take over the training with Toby's help, so they'll bond with you; teach Mr. Jake how to call the puppies then crate them. I'd suggest your next step after that would be to train them to ask to go outside, so they'll be housebroken. Toby can help with that. He noses the door when he wants out, and we'll ask him to go to the back door. He'll encourage the puppies to copy him. This training is a little different. Don't reward them with a 'good boy' or a treat, or they'll drive you crazy to go out for their treat."

"I don't think I'm ready to take over yet. I need you to help," Melissa said.

"Oh, you're ready, and Mr. Jake will jump right in. Duffy and Finn are smart..." Riley yawned midsentence and placed her hand over her mouth. "I'm sorry. I must be tired." She placed her Irish blessing bookmark that Melissa had given to her into the book she was reading.

"Go on to bed. I've got a few more pages to read then I might read another chapter," Melissa said.

"Good night." Riley headed to her bedroom, and Toby and Princess followed her. Before she climbed into bed, she pulled her phone out of the nightstand and checked it. Zero charge. She plugged in her phone to charge overnight then climbed into bed. When she closed her eyes, she smiled at the thought of the sailboat and Deputy Ben with his veterinarian lab jacket that flapped in the wind.

CHAPTER FIFTEEN

He stared at the pack of cigarettes on the table. *I promised myself I'd wait until after Mildred called.* He chuckled. *She hates it when I call her that.*

He picked up the pack, pulled out a cigarette, and stared at it. *Quitting is hard.*

He lit the cigarette and inhaled in relief. *Life's short.*

After he smoked his second cigarette, his phone rang; he let it ring several times. *She made me wait. She can wait.*

When he picked up the phone, Millie growled, "I almost hung up."

He narrowed his eyes. *Liar* was on the tip of his tongue, but instead, he said, "I got your text that you were going to call. What's so urgent?"

"Where's the carrier?"

"In a crime lab somewhere would be my guess. One of the GBI forensic teams has it," he said.

"Damn. Well, that's a loss that would have been a nice bonus for our trouble, but no one can trace the product to either one of us. What about the invoices?"

"I don't know. I thought they'd be with the carrier, but evidently not."

Millie's voice turned hard. "Those invoices identify both of us. I can't believe how stupid Truman was. If he'd had the sense to use numbers instead of names, we'd have been saved a lot of extra work."

"So, what's the plan?" The man tapped out another cigarette and lit it. After he inhaled, he leaned back and exhaled slowly. *My reward for listening to her drivel.*

"There's a possibility Marcy's scatterbrained cousin has the invoices."

"If she does, she doesn't know what they are; otherwise, she'd have contacted you. I'm not sure she knows who I am. She was after the carrier, so she must have known what was in it."

"That's at least something. Follow up with her."

"What about Riley?" he asked.

"I told you. Forget about Riley."

He sneered. *Right. I'll just write her off.*

After they hung up, he lit another cigarette. *Riley's disappeared.*
Maybe Luanne can find Riley for me.

CHAPTER SIXTEEN

Millie reached for the bottle of Bourgogne wine and refilled her glass. She sipped her wine while she nibbled on goat cheese and bread. *He's not interested in the invoices at all; he's become fixated on Riley. His usefulness and time is up.*

She picked up the phone. When a woman answered, Millie said, "I think I know who has the invoices, but I've got a big stumbling block in the way."

"What do you want me to do, boss?"

"Get the invoices. Marcy's cousin has them or knows where they are. Her name is Luanne Nichols, and she may be in the Atlanta area. She comes across as a bimbo, but don't let her fool you; she's actually very sharp. I think my stumbling block is getting sloppy and may self-destruct with a little assistance. I'll take care of that."

"You care anything about this Luanne?"

"No, not at all. Do what you have to do."

"Thanks, boss. Makes my job easy. The usual?"

"Yes, your usual fee plus expenses and a bonus if we have the invoices before the end of the week."

"You're always generous, boss. Thanks."

One more call.

"Hi Sam, this is Millie. I've been trying to get in touch with Riley. Do you know where she is?"

"She's safe."

"Is she at least close enough that you can keep an eye on her? I'm really worried."

"Don't worry, Millie. She's fine."

He disconnected.

Stupid, infuriating sheriff. She fumed as she poured another glass of wine. *I'm family. I have a right to know where my niece is. How can I set up that jerk of a stumbling block for a fall if you won't cooperate?*

She sipped her wine while she called room service. After she accepted the concierge's recommendation for her evening meal, she scanned the Paris skyline. *It's time to see if I can help bring down Mr. Big Shot.*

She picked up her phone and made another call. When the young man answered, she smiled. "Are you keeping a close eye on my niece? Is she safe?"

"I spoke to her earlier today. She's fine."

She left town, you dolt.

"That's good news. Do you happen to know Ben Carter?" she asked.

He snorted. "That junior deputy? Yeah, I know him."

"His mother's an old friend of mine, so don't disparage him too much." She chuckled. "She thinks the world of him, but when we talked today, she told me that she's a little worried he's seeing too much of Riley. He's engaged, you know."

"I didn't know that."

Millie smiled at the surprise in his voice. "The wedding's only a month away. It'll be a big affair. Jacob Carter has a lot of family that live near Carson."

"Does Riley know?" he asked.

"I'm sure she doesn't, which is exactly why I wanted to put a bug in Riley's ear," Millie said. "Is she staying at the cabin?"

"I don't know. What cabin is that?"

Millie held back her sigh. *You should have already known this.*

"It belonged to my mother. I'll send you the coordinates, if you want to check. So, any ideas of who is stalking Riley?"

He cleared his throat. "My team is getting closer to finding out."

"I just feel like it's someone that has recently shown up in Barton. What do you think?" Millie sipped her wine.

"I'm a little ahead of you." He chuckled. "I've been looking into that."

Sure you have.

Millie chuckled with him. "I should have remembered what a professional you are. Thank you so much for everything you and your team are doing."

"All in a day's work," he said.

Millie rolled her eyes. *You are so full of yourself, bud.*

"Keep me posted," she said before she disconnected.

She smiled and rose to answer the tap at the door. *I'm suddenly starving.*

CHAPTER SEVENTEEN

It was still dark when Toby whined and woke Riley. After she stretched, she yawned. "I hear them now; the puppies are whining. Thank you, Toby, we'll take them outside."

Riley pulled on her jeans, socks, and boots before she picked up her poncho then hurried to the kitchen and turned on the light. Duffy and Finn danced when they saw Toby and Riley. Riley let the puppies out of the crate then opened the back door, and Duffy and Finn dashed outside with Toby.

Riley checked their crate. *Dry. Good boys.*

Princess strolled to the kitchen and stretched before she meowed.

"It's early, but I guess it's not too early for breakfast after the boys come in."

Riley opened the back door, and Princess pranced outside.

Melissa hurried into the kitchen; her eyes widened when she saw Riley standing by the back door. "I thought I'd left the light on," Melissa said. "I'll get our coffee going. Did the puppies wake you up?"

"Toby woke me because the puppies were whining. Really good news: their crate is dry. Everybody's outside; when they come in, you can feed Duffy and Finn, and I'll feed Toby and Princess."

While the coffee perked, Melissa asked, "How do I do that?"

"They're a little young, but we'll establish their routine. I'll show you."

Riley stacked two puppy food bowls with one hand and chuckled. "Pretend I have one bowl in each hand. The best place to feed them may be close to the washer and dryer because it's out of the way and convenient to the pantry where their food is."

Riley stood near the washer and held up two bowls. "The red one is Finn's, and the black one is Duffy's. They'll know their own bowls after a few feedings, so it's important to be consistent." She held the bowls to one side. "Hold the bowls, so the puppies have their own space. If you have two small rugs or pads, that would define their personal areas."

"I have some bathmats that are in excellent shape, but the colors are out of date. Shall I place them on the floor now?" Melissa asked.

Riley nodded then waited until Melissa returned.

"Those are perfect," Riley said as Melissa put down the neon yellow and the purple swirl bathmats.

Riley held the bowls to the side, and said, "Sit," before she set the bowls on the mats.

"That's it. They won't sit because they haven't learned it yet, but after they do, they'll sit for you while you place the bowls on the mats."

"It helped to see you do it. I can feed them when they come inside. Do I call them first?"

Riley nodded. "They may come to see what you're doing when you dish up their food, and Toby and I might have to adjust them to the right rug, but it won't take long for them to learn."

Melissa poured their coffee. "I'm really glad you're here."

"You'll be the expert by the end of the week." Riley sipped her coffee. "Ready?"

"I think I am."

Riley opened the back door, and Princess sauntered inside. Toby led the puppies in, then when Melissa picked up their food bowls, Duffy and Finn raced across the kitchen to see what she was doing. After she filled the bowls, she followed Riley's example then set down their bowls after Riley and Toby put the right puppy at the right spot.

Melissa watched while Duffy and Finn gobbled down their food. "Oh, no. They're licking each other's empty bowls. Do I stop them?"

"No, they're just checking to see if the other one missed anything. That's fine. It's good to see that neither one started a fight over the food."

While Riley fed Toby and Princess, Melissa cooked breakfast; Jake came into the kitchen and poured himself a cup of coffee.

"I'll mow right after breakfast," he said. "We're supposed to get some rain later this morning, and it will be harder to mow."

While Melissa cooked, Riley slipped on her poncho before she opened the back door. Toby, the puppies, and Princess followed her outside. While she watched the horizon brighten as the sun rose, Jake joined her.

"It's a jungle out here," Jake said. "I see Toby but not Duffy and Finn."

"They're there somewhere," Riley said. "Sometimes I think I see the grass part."

"Sheriff Dunn told me about the attacks on you and the break-in at your house. Do you feel safe here?"

"I don't know. I did, but now I'm nervous because Ben had to leave so suddenly."

"I understand. Ben didn't give me any hints either, so I guess you just lay low." Jake smiled. "I have a feeling that's not your best skill."

"You're right."

Toby trotted to the door, and Duffy and Finn followed him.

"I'm ready to go inside too." Riley shivered. "It's cold."

"What about Princess?" Jake asked after they were inside.

"We'll see her when it's time for supper," Riley said.

After breakfast, Riley returned to her room to put away her poncho and make her bed. She checked her phone. *Only fifty percent charge. I really ran it down.* She frowned. *A text?*

She checked the text, and her eyes widened. *It's from Luanne.* "Sent draft." Riley shook her head and strolled to the kitchen. *Wonder if she texted me by mistake?*

"I have to go into town to get new blades for my mower. You want to ride along, Riley?" Jake asked.

Riley bit her lip. "I'm not sure."

"I have a big floppy sunhat you can wear, if you're worried about being recognized," Melissa said. "Your hair and your sling are your most recognizable characteristics right now, and your poncho covers your sling."

"I'd love to get out," Riley said.

"Good," Jake said. "What about Toby?"

"He'll probably go with us." Riley rushed to her room and slipped on her poncho. She sneaked a peek at her phone. *One hundred percent.* She shrugged then stuck it into her back pocket and placed the charger in the drawer. *I'll have it if I get into trouble.*

After Jake parked on the street in front of the hardware store, he asked, "Are you staying in the truck? I'll leave the engine running for the heater."

"No need to do that; I'll be fine." Riley lowered her window two inches. "I wouldn't mind a little fresh air."

Jake nodded. "It is warming up, isn't it? I shouldn't be too long."

After Jake went inside the store, Riley listened to the birds and the distant, mournful sound of a train's airhorn. Her eyes widened when a young man with dark blond hair sauntered down the sidewalk then stopped a man who was going into the post office. *Eli Reeves. What's he doing here?*

The man pointed at Jake's truck then Eli nodded.

"Down, Toby." Toby flattened himself on the back floorboard while Riley pulled down the brim of Melissa's sunhat then put on Jake's sunglasses and watched Eli. When Eli reached the hardware store, he stopped for a moment and glanced at Jake's truck before he opened the door for a middle-aged woman who was coming out.

"Thank you, young man," the woman said, and Eli's smile included his signature dimples.

When Eli went into the store, Riley watched through the wide storefront window as he picked up a small item from a shelf before he approached Jake and spoke to him, and the two men shook hands. The two men talked then laughed; Eli peered out the window, and Riley turned to watch a woman climb out of her car that she had parked next to Jake's truck.

Riley nodded at the woman as she hurried past her, and the woman returned her nod. The woman went into the nail salon that was next door to the hardware store. Eli motioned toward Jake's truck. Jake nodded, then they laughed again.

When Eli came out of the store with a small sack in his hand, he absently waved in the direction of Jake's truck. Riley dipped her head in a nod, but Eli was already headed back the way he came. Riley glared at Jake when he came out of the store with a large sack.

Jake climbed into his truck and started the engine. While he backed out of his parking space, he said, "That was a good move putting on my sunglasses. Eli Reeves from the GBI approached me in the store and asked me if I was Ben's father and said he knew Ben. Is that true?"

"Yes, it is. He's been in Barton several times on different investigations," she said.

Jake nodded as he drove toward his house. "He told me you had disappeared and wanted to know if Ben had ever mentioned you. I told him Ben has mentioned several girls the past few months, but he wouldn't have discussed a case with me. We laughed about Ben and girls. When he asked me about Ben's wedding next month, I told him that was up to the women because I just did as I was told. He looked at me like I was pretty wimpy, and I laughed and told him to get back with me after he was married, and he kind of bristled." Jake chuckled.

Riley's mouth was open as she stared at Jake. After she closed her mouth and shook her head, she asked, "Excuse me? Ben's wedding?"

Jake glanced at Riley. "He's obviously an idiot."

"You're right. It just sounded so bizarre."

"No kidding. It took everything I had to go along with it. He looked out the window then asked me if that was my wife in my truck, and I told him she wasn't a hardware store fan, so I'd be buying flowers on the way home. We laughed again. You didn't know I was so funny, did you, Riley?"

He wiggled his eyebrows, and Riley giggled while Jake continued, "He asked if it would help if he chatted with my wife, and I told him she'd like that, and if he'd wait a bit while I finished shopping, I'd introduce him. He told me he was on a tight schedule, and he'd have to take a rain check."

"Wow, you called his bluff," Riley said.

Jake exhaled. "It was a chance I took. I was certain he followed me into the hardware store and was on a fishing expedition."

"Can you let Sheriff Dunn know?"

Jake nodded. "I'll send him a text after I get home unless you think I should do it now."

"Is there a flower shop nearby?"

"I don't know, but I can buy flowers at the grocery store. Good idea."

Jake parked at the grocery store, and Eli cruised past his truck. When Jake came out of the store with a box of pastries and a vase of flowers, Eli parked and waited. Jake climbed into his truck and Riley leaned close and whispered, "Eli followed you to the grocery store," as she kissed him on the cheek. Jake grinned and handed her the vase then pulled away from the lot and headed home.

"He's not behind us," Jake said.

"He was just checking your story."

"What was he doing in Carson, why did he follow me into the hardware store, and did you really disappear?" Jake asked.

"I don't have any answers. Maybe next time, you can send him out to the truck when Melissa's waiting. She'll have a story for him."

Jake guffawed. "You're right about that. She'll be mad she missed the opportunity today, but she got flowers and some kind of fancy dessert thing out of the deal. I don't even know what it is."

Riley peeked into the box. "It's pretty." She pulled out a card. "Is this what it's supposed to be?" She read the card aloud. "*Mille-feuille with roast strawberries and mascarpone.*"

"I guess; doesn't it sound fancy?" he asked.

"Sure enough does," Riley giggled. "It's definitely hardware store worthy. Melissa will think we robbed a bank or something because this looks like we got ourselves in a terrible mess."

"She'll be okay with that. She'll just tell the coppers a good cover story."

Riley laughed. "I'm not sure Ben would appreciate being called a copper, but I'll give it a try sometime when he irritates me."

Jake narrowed his eyes. "Only if you do that when I'm around because I want to see his reaction."

After they were out of town, Riley said, "If you give me your phone, I'll send the sheriff the text for you."

"Here you go." Jake handed the phone to Riley.

Riley tapped the text. "I said, 'Eli R in Carson asked me about RM disappearance.' What do you think?"

"That's perfect. Send it."

"Done. He'll probably call you back about the time we get to your house. Ask him about Ben for me and ask him when I can talk to Ben."

Jake phone rang before he reached the end of the driveway. He stopped and answered. After he told the sheriff about what Eli Reeves had said, he asked, "What about Ben? How is he?"

Jake nodded while the sheriff talked. "So, when can he and Riley talk?"

Jake glanced at Riley and nodded. "You're absolutely right. Take care."

After he disconnected, Jake said, "The sheriff said Ben's fine, and he's working long hours. He said he'd try to think of a way Ben can talk to you because Ben's driving him crazy, and he bets you're the same."

Riley smiled. "That was the 'absolutely right,' wasn't it?"

Jake chuckled. "Sure was. Ready to surprise Mick? I'll carry the flowers and the box inside. I'll leave you to tell her what happened while I get my mower put together, so I can cut the grass before it rains."

When Jake, Riley, and Toby went inside, Melissa's eyes widened. "What on earth? I thought you went into town for mower blades."

"Riley will explain it." Jake kissed Melissa on the cheek then went out the back door; Toby and the puppies followed him.

"These flowers are my favorite." Melissa put the flowers in the middle of the kitchen table before she peeked into the box. "Wow. I'll bet your story will top any of mine. This is a beautiful dessert; I'll put it into the refrigerator while you tell all."

Riley told her about Eli Reeves, his questions, Riley's impersonation of Melissa, and the stop at the grocery store while Melissa put the dessert in the refrigerator.

"I am so sorry I wasn't on the floorboard with Toby to witness all of that. I know it must have been stressful for you, though. Are you okay?"

"I'm actually fine in spite of all that drama."

"Do you want any hot tea? I'd like to get my vacuuming done before lunch. You can be wherever you like. I can work around you."

"I can brew my tea, if you want to get started."

"Okay, after I have the living room dusted and vacuumed, you can sit and read there if you like. I do the downstairs floors on Tuesday, and the upstairs floors on Wednesday. I sweep the stairs before I do the downstairs, so they're done. The puppies weren't happy because they wanted to be with me but couldn't maneuver the stairs quite yet."

While Melissa cleaned the living room, Riley sat with her tea at the kitchen table and sneaked a peek at her phone. Her eyes widened at the text she received from Claire. "PA not OK. Call when u can."

Riley stuck her phone back into her pocket and sipped her tea. *How many bad guys can there be?*

She threw on her poncho and went outside. Jake had finished installing his new blades and was wiping his hands with a shop rag. "Good, you're here. The puppies need to go inside. I don't trust them around the mower."

"I'll take them. I really need to talk to Ben. What do I do?"

Jake narrowed his eyes. "I'll tell you what I told Ben more times than I can count. Talk to your mother."

Jake picked up his tools and carried them to the barn while Riley and Toby headed to the back door, and Duffy and Finn followed them inside.

"What kind of response is that?" Riley fumed as she removed her poncho. "Talk to your mother. My mother is..." She smiled. "Ben's mother, of course."

When Riley strolled into the living room followed by three dogs, Melissa unplugged her vacuum to move it to the next room. "Nice parade you've got going there, Riley. You look like you're on a mission."

"I kind of am. I need to talk to Ben. Jake told me he always tells Ben to talk to his mother, so here I am."

Melissa nodded. "Well then, let's think of something. Do you need to talk to him in person or on the phone?"

"In person would be ideal, but the phone would be good too."

"How much time do you need?"

"Not long. I have something I need to tell him, then he'll need a little time to yell at me."

Melissa laughed. "That's Ben, for sure. So, I have another question. Could I call him and tell him for you? You could be with me to prompt me or answer any of his questions. I'll put it on speakerphone, so you could hear if you can stay quiet. Never mind. You won't."

"He might not yell at you," Riley said. "That's a plus." Riley wrinkled her nose. "Except he'll just save it for later."

"Maybe not," Melissa said. "So, what am I telling him?"

"First, you need to know that the sheriff said that I'm not supposed to have my phone, but Ben gave it to me but told me not to turn it on except for emergencies."

"Got it."

"I knew you would. I got a text from my friend, Claire, who works at the clinic, a few minutes ago. Her text said that Doc Preston Ansell was not okay and for me to call her when I could."

"Do you know what Claire meant?"

"There were doubts about Doc Ansell's credentials, but I thought all that had been resolved. Something else must have come up. I need to let Ben know to call Claire."

"I'll call Ben, but his phone may ring around to voice mail."

Riley bit her lip. "If you mention Claire's name, he'll know to call her, and be sure to tell him that we're okay because his first thought will be that something's wrong here."

"Got it." Melissa called Ben then smiled and nodded at Riley when he answered.

"There isn't anything wrong. She's fine. If this isn't a good time for a quick chat, call me later."

Melissa listened then said, "Okay," before she hung up.

"He'll call me back in an hour."

"Good." Riley smiled. "Thank you."

"I still want to vacuum, but in case he calls back early, would you follow me around with my phone?"

"You don't trust me alone with your phone, do you?" Riley scowled.

Melissa smiled. "Of course not."

"My bedroom then the hall and your bedroom," Melissa said as she loosely wrapped the cord then dusted the master bedroom.

"I could dust my bedroom while you vacuum in here," Riley volunteered.

Melissa narrowed her eyes at Riley then handed Riley her duster. "Okay, give me my phone then go ahead. We'll save a lot of time. I'll place the phone where I can see it."

Busted.

When Melissa turned on the vacuum, Toby trotted to the kitchen, and Dusty and Finn followed him.

Riley dusted her room then dusted the lamp and table in the hallway before she hurried to Melissa's bedroom.

Melissa turned off the vacuum. "Done. If you'll return the duster to the utility, I'll meet you in your bedroom. I'll vacuum the hall on my way there."

When Riley returned to her bedroom, Melissa handed her the phone and finished vacuuming. After she turned off the machine, Melissa said, "Thank you for your help, Riley. I can't believe how fast we cleaned the first floor; although, if it weren't for Toby, it might have taken me a little longer to vacuum because Duffy and Finn looked ready to pounce on the vacuum cleaner."

Riley giggled. "You're right. They were definitely up for the challenge."

After Melissa put away the vacuum, Toby and the puppies walked to the back door, and Melissa opened the door for them. Melissa grabbed her jacket and went out with the dogs while Riley rushed to her room for her poncho. When Riley joined Melissa outside, they strolled to the garden, and the puppies followed them.

"Feels good in the sunshine," Riley said, "even if it is cold."

When Melissa's phone rang, she put one index finger to her lips then answered with the speakerphone on.

"Hi, Mom. I have just a few seconds."

"That's fine. Claire says hello. Everything's fine here."

"That's great. Thanks for letting me know. Love ya, cutie."

Ben hung up.

Melissa and Riley stared at each other then burst out laughing.

Melissa wiped away her tears of laughter. "That deputy man is good, isn't he?"

Riley caught her breath. "You were slick, and so was he. He'll go by the clinic to see Claire or call her as soon as he can, and wasn't that a great way to tell me hello? I feel a lot better."

"Good. Your new official code name is cutie, except it's spelled capital Q, capital T."

"Love it." Riley giggled.

"What do you love?" Jake asked as he rounded the corner.

"Well, for starters, I love it here." Riley side-glanced Melissa.

"Jake, you heard everything, didn't you?" Melissa narrowed her eyes and crossed her arms.

"Who, me?" Jake asked. "Wouldn't that be eavesdropping? Isn't that against some rule?"

"Sure, just like the rule of no cookies before dinner," Melissa said.

"You hurt me to the quick." Jake put his hand on his chest and sighed before he headed back to the barn then turned around and winked at Melissa.

Melissa glared. "Let's go inside."

Toby and the puppies rushed to go inside with them. After they were in the kitchen, Melissa chuckled. "I couldn't laugh in front of him because then he would have won."

"Did he hear everything?" Riley asked while she hung up her poncho near the back door.

Melissa refilled Toby's large water bowl and the puppies' smaller one.

"No, but he didn't need to. He knew we were up to something because we were standing outside in the cold."

Riley snickered. "We gave ourselves away."

"I canned some old-fashioned vegetable soup last spring. What do you think about hot soup and buttermilk biscuits for lunch?" Melissa asked.

"That sounds wonderful," Riley said.

"I had planned to make chili for supper and have already started the beans, but would chili go with our fancy dessert? We could put grated cheese on top to have gourmet chili."

"The fancy dessert would cool down the spicy from the chili. Sounds perfect to me," Riley said.

"Why don't you relax a bit? I'll let you know when lunch is almost ready, so you can find Jake and tell him to come inside."

While Riley was reading her third chapter, Melissa came into the living room. "Fifteen minutes."

"I'll let Mr. Jake know," Riley said. She hurried to the kitchen and slipped her poncho over her head then went outside. Toby and the puppies bounded to her.

"Want to help me find Mr. Jake, or are you ready to go inside?" she asked.

Duffy and Finn climbed the three steps to the door, and Riley giggled then opened it for them. "The puppies wanted to come in. Toby's going with me," she said.

Toby led Riley to the barn. Jake was sitting on a small wooden box with several small parts scattered next to his tractor. "Hey, Riley. Mick send you?"

"Lunch will be ready soon."

"What's on the menu?" he asked while he tightened a bolt.

"Melissa's old-fashioned vegetable soup and buttermilk biscuits," she said.

Jake wiped his hands on one of his newer shop rags and stared at his tractor. "It's been sitting a while. It can wait a little longer, let's go inside."

On the way, Jake said, "I heard back from the sheriff. He wanted to know more about Eli Reeves. I told him everything I could think of which was pretty much a repeat of what I told him before. He wanted to know if I was positive that Reeves didn't recognize you. I told him I'd check with you. Are you positive, Riley?"

"I'm positive. He didn't look at me when he went into the hardware store, came out, or when he waved, and Toby stayed out of sight on the floorboard. He was essentially waving in the direction of your truck in case anyone was watching. I nodded to acknowledge his wave, but he was already halfway down the street. He was in a big rush."

"I forgot to tell the sheriff about Toby. That's a good point. You go on inside; it's cold out here. I'm going to call the sheriff back. I won't be long."

Riley hurried inside. "Brr. I think the temperature is dropping."

"Wouldn't surprise me; we have a cold front heading our way, and it's bringing rain with it," Melissa said. "We'll make sure to have a roaring fire for you to chase away the chills. I'm making a fresh pot of coffee. Would you rather have hot or sweet tea?"

"Sweet tea would be great," Riley said. "You have plenty of candles if the lights go out, right?"

"Sure do, and better yet, we've got our kerosene lanterns that are much brighter."

Riley exhaled. *Warm, dry house, plenty to eat and drink, comfortable place to sit and sleep, and a clean bathroom. Total luxury.*

Melissa hugged her. "I'm so sorry, Riley."

Toby leaned against Riley and whined, and Riley's mouth quivered. "Toby understands too."

Melissa poured Riley's tea then placed her glass on the table before she pulled out the biscuits from the oven. She used her oven mitt to grab one and toss it onto Riley's small plate.

"Split your biscuit and butter it while it's hot."

Riley sat at her place, put a large pat of butter inside her biscuit, and smiled as the top of the biscuit slowly lowered as the fat butter pat melted and drizzled over the side of the biscuit.

When Jake came inside, his cheeks and nose were red. Princess darted inside before he closed the door.

"It's going to be that cold and wet, Princess? I guess we'll have to find an indoor project for us this afternoon." Jake said.

Princess meowed then strolled to the stove and flopped down next to the oven. When the puppies crept toward her, she hissed then closed her eyes, and they raced to Toby.

While Jake let the faucet run until the water was warm, he said, "Smart boys. Might as well learn to hone your skills of discretion now."

Melissa handed Jake his plate with two biscuits. While she dished up the hot soup, Jake buttered his biscuits. "Riley, Sheriff Dunn was definitely unhappy about Eli Reeves showing up in town. I told him that I had the feeling Eli Reeves had followed me to the hardware store. To quote the sheriff," Jake's voice dropped to a deep growl, "'if Reeves traced Riley to Carson, anybody could trace Riley to Carson.'"

Riley smiled. "That was a very good impression of the sheriff."

Jake grinned. "I take it Sheriff Dunn doesn't have a high opinion of our friend, Eli Reeves, and intends to find out exactly how Reeves knew to come to Carson to look for you."

Melissa narrowed her eyes. "You and the sheriff need to figure out what you want to do, but Riley is warm and safe here. If it takes an army to protect her, so be it. She has to be warm, dry, and safe at all times."

"I hear you, honey. I told the sheriff I didn't know what he had in mind, but it better be a darn good plan to get past you."

"Good. Let's eat," Melissa said.

After everyone finished their soup, Melissa asked, "Anyone interested in a little lunch dessert?"

Riley grinned as Jake said, "Absolutely."

Melissa placed moderate portions of Mille-feuille on three plates while Riley pulled out three forks.

"If we don't like it, I'll have time to make a peach pie," Melissa said before she took a bite. "Oh, this is really good."

"Sure is," Riley said, and Jake nodded.

While they were still eating their dessert, Jake's phone rang. "It's the sheriff. Dang it."

"Hello, Sam." Jake listened.

"I agree," Jake said. "I don't think there will be any objections, but if there are, I'll let you know. Thanks."

CHAPTER EIGHTEEN

After he hung up, he poised his fork for another bite, and Melissa jerked the plate away. "Oh, no you don't. Talk, or I'll give the rest of it to the puppies, and they'll be pooping rich dessert all afternoon."

Riley's eyes widened, and Jake guffawed. "You are truly the master of destroying a good dramatic opportunity that promised to be complete with tension and suspense."

"Talk, farmer man, or the plate goes on the floor." Melissa glared as she lowered the plate, and Jake returned her glare.

Riley looked from Melissa to Jake then back.

Melissa laughed and returned his plate. "You win. I went too far with the puppies, didn't I? You knew there was no way I'd let them have something that would upset their stomachs. I should have threatened to eat it myself. So, what did the sheriff say?"

"You've still ruined the whole thing," Jake said.

"Fine. I'll make the peach pie."

Jake's eyes twinkled. "He's sending Ben here."

Melissa squealed, and Riley whooped and knocked over her chair as she jumped up. The puppies scattered, Toby howled, and Princess danced with Riley.

After Riley righted her chair and returned to her seat, Jake cocked his head. "Unanimous, I see."

"Oh, yes." Riley said as Princess hopped up on her lap and purred, and Toby leaned against Riley while she scratched his ears. "When will he be here?"

"He's under strict orders not to speed, but he's already left. According to the sheriff, Ben never unpacked and has been sleeping in his truck."

"Will he make it here before the storm hits?' Riley's tone matched the worry that spread across her face.

"Good point. I'll check." Jake strode out the back door, and Toby followed him.

"After I put away the soup, we need to clean the upstairs," Melissa said. "Will the stairs be too hard for you?"

"Not at all. How can I help?"

"Clear the table, then we'll tackle the upstairs rooms. I'm actually glad we have something to do to keep from going crazy."

When Jake and Toby returned, Jake said, "It'll be close, but he might make it."

"We'll be upstairs," Melissa said.

"I'll bring in more firewood," Jake said, and Toby and the puppies followed him.

Melissa handed the duster to Riley. "I got tired of hauling the vacuum from one floor to the other, so I have another one upstairs. While you dust the guest bedroom, I'll give Ben's bedroom a quick dust then vacuum. We're just getting this out of the way, so I don't think I have to do it tomorrow. I have a bed in the third bedroom, but it's become a storage room."

After they cleaned and were on their way downstairs, Melissa said, "I'm going to make that peach pie."

Riley went to the living room and was reading her book when Jake came inside and stacked a few logs near the hearth.

"If we need more, I've stacked it on the front porch then covered it with a tarp to keep it dry." After he added a large log to the fire, he asked, "Are you and Ben just friends or something more?"

Riley put down her book and furrowed her brow. "I hadn't really thought about it. He's the best friend I've ever had."

Jake nodded. "So, what do you think about in between being kidnapped, almost drowned, your car exploding, and staying alert to avoid a crazed killer?"

Riley furrowed her brow then giggled. "Ben."

Jake chuckled. "Thought so."

Melissa called from the kitchen. "I can't finish this pie unless you two talk louder. I think I missed something."

"You tell her," Jake said. "I need to check on Toby, Duffy, and Finn and make sure the driveway's clear."

As they strolled to the kitchen, Riley asked, "What's wrong with the driveway?"

"Nothing," Jake said as he went out the back door.

"So, what was so funny?" Melissa asked.

"Mr. Jake tricked me." Riley told her what he'd asked her.

"And you answered, 'Ben,' didn't you? He's a wily old guy, that's for sure." Melissa chuckled. "He's just happy that you and Ben are such good friends. I'd say that he doesn't mean to push you, but he's an incurable romantic with the soul of a matchmaker. It's all part of what makes him such a likeable old cuss."

Riley giggled.

Melissa put the pie in the oven. "Ben will be here before the pie finishes baking. Would you like for me to wash your hair? We have time before Ben arrives if we blow dry it."

"What a good idea. How can we wash it?"

"I'll grab the shampoo, conditioner, and some towels. We'll wash your hair in the kitchen sink."

After Melissa washed and rinsed Riley's hair, she combed out the tangles. While Melissa blow dried Riley's hair, she said. "I didn't think this through; I'm not a hair stylist. Is a ponytail okay?"

"Perfect. I really appreciate this," Riley said.

"There you go. Check the bathroom mirror."

"Thank you so much. I'm sure it's fine." Riley threw on her poncho and dashed out the front door.

Jake grinned when she joined him at the driveway. "He's that close? I take it your Ben radar alert went off."

"Yep, and there's a truck that's headed this way on the road." She hugged herself under her poncho in excitement, and Duffy and Finn caught her mood and danced around her.

Toby barked at the crunching sound of tires as a vehicle rolled its way down the long driveway to the house, and Jake smiled. "I sure hope Ben's ready to be mobbed."

After Ben parked and jumped out of his truck, he raced to Riley and lifted her off her feet in a bearhug. "I missed you more," he whispered as he held her tight then kissed her soundly while Toby leaned against the two of them, and the puppies clamored for Ben's attention.

"Hey, Dad. Thanks for the welcome home party." Ben kept his hold on Riley while he scratched Toby's ear and peered at Duffy and Finn. "Hi, puppies."

A gust of cold wind from the incoming front blew through, and Jake said, "I'll help carry in your gear. We're about to get hit with that storm. Take the dogs inside, Riley."

When Riley ran toward the house, Toby, Duffy, and Finn raced along behind her. She opened the door, and the dogs dashed inside.

"Ben's here." Riley inhaled the sweet aroma of baking peaches. "The pie smells wonderful."

Melissa peeked into the oven. "He beat the pie by ten minutes."

When Ben, Jake, and the dogs came inside, Jake and Ben set Ben's bags and gear on the floor before Ben hugged his mother. Princess planted herself in front of Ben and yowled; after he stroked her back, she rubbed against his leg. When the puppies approached, she hissed, and Duffy and Finn ran to Melissa.

"She's kind of possessive," Melissa said. "She'll let you say hello in a minute."

Princess flicked her tail then strolled to Riley, and the puppies rushed to Ben.

"Did you name them yet?" Ben asked as he bent down and rubbed puppy bellies.

"The black one is Duffy, and the golden one is Finn," Melissa said.

"Sounds like a couple of Irish pups to me," Ben said.

"Exactly," Melissa said.

Ben glanced at the crate. "They're already crate-trained?"

"So far, so good," Riley said.

While Melissa pulled the pie out of the oven, a boom of thunder shook the windowpanes, then a blast of wind slammed the downpour of rain against the side of the house. When a second thunder roar crashed, Princess darted into the puppies' crate. Finn rushed the side of the crate and barked at her while Duffy carefully pulled out their baby blanket.

"You made it just in time, Ben," Jake said as another roll of thunder shook the windows.

"It chased me the whole way," Ben said. "I probably shouldn't text the sheriff that I'm here for another ten or so minutes."

"Did you have lunch?" Melissa asked. "It will take me two minutes to warm up some soup for you."

"That sounds good. I planned to pick up a sandwich on my way, but the storm behind me kept getting darker and closer."

Melissa dished up a healthy serving of cold soup into a pot she'd set on the stove and turned on the burner before she set the foil-wrapped biscuits into the warm oven. "After I warm up Ben's soup, I'll see if I have something that will be yours, Princess."

"I can stir," Riley said.

"Thank you. I'll check the storage room."

"I'll follow you, Mom, and put my things in my room." Ben strode to his bags.

"I'll help you with your things." Jake picked up the bag that he'd brought inside.

After they had gone upstairs, it wasn't long until Ben returned to the kitchen in jeans and a long-sleeved, blue plaid flannel shirt.

"I turned on the burner for the kettle in case you wanted hot tea." Riley stirred the soup.

Ben came up behind her and wrapped his arms around her and snuggled her neck. "This is what I want. I don't like being away from you. It doesn't work."

Riley turned and met his gaze. "No, it doesn't work at all."

Ben leaned down and kissed her, and she wrapped her arm around his neck and pulled herself close to him while she returned his kiss.

When they broke apart, Ben smiled. "Nice."

Riley turned back to the stove. "I think your soup is hot."

"So are you," he whispered as he kissed the back of her neck and sighed before he poured his soup into a bowl.

Riley sat with him at the table. "Toby and I decided that good friends kiss. I told your mom that you're my best friend." She put her hand on his arm, and he met her gaze.

"Best friends kiss the best," she said.

Ben smiled. "Agreed. Did Dad talk to you?"

"He did, and your mom told me that he's an incurable romantic."

"Mom's not wrong. He talked to me too," Ben said.

Riley frowned. "The thing is that I've had school friends and work friends, and I have no idea where they are now, and that's okay, so..."

"You're worried that we're, what? Disaster friends?" Ben asked.

"Something like that."

Melissa and Jake came down the stairs.

"We'll talk more later," Ben whispered, and Riley nodded.

"We found you a nice, sturdy box, Princess," Melissa said. "If we set it with the sides up, the puppies won't be able to get into it for a while, or we can set it so that you have a roof, and you can tell them to stay out, and I found an old, soft towel.

Melissa put the large box with the top open and Princess tipped it over. "A roof is nice," Melissa said.

"What's our plan, Ben?" Jake asked when he came downstairs.

"It's fairly simple. We just keep Riley safe." Ben kept eating his soup after he crumbled a biscuit and dropped it into his bowl to soak up the hot liquid.

Jake nodded. "Good plan. Any ideas how we do that?"

"So far, the best I can come up with is to circle the wagons." Ben shrugged.

"Can I ride shotgun?" Melissa asked.

"You and your shotgun watching out the kitchen window actually sounds like a good idea, honey," Jake said. "Do we move Riley upstairs?"

"Either that or I move downstairs," Ben said.

"Either way would work from a bed standpoint," Melissa said.

"My knee is fine, so I could easily move upstairs to the guest bedroom," Riley said.

"Or we could swap bedrooms," Ben said. "We have options."

"We had a small dessert, Ben. Care for a taste of a French pastry your father, the connoisseur of all things sweet, found?"

Ben narrowed his eyes. "Do I have to run upstairs and put on my suit?"

"Do what you want; I wore mine," Jake said.

"You don't even own a suit." Melissa laughed as she dished up the pastry for Ben.

"This is fancy," Ben said.

After Ben ate his dessert, Melissa said, "I'm sure you and Riley have a lot to talk about. I need to work on supper, so I'd appreciate it if everyone cleared out of the kitchen unless you intend to help me chop vegetables and char and peel poblano peppers."

"I'd like to unpack a few things. I've been living out of my duffel bag for a while. Willing to supervise, Riley?"

"Watching people work has become my newest hobby," she said.

"I have a project in the barn," Jake said.

"Really? And what is that?" Melissa asked.

"I'll know when I get there." Jake strode to the back door and put on his hat and raincoat then dashed outside.

Ben carried his dishes to the sink. "Leave them there. I'll take care of them," Melissa said.

As they headed upstairs, Ben said, "I only got bits of information from the sheriff. Let's talk."

Riley relaxed on the old, leather chair in Ben's room. While he hung up his uniforms, she told him about Eli Reeves showing up at the hardware store.

"Wow, no wonder the sheriff went on a tear about Reeves. After he talked to Dad, he called Marc and asked him what Reeves was working on. I got the impression Marc was very closed-mouth until Sheriff Dunn told him about Reeves showing up in Carson. More interesting GBI stuff: Doc Thad got a call from GBI, that was legitimate because he checked, and the GBI agent told Thad to stop digging into Preston Ansell's records. At my urging, Doc Thad called Sheriff Dunn, but the sheriff didn't know anything about it and intended to talk to Marc. When the sheriff called Thad back, the sheriff told Thad that he didn't have any details he could share, but he would personally recommend against hiring Doctor Ansell."

"The sheriff would never say anything like that about someone unless he had a good strong reason," Riley said.

Ben nodded. "I dropped by to see Claire, and she told me about Evy. Claire would be a great interrogator, wouldn't she? Anyway, Pia has a good friend in Miami that she called to ask about the Ansells, and her friend didn't know a Doctor Preston Ansell, but he did know of a Doctor Peter Ainsdale, but Pia's friend said Ainsdale was single."

"Then the similar initials must be coincidental, right?" Riley asked.

"You'd think so. There were rumors that Ainsdale lost his veterinarian license a couple of years ago after a drug conviction, but I couldn't find a record of anything. Doc Thad thinks Doctor Preston Ansell didn't exist until he managed somehow to get a Georgia veterinarian license."

Riley furrowed her brow. "That would kind of explain why Doc Thad was told to forget about Doctor Ansell then, doesn't it?"

"Maybe, if he's under an investigation, or it may just muddy the waters. Doc Julie Rae called one of her friends in Atlanta who knew some people who might know Preston Ansell. The friend is supposed to get back to Doc Julie Rae today, and Doc Thad will let me know how that goes." Ben shook his head. "Back to Claire. She took a picture of Doctor Preston Ansell when he was walking to the clinic from the parking lot, so Doc Julie Rae intends to show it to her friend."

Riley snort-laughed. "Claire did what?"

Ben rolled his eyes. "For the record, your friends are crazy. I feel like you somehow cloned yourself."

Riley smiled. "You're my best friend. Does that make you my best crazy?"

Ben's crooked smile widened. "Yes, it does. Crazy about you, just like they used to say in the corny, old movies."

Riley leaned her head back against the chair. "I am so glad you're here."

After he had finished putting his clothes away, he folded his duffel bag and put it on the top shelf of his closet. "So, what else do you have?"

"I got a strange text from Marcy's cousin Luanne today," Riley said. "I'm not sure she meant to send it to me because it didn't make any sense."

Ben frowned. "I forgot to yell at you because you weren't supposed to turn on your phone unless it was an emergency."

Riley raised her eyebrows. "Well, go ahead then. I'll wait."

Ben laughed. "Dang it. You are so cute." He rolled his eyes. "Okay, I'm done. Luanne's text."

"It said, 'sent draft.'"

"Is that all? Does that mean anything to you?" Ben asked.

"Not a thing. I can't imagine a draft of what. I almost forgot about it."

Ben drummed his fingers on the top of his dresser. "I guess this draft could be in the mail or in an email."

"I don't know. I really wanted to respond to her and ask what the draft is or if she meant the text for someone else."

"Bad idea. What if I..."

"Worse idea," Riley said.

"You're probably right. Okay, get your phone. If I get nervous about this, though, you're going to have to sleep in my closet."

Riley rose and peered inside his closet. "I think I could very easily fit in there."

When she turned and saw Ben's scowl, she said, "Phone, I'll be right back."

She stifled her snicker as she went downstairs to her bedroom then returned to Ben's room.

He was still scowling. "You have your phone in your back pocket. Why did you leave?"

"You told me to get it, and I didn't want to irritate you any more than I already have. So, how do you know it's in my back pocket?" She crossed her arms.

"Because I had to watch you very carefully while you went down the stairs because your back pocket is so cute."

Riley burst into giggles. "You totally caught me off guard. Well played, Deputy."

She was still giggling as she composed her text to Luanne: "To my email?"

She showed her phone to Ben. "What do you think?"

Ben frowned. "This is worse than my worse idea. Check your email first. If there's nothing there, the text was meant for someone else, and you can ignore it."

"That's smart." Riley shuddered. "The storm is even noisier upstairs."

"I've never noticed before. That means it will be hard to hear if anything's going on downstairs during a storm. We're staying on the first floor," Ben said.

As they descended the stairs, Melissa shouted from the kitchen, "Benjamin Jacob! Riley Malloy!"

Riley froze. "Are we in trouble?"

"Sounds like we are. Come on. We're strong together."

"I hope so because it sounds bad."

When they hurried into the kitchen, Jake stood behind Melissa with the palms of his hands facing them as he motioned for them to slow down.

Melissa's face was red as she waved her phone. "Explain yourselves. Why am I just now hearing this? Why didn't you tell me?

Do you have any idea of how many phone calls I have gotten in the past twenty minutes? What were you doing upstairs? Planning to run away?" Melissa took a breath, and Jake broke in.

"Mom's received almost twenty phone calls from irate friends that weren't invited to the wedding."

Ben and Riley stared at each other then at Melissa, who burst into tears.

"What wedding? Who's getting married?" Riley asked.

"Don't pretend you don't know, Missy, and I need to know what your middle name is," Melissa growled.

"Mom, wait a minute. Dad, who's getting married?" Ben asked.

Melissa stomped her foot. "No pretending from you either, Benjamin Jacob, and Miss Riley Malloy, I need to know your middle name, so I can properly yell at you."

Jake furrowed his brow. "Melissa, could you slow down one minute? I need a fresh cup of coffee or hot tea. What about you?"

Melissa turned to the sink and filled the tea kettle with water. "If I find out you knew anything about this, you are in hot water yourself, Jacob."

"Mom, I'm not getting married next month." Ben rolled his eyes.

"I'm not either." Riley narrowed her eyes as the turned to Ben. "Who is this person you aren't marrying?"

"What?" Ben's eyes widened then Jake laughed.

"The entire town called your mom to tell her that Ben is getting married next month, and since he has no other prospects, the natural assumption was that he was marrying Riley," Jake said.

"That's kind of sad when you say it like that," Riley said. "Ben probably has lots of prospects, but he's busy right now with crime and things."

Ben hugged Riley. "You're awesome. In fact, you're so awesome, I'd marry you if I weren't already getting married."

He winked, and Riley laughed.

Melissa stared at them then exhaled. "The story going around is that Ben is getting married next month. I'm sure some of the people who called embellished some of the details, but I won't go into them. The story is that a friend of Ben's was in town today and stopped at the gas station and was talking about Ben's wedding next month. Ben's friend mentioned Riley, but according to the one person I trust who pays attention to what people say, Ben's friend said that Riley didn't know. Everyone else who called me said Ben was getting married to Riley, and they were quite pleased with themselves to be the first to tell me."

"A friend of Ben's?" Jake asked. "Definitely Eli Reeves, and if he wanted to cause an uproar, he was successful."

Riley sat at the table. "What on earth for?"

"I'd say he's jealous. Was he an old boyfriend, Riley?" Melissa asked.

Riley snorted. "Not hardly. According to our new vet tech, Eli has a reputation for conquer and dump. Eli Reeves is with the GBI and came to Barton to ask me about the Trumans and their criminal activities after I left Pomeroy. He was essentially my contact with the GBI. He's been around lately because he's investigating something, but I don't know what. Something important, if you listen to him. I don't believe much of what he says."

"Well, shoot." Tears welled up in Melissa's eyes. "I was looking forward to the wedding."

"Honey, if you scare them any more than you have, they'll have to elope, and you'll make me chase them down. Let's not do that."

Melissa laughed. "That might be fun. So, Riley, what is your full name?"

"Riley Erin Malloy, but if you're going to yell at me like Grandma did, she pronounced Erin 'Eire-ann' when she was really angry."

"I'll do my best," Melissa said.

Riley's phone rang, then Ben's phone rang.

"It's Claire. I'll bet Eli's in Barton." Riley shook her head.

Claire spoke as soon as Riley answered. "How could you do this? Ben's getting married to some bimbo, and you didn't call me?"

"Oh, man. It's the sheriff. I'm fired," Ben said.

When Ben answered, he held the phone away from his ear while the sheriff shouted, and he took his phone into the living room. Jake shook his head and followed him.

"Claire," Riley broke in. "Eli was in Carson and left the whole town in an uproar by starting a rumor that Ben was getting married next month."

"Eli Reeves? That's who came by the office and told us the same thing. He said Ben was getting married, and you didn't know about it. He thought it was awful that Ben's been stringing you along. He suggested it might be better if we told you before you hear it from someone else. It's not true?"

"Nope. Ben's not getting married."

"And your heart's not broken?"

"No. Would it be okay if Ben's heart was broken?"

Melissa cleared her throat, and when Riley glanced at her, Melissa snickered.

Claire giggled. "That wouldn't go over well at my house. Thad and Ben are friends. I'm glad you're okay. While I've got you on the phone, I got another Evy call. She was wondering if I knew who Marcy was, and I told her about the cat. Then she asked about Marcy's cousin, and I reminded her that I didn't know Marcy personally, so I wouldn't know any of her relatives. Very curious."

"Yes, it is."

"Ben told me about Ansell," Riley said. "Did you send the photo to the sheriff?"

"Sure did. Right after Thad found out I had it." Claire snickered. "Oh, one other thing: Doc Julie Rae's friend in Atlanta hit a blank wall and couldn't find anyone who knows Preston Ansell. Pia and I were not surprised. I'll keep you posted."

After Claire disconnected, Riley said, "Eli spread his lies in Barton. What was the purpose? Distraction? No, I've got it. I have to talk to Ben."

Riley rushed to the living room. "I need to talk to the sheriff. Don't go anywhere. Either of you."

Ben said, "Sorry sir, but I have to hand off the phone to Riley. She wants to talk to you."

"Sheriff, I know what's going on. Eli Reeves spread the same story about Ben in Carson, and now everyone in two towns and probably the entire region knows where I am. Or if they don't, they will by the time the day is over. The phones have been on fire here, and Claire told me it's all over Barton. Anybody can find me. Anybody. All they have to do is walk into either town and ask. Whoever was looking for me just got a big boost. I don't believe Eli realizes what he did though, but he must be taking orders from someone who does."

"You sure about this, Riley?"

"It's the only thing that makes sense."

Melissa came into the living room and sat next to Riley.

"What do you want me to do?" Sheriff Dunn asked.

"It's time for me to disappear for a while. I have an idea, but I need to talk to Ben, Jake, and Melissa first. One of us will get back to you."

After Riley disconnected, Ben said, "I don't like it."

"How can you say that, Ben? Riley hasn't said anything," Melissa said.

"You'll see."

"Ms. Melissa, how long would it take for you to spread a counter-rumor?" Riley asked.

"You mean like a better rumor that will take the place of the first one? Two phone calls, but you have to call me Melissa or Mick because otherwise, I'd feel funny the next time I yell at you and Ben."

Riley peered at Melissa. "I'll have to think about it, but two phone calls is outstanding. We need for the rumor in Carson to be that I left to go home, then we need the rumor in Barton to be that I left Carson and disappeared. Claire and the sheriff can take care of the Barton rumor."

"So, where will you go?" Ben asked.

"Nowhere. I disappear here."

"How do you do that?" Jake asked.

"I'm definitely open to suggestions, but my idea was that we make a big show of Jake driving me out of town then we come back without anyone knowing I returned. I'll have to stay in the house in case anyone is smart enough to think of using a drone to see if I'm on the property. It might make sense for me to be upstairs with all my things in the spare room. I won't be able to have any lights on at night, but I can deal with that. If I want to read, I can read in the closet with a flashlight and a book. There may be details to work out, but we can do that later."

"What is the purpose of your disappearance?" Ben scowled.

"To buy a little time for us to figure out why someone is after me."

"If you ask me," Jake said, "Eli Reeves is somehow key. If Riley's right, he was an unwitting catalyst, so who put him up to it and why? Who would Reeves talk to? Maybe he thinks the sheriff is an ally."

"That's an excellent idea, Dad," Ben said. "As far as Reeves is concerned, the sheriff has no ties to Riley, and the sheriff certainly has a way about him that gives people, even bad guys, the impression that he's on their side."

"So when does Riley leave?" Melissa asked.

"As soon as we can get her bags loaded," Jake said. "Riley, I'll stop for gas to be sure you're seen leaving town, and if anyone is watching the house, I'll return from the other direction with you hidden."

"I agree," Riley said.

"You'll need to be gone about two hours, Dad," Ben said.

"I can do that. I can stop at a couple of pawn shops before I turn back."

"Two hours means it will be after dark before you get back," Melissa said.

"Even better," Riley said.

"Let's get busy. Not that I like it at all, but we can refine as we go," Ben said. "I suppose I can't go with you, can I, Riley?"

"How can you ask that, Ben? You just dumped that poor girl," Melissa said, and Ben rolled his eyes.

"Yes, Mom."

"I need to talk to someone because I'm so distraught. I was really fond of Riley." Melissa flounced to the kitchen, and Riley giggled.

CHAPTER NINETEEN

"I'll take my things upstairs," Riley said.

"I'll move them if you'll supervise. I have an idea for your running away luggage too," Ben said.

Jake picked up his phone as Riley and Ben left the living room.

"I'll call Claire while I point," Riley said after she and Ben reached her bedroom.

When Claire answered, Riley said, "The rumors were true; Ben is getting married next month, and I'm leaving the Carters' as soon as we get Mr. Carter's truck loaded with my things."

"Gotcha," Claire said.

Riley smiled. *Claire's awesome.*

"Do we know where you're going?" Claire asked.

Ben asked the same thing. I should have an answer.

Claire continued, "It's okay. I know you'll be comfortable at your professor's beach house while you recover from this terrible blow."

"Thank you, Claire. I'm so glad you understand, and I'm looking forward to some beach time; there's no better place to think. You're totally awesome."

Riley glanced at Ben who nodded before he carried her full duffel bag and backpack upstairs.

"I'll keep this as quiet as you probably planned."

Before they disconnected, Claire said, "Be safe. I'm here for you."

"I know you are. Thank you; good friends like you are really rare."

Riley felt her eyes well up as she hurried to the living room; Jake was still on the phone with the sheriff.

"Are you okay?" Jake asked.

"Of course not, your son just dumped me for some man-stealer." Riley grinned. "Can I talk to the sheriff?"

Jake handed her his phone.

"Sheriff, I just got off the phone with Claire; she's going to make sure the right people know that I'll be at my favorite professor's beach house to heal my broken heart."

"I like it. Nothing like sea air to clear your head. Thanks for letting me know, so I can back up Claire."

"Thanks for everything, Sheriff." Riley handed the phone to Jake.

"Guess that's it, Sheriff. I'll keep you posted." Jake disconnected.

"The sheriff's going to chat with his good friend Eli over dinner. Let's get moving, Riley. Be sure to pack your beach clothes, except no bikini."

Riley giggled. "You've got the dad-itude down pat."

Jake beamed.

Ben came downstairs with two flattened boxes. "If we open these up and put them on the backseat, they can be your things you packed. Before you return, flatten the boxes, and Dad's truck will look empty. This is probably unnecessary, but I'd feel better. Are you sure I can't go with you to the beach?" Ben gazed at Riley. "Maybe we need some time to reconcile or something because I'm definitely dumping ole what's-her-name."

"Too late, Ben," Melissa said as she came into the room. "You can't expect a stroll at midnight on a moonlit beach to make any difference after what you've done."

"Dang. I'm not crazy about being such a jerk, How do I recover my good reputation after this is over?" Ben asked.

"Don't worry about it," Melissa said. "We'll just put a twist on the twist. No one will be surprised when it turns out that ole what's-her-face started the wedding rumor out of spite."

"Oh, that might not be good; Won't people think it was Pamela something?" Riley asked.

"Pamela Suzanne," Melissa said absently. "People might definitely consider her as a prime candidate to start a spite rumor, but new rumors will pop up, and all this will all be forgotten by the end of the month."

Jake shook his head. "I don't understand all of this, and I'm okay with that. Are we ready to leave after we get the boxes in the truck, Riley?"

"I'll do one more sweep of the bedroom and bathroom to make sure we got everything."

When everything was loaded, Ben held Riley then kissed her tenderly before she left the house. "Be safe. I officially don't like this."

After Riley and Jake walked to the truck, Riley's eyes welled up. The tears slipped down her cheek as Jake turned the truck toward town.

"What's wrong?" Jake asked.

"I was thinking about the beach and how nice it would be to walk on the sand with Ben without worrying about who might be watching. Is that what normal people do?"

"I'm not sure I know anymore," Jake said. "We'll have to try out that normal thing one day, but I'm warning you in advance that Mick will rent a big house that allows dogs and a barn cat, so we can all go to the beach. Don't think about that, though, because we'll have a great time. You need to keep crying."

"The beach house was Claire's idea. She knew I hadn't thought of where I was going to disappear. She's a wonderful friend." More tears slipped down Riley's face, and she bit her lip.

When Jake pulled into the gas station next to the pump, Riley looked away when people stared at her, and she felt her cheeks grow warm. "They're angry at Ben. I should have thought of another way because this is awful for him."

Jake shook his head and climbed out of the truck. While he refilled, a man approached him, and the two men spoke quietly.

She sniffed back her tears and pulled out her phone to turn it off but changed her mind. *Everybody knows I'm in Carson; I can text Claire.*

"Left. This is very sad."

Claire responded, "I know. Be tough."

I feel like I've thrown my best friend under the bus. How can I be tough?

Jake went inside the store and stood in front of the refrigerated case then pulled out two bottles of water. As Jake stood in line to pay, a woman stared at Riley then tapped on Jake's arm and spoke to him. While Jake answered her, others nearby stopped to listen then shook their heads.

After Jake hurried out to the truck, he climbed inside and opened a bottle of water before he handed it to Riley then started the engine.

"Word has already gotten out," he said. "I had my concerns, but now I'm certain that you'll be safe at our house."

"They think Ben's terrible, don't they?" Riley wiped her cheek with her shirtsleeve to dry her tears.

"One woman wanted me to tell you that Ben will come to his senses, and you shouldn't lose hope." Jake shook his head. "Overall, people are being very sympathetic."

Riley shook her head. "That is so sweet." She sniffed back her tears as Jake headed south on the interstate.

Thirty minutes later, as cars sped past them, Jake shook his head. "Now I remember why I rarely travel on the interstate. I'm going five miles over the speed limit, but you'd think I was crawling. I'm taking the next exit."

"Good timing on my part. There's a popular hardware store down the road, and I've never taken the time to visit it. Ready to look at all kinds of things you never imagined you've always needed?"

Riley smiled. "That does sound like more fun than the interstate."

When they went inside, Riley inhaled the surprising aroma of cinnamon and apples and gazed at the homey display of candles in wooden crates. She went from box to box and marveled at the variety of fragrances and sizes of candles. *I'll bet Ms. Melissa would like some emergency candles that could double as decorations.* She rounded the corner and found a row of glass lanterns, vases, tubes, and globes for candles. *Mr. Jake was right. I didn't know I needed candles and glass lanterns and vases.*

"Are you ready to go?" Jake asked, and Riley sighed. "You were right. I didn't realize how much we need candles on every horizontal surface in the house."

After they were back on the road, Jake said, "That store sure lived up to its reputation."

"I wouldn't know because I couldn't get past the candles," Riley said.

"We'll have to go back sometime and take Mick and Ben. There's a Western wear store on the way back that I've always wanted to visit. People say if they don't have what you want in the store, they get it; and if they can't get it, they'll make it."

"What are you going to look for there?" Riley asked.

"They have saddles. I don't need a saddle because we don't have a horse, and I certainly don't need a horse, but I need to see the saddles."

"I think I might like to look at the hats. I need sunglasses and a sunhat, but I'd rather have a Western hat," Riley said.

"I'll bet you'll find something there," Jake said. "Ben and Mick are going to be jealous because they didn't get to run away."

Riley snickered. "If I find sunglasses, I may tell Ben I found them at the beach."

Jake laughed. "Maybe they'll have seashells."

A wizened old man with an enormous white moustache approached Riley as she stared at the wall of Western hats.

"Hat for yourself, Missy?" he asked.

"Yes, sir."

He pulled out a tape measure from his pocket. "Sit up here on the stool, so I can see what size you need."

After he measured the circumference of her head, he asked, "For riding or sun protection?"

"Sun protection."

"And warmth too, am I right?" He strode to a section of hats and selected a chocolate brown felt hat then handed it to her.

When Riley put it on, she widened her eyes. "This is comfortable."

The old man smiled. "Looks good on you too." He handed Riley a hand mirror. "What do you think?"

Riley peered in the mirror. "I like it a lot."

Jake joined them. "Looks like you found your hat. How do you like it?"

"It's really comfortable."

"I'll give you a hat box to store it. Don't ever place it down on the brim. Other than that, bring it here when you need it cleaned or reshaped, and we'll take care of it for you."

"This will be my treat," Jake said.

Riley shook her head. "You don't have..."

The old man held up his hand and interrupted Riley. "Missy, don't deprive your old dad the privilege of buying your first cowboy hat for you."

"Right," Jake said.

Riley rolled her eyes. "Okay. Thank you, Dad. I love it."

After they were back on the road, Jake chuckled. "You called me Dad. Mick's going to have a conniption."

Riley snorted. "No way was I going to blow our cover, and you knew it; you're as bad as Ben, or is it vice versa?"

When they were twenty minutes away from the Carters' house, Jake pulled into an abandoned gas station's parking lot.

"Time to fold up those boxes."

After Jake flattened the boxes, Riley lay down on the floorboard and handed her new hat to Jake. "Will you put my hat into its box?"

"Sure will, then I'll put the box on the floor in front of the passenger's seat," Jake said.

When they were back on the road, he said, "I've had more fun today than I've had in a long time. Mick and I need to wander off for an afternoon to explore new shops."

"I highly recommend it," Riley said. "I've never taken an afternoon off to explore my entire life. I think that needs to be a new goal for Ben and me."

"As soon as you're reconciled," Jake added.

Riley snickered. "Right."

When Jake pulled into the driveway, he said, "I've turned off the interior lights, so you won't get out in a spotlight. I texted Ben when we turned at the driveway, but I'm sure Toby alerted him. He'll be waiting to scoot you inside."

When Jake stopped the truck, Ben opened the door and whispered, "Back door."

After Riley climbed out, Ben quietly closed the door then put his arm around Riley as they rushed to the back of the house that was dark inside. When they were inside, Melissa waited for them in the dark kitchen. She turned on the kitchen light after they hurried past her and upstairs to the dark second floor. "How was the beach?" Ben asked.

"Except for the circumstances, we had an enjoyable afternoon."

"I still wish I could have gone." Ben sighed. "Supper will be ready soon. I'll sit at the table for a bit then bring our plates upstairs. Mom and I hung insulated curtains on all the upstairs windows. They won't necessarily block any light, but they will definitely keep anyone from seeing inside. My bedroom's upstairs, so my bedroom light going on is fine, but we don't want to take any chances because we aren't sure about shadows. We didn't have time to check."

Ben helped her remove her poncho then held her tight. When Riley tilted her head back, he leaned down and kissed her. "I'm glad you're safe."

"Before you go, do you mind helping me with my boots?"

After Ben helped her remove her boots, she sat on the soft chair. "Thank you for moving your chair to my room. I really appreciate it."

"Good. I'll be back a little later. Do you need anything?"

"I'm fine."

Ben kissed her forehead then went downstairs. Riley leaned back in the chair and closed her eyes as she listened to the distant voices coming from the kitchen.

She and Ben drifted in the sailboat, and the boat slowly bobbed and floated toward the shore. Angry shouts from the top of the hill startled her, and while she squinted to see what caused the commotion, an angry mob charged down the hill.

Riley jumped to the cannon on the bow, and Melissa loaded the cannon with cookies then shouted, "Fire." When the cannon boomed, people dropped to the ground to pick up cookies; Jake unfurled their sail, and Ben jumped to the helm.

"Riley, Riley, wake up. Are you okay?" Ben asked as he brushed the hair away from her face.

Riley stared at him then looked around. "Where's the sailboat?"

"I think you were dreaming," he said. "Would you like to eat now or later?"

"Let's eat now," Riley said.

While they were eating, Riley said, "It's nice that there's enough light from downstairs to be able to see our food. I guess I expected it to be pitch black."

"Mom said she'd come upstairs after we have dessert and help you take a bath. She found the bath bombs that were in the downstairs bathroom and will bring them up with her."

"I was weepy all the way to town because Claire was so nice, and I was worried about you. That's really nice of Melissa."

"Why were you worried about me?"

"I should have come up with a different idea. I'm so worried that everyone is mad at you."

"Are you mad at me?" Ben asked.

She narrowed her eyes to examine his face. "Are you kidding?"

"No, I'm not."

"Why on earth would I be mad at you? You're my hero."

"I am?"

Riley heard the surprise in his voice and smiled.

When Melissa's phone rang, Ben said, "Mom's been getting condolence calls all afternoon."

"That's terrible," Riley said.

"Let's get closer to the staircase, and you can listen."

"Oh yes, I miss her already. She's absolutely perfect for Ben, and I'm sure you're right. It must be a terrible misunderstanding,"

After Melissa disconnected, she strolled to the staircase then stood in the living room doorway. "Are you ready for dessert, honey?"

"Sure am," Jake said. "Looks like Toby and the puppies are too."

When Toby reached the bottom of the stairs, he raced to the top and to Riley while Jake and the puppies followed Melissa to the kitchen.

Riley scratched his ears. "Good boy, Toby. You found me again."

Toby flopped down at her feet.

"You might need to help with the puppies, but after they're in their crate, come up here with me," Riley said.

"I'll take our plates downstairs then be right back with warm peach pie and ice cream," Ben said.

After they ate dessert, Toby followed Ben downstairs to take the puppies outside, and Melissa came upstairs.

"Do you want to pick your bath bomb, or shall we be random?"

"Random sounds fine to me. I think my decision brain cells need a little recharging. I'm exhausted."

"I can imagine," Melissa said.

Melissa adjusted the water for a warm, but not too hot, bath, before she dropped in the bath bomb.

"Wow, this is nice," Melissa said as the aroma of lavender and chamomile filled the bathroom. "I've always heard that lavender was the best fragrance for a good night's sleep."

Riley climbed into the bath, and Melissa whisked away Riley's clothes and returned with one of Ben's old shirts and Riley's pajama bottoms.

After Riley dried and dressed for bed, she slid under her covers, closed her eyes, and listened while Toby came into her room and flopped down next to her bed.

When Ben tiptoed in later, she said, "I think this is a magical bed that soaks away stress."

Ben chuckled then kissed her. "Good night, sweetie."

"Good night, my hero." Riley rolled over and sank into her magical bed.

* * *

The next morning, Toby nudged Riley's elbow, and she sat up and smiled. "Good boy, Toby."

He trotted down the stairs and to the kitchen. Riley inhaled. *Mmm, coffee.*

She heard the stairs creak, and Ben peeked into her room. "I brought you coffee. Toby said you were awake."

Riley swung her feet to the floor. "Coffee sounds great. How did you sleep?"

"Surprisingly well. Mom said it was because I wasn't worried about you, for a change, and I think she's right."

Riley sat in the soft chair. "This whole thing has been a lot of stress for everyone, hasn't it? I'm really sorry about that."

"There's really nothing for you to feel sorry about. Princess checked on you last night, did you know?"

"She must have been very careful not to disturb me because I didn't hear her." Riley scanned her room. "Is there another chair we can have in my room, so you can sit with me? There seems to be plenty of space."

"I'm sure there is. I'll check with Mom. Breakfast will be ready soon. You know, that was my favorite shirt in high school. I didn't even know Mom had kept it."

"Really?" Riley rubbed the front of the cotton shirt. "It is really soft."

Ben bit his lip while he stared at her then swallowed hard and nodded.

"Breakfast," Melissa called out.

"Mom's talking to the living room again." Ben chuckled. "I'll be right back."

Melissa came into the bedroom with scrambled eggs and green chilies and two buttered biscuits on each of their plates. After she set their breakfast on the table next to the soft chair, she pulled out forks and napkins from her pocket. "Ben's coming up the stairs with another chair. Enjoy your breakfast."

As Melissa left, Ben carried in another soft chair and placed it next to the table. "I'm glad Mom said this chair can stay upstairs because these sturdy, old chairs are heavy; I got my morning workout."

"We're all getting a workout." Jake stood at the door. "Coffee anyone?"

He carried the coffeepot in one hand and held two cups in the other. "This is yours; Melissa's making a small pot for us."

Ben took the pot and cups, and Jake hurried downstairs.

"I think your dad plans to disappear to the barn right after breakfast," Riley whispered.

Ben poured their coffee. "I may have to join him."

"What are your plans for today?" Ben asked as they ate.

"I'd like to check my email, but I'll need the Wi-Fi password, won't I?"

"I'll get you a small table and chair for your laptop then ask Mom for the Wi-Fi password; it's a combination of letters and numbers that make sense only to her. My phone and computer connect automatically, so I never think about it."

Ben left then returned with a small folding table and a folding chair. "Will these work?"

"Perfect, thank you," Riley said.

Ben set up the table and chair then gathered their dishes and the empty coffeepot. "I'll be back in a bit with the Wi-Fi password."

Riley put on one of her new front-snap shirts from the pawn shop then pulled up her jeans. After struggling with the zipper, she lay on the bed and zipped then buttoned her pants. She pulled out a pair of socks then sat on the chair to put them on. She stuck her pistol into the waist on her right at the back of her jeans before she padded to the bathroom to brush her hair.

When she returned to her room, she sat down and shook her head. *Getting dressed is definitely a workout.*

Melissa came into her room. "Jake, Toby, Princess, and the puppies went to the barn. Jake has a new battery for his old tractor to install after he takes the old one out. I think Ben joined him to help. I wrote down the password for you."

Melissa handed Riley a sticky note, and Riley read it then nodded. "Thanks, I want to check my email."

Riley pulled out her laptop from the closet and turned it on while Melissa waited to be sure Riley got onto the internet.

"I'm connected," Riley said, and Melissa headed to the stairs.

When Riley opened her email, she raised her eyebrows. "Luanne forwarded an email to me that Marcy sent to her."

"Did you say something, Riley?" Melissa called from the bottom of the stairs.

"Just talking to myself. Sorry," Riley said.

"Holler if you need me." Melissa continued to the kitchen.

Riley read the email from Luanne. 'Marcy was right. I don't understand this. I'll call you because you have to explain it to me.'

Riley continued reading as she scrolled to the email from Marcy to Luanne: 'Save this for me. You don't need to bother with reading it. It's too technical for you. No one except my old friend Riley would understand it.'

Riley saved the document to her laptop before she opened it, and she stared in disbelief at her screen as she scanned page after page. *This is a copy of the invoices we used to compare to the physical inventory and found the discrepancies. There's something in these invoices.*

She shrugged. "What else do I have to do besides read?" Riley started at the first page.

* * *

When Ben reached the barn, Jake was on the phone. "He's here, now." Jake handed the phone to Ben. "It's the sheriff."

"Jake caught me up on his travels yesterday, and I feel like Riley is finally safe, at least for a while. I took Eli Reeves out to dinner last night. He was definitely happy to explain how smart he is. According to him, his skill and charm allowed him to win the confidence of someone who is close to Riley, and this person is keeping him in the know as far as Riley's whereabouts are concerned. He claimed that he has to know where she is, so he can save her from the bad guy, but I think he's either leading the bad guy to Riley or is the bad guy himself and was enjoying his little subterfuge of fooling me. Whatever's going on, his interest in Riley isn't casual or at all professional. He's convinced that Riley is smitten by him, I know that's an old-fashioned word, but it fits, and she's just being kind to you. You are definitely in Eli's way."

"Good," Ben growled.

"His confidante told him about your impending wedding, and Eli seemed to believe it. He was proud that he let everyone in Barton and Carson know what a scoundrel you are. He told me about going to Carson and talking with Jake and bragged about his skillful interrogation of him. Eli was certain that if Riley was in Carson, Jake didn't know anything about it. He's definitely a hazard whether he's the bad guy or an unwitting dupe because he's driven to find Riley. I have a meeting with Marc later this afternoon. I want Eli Reeves out of the picture. Marc will find a way to occupy him or divert him, for at least a few days."

"Who do you think is supplying Reeves with information?"

"That's troubling. When I told him I didn't think he had a confidante at all and was just being modest, he considered going with it before he decided to impress me with his ability to gain the confidence of someone he hadn't met. He did hint that it was someone I knew well, and I would be surprised when he told me after he had everything solved, and Riley's eyes were opened to his brilliance. I know it isn't you, and I checked out Jake earlier, and it isn't him."

Ben's eyebrows raised. *The sheriff's definitely covering all the bases.* "Do you believe that it's someone he hadn't met? What about Marc?"

"Could be someone he hasn't met, but it was hard to decide what was really true, a lie, or only true in his deluded mind. I considered Marc briefly, but he and I have history, and I'd be dead if it were Marc because I know too much. I haven't checked out the staff at the vet hospital yet. They aren't likely, but I do wonder if Eli's contact is getting information from someone in Barton in the course of casual conversation."

Ben shrugged. "Keeping an old friend informed of what's going on in Barton?"

"What? Say that again; you might have something there."

"Barton's a small town where everyone knows everyone else's business. It would be natural for someone to mention Riley and what's going on, especially if the person was from Barton and knew Riley or at least of Riley. You know, 'thought you'd like to hear the latest.'"

"Could our informant be manipulating Eli? It would be easy to do. Now, I'm not so sure we have an informant. I think we're talking about a bad guy," the sheriff said.

"Close to Riley, and you know him," Ben said.

"Wait. Reeves never said, 'him.' Always 'someone.'"

"He was being clever?" Ben snorted. "Never mind. Sorry I said that."

The sheriff chuckled. "It was a stretch. Anyway, that's all I've got. Talk to Riley. She may have a different perspective."

Ben nodded. "She usually does."

After the sheriff hung up, Ben exhaled then told his dad about his conversation with the sheriff.

Jake stared at Ben. "I hate this entire thing. Is police work always like this?"

"Only if you mix in Riley."

CHAPTER TWENTY

While she rifled through the pink backpack, she glanced with disdain at the blood on the floor of the abandoned house and the lifeless body she had tied to the chair. *You sure were a screamer, Miss Luanne.*

She removed the SIM card from Luanne's phone and pulled out an overstuffed manila envelope from the backpack. "Here they are, sweetie. Just like you said. Thanks for the help."

She stepped carefully to avoid getting any blood on her shoes as she headed to the door. After she was outside, she strode into the woods and used the knife to dig a shallow hole. She dropped her knife into the hole. She tossed the useless phone as far as she could, removed her oversized surgical gloves, and dropped them on top of the knife before she kicked the dirt over the hole and tamped it down then kicked leaves and a branch on top of the hole.

After she was in her car, she headed down the lane to the country road. When she reached a small town, she parked in a grocery store lot, and called Millie.

"I've got the invoices from Luanne," she said.

"That was fast," Millie said.

"It was what you wanted. Do you want me to mail or fax the invoices to you?"

"Mail them to the usual mail drop."

"They'll be on their way as soon as I can find a post office."

"Text me the tracking number, and I'll authorize the funds immediately."

"You're efficient as always, thank you," she said.

After she disconnected, she made another call.

"Marcy had an electronic copy of all the invoices and sent a copy to Luanne; Luanne forwarded the email to Riley because she thought she had something valuable but didn't understand the invoices."

"You do good work, you know that?" he said.

"Of course. Are you taking over now?" she asked.

"On my way. Did you get paid?"

"Not yet. I need to send the folder with all the paper copies of the invoices to Millie's drop box and text her the tracking number. I'm in a small town, so it should be easy to find a post office. Aren't you worried about someone else seeing that email from Marcy?" she asked.

"Not at all. Millie's convinced Truman recorded the purchasers' names on the invoices, and he did but not in a form anyone could understand," he said. "According to Marcy, Truman used his own code that no one else could interpret except a select few of his staff. That's why she understood the value of the invoices she had saved and planned to cash in. If she'd been satisfied with the packet of drugs she had stolen from Truman, we've have never known about her and the invoices, but she got greedy. She said Riley's the last of his staff still alive who can interpret the names. With Riley gone, we're safe."

"Good. Do you know where you're going? I understand there's a plethora of conflicting information," she said.

"You got that right, but I know where I'm going. I'll text you the address."

* * *

Millie's phone rang again. *At least these people are calling me during daylight hours here.*

"Millie, I'm so distraught over Riley. Have you heard anything from her?"

"No, Helen, and I'm worried to death. Do you think I should drop everything and come to Barton?"

"I can't think of what you might possibly do here other than fret. It's probably best that you're busy at work. I'm sorry; I wasn't thinking. You must be busy. Do you want to call me back later?"

"No, that's fine. I'm on a break, so now is a perfect time to talk."

"Did you hear about the trouble with Ben?"

"No, is he okay? What happened?"

"He's fine; well, maybe not fine, but none of us knew that he was going to be married next month. We're all terribly shocked. He's such a nice young man."

Bingo! "Oh my goodness. There must be some type of terrible mistake."

"I'm sure you're right. Riley must have been heartbroken because she just up and left him. She's gone to the beach, and of course, I've forgotten which beach, or maybe no one really knows. She needs a little privacy and time to get over him; the beach is the place I would go to mend a broken heart."

"Well, that's good news. She was always level-headed. I'm sure I'll hear from her soon, but if I don't, I'll take the next flight. Keep me posted. I really appreciate it."

After Helen hung up, Millie smiled. *Well done, Eli, and now Riley's safe, and so am I.*

CHAPTER TWENTY-ONE

Riley smiled when Ben strolled into her room. "My eyes are crossed from reading and cross-referencing Doc Truman Senior's code. Here, look at this."

Ben frowned at her screen. "It's not even letters; it's symbols. Does each symbol correspond to a letter?"

"You'd think so, wouldn't you? It's more convoluted than that. Each symbol corresponds to a different symbol that corresponds to a number that corresponds to a third symbol that corresponds to a letter. I created a cheat sheet for Marcy and me. Once I got the hang of it, it wasn't all that hard, but I'm a little out of practice."

"That's interesting. Do you still have your sheet?" Ben asked.

"Thank goodness I do because it would take a lot of work to recreate it." Riley flipped her screen to her other open document and showed Ben her cheat sheet.

Ben peered at her screen. "Wow. That's amazing. Is it okay if I don't try to help you?"

"I wouldn't put you through that torture. So, what did the sheriff say?" Riley asked as Ben strolled to his chair, sat, and waited while Riley closed her laptop and joined him at the small table.

"Sheriff went out to dinner last night with Eli Reeves. I'll try to keep this factual and leave my opinion out of it," Ben said. "According to Eli, someone close to you is keeping him informed about where you are and what you're doing. He's convinced you have a crush on him but are in denial because of my magnetic charms. Actually, you're getting this completely from my point of view, after all."

Riley smiled. "It wouldn't be nearly as interesting without it."

"Thanks, I'm not sure I could tell it any other way. Your close friend told him about my wedding next month, and Eli took the hook and ran with it. I believe it because I'm not sure Eli would have thought of it himself, and it was a perfect way for that so-called friend to feed Eli's ego. The sheriff will meet with Marc later and fill him in. Sheriff wants Eli out of the picture for a while. What do you make of all this?"

"Eli's been played by this friend of mine. Who does the sheriff think this friend is?"

"He doesn't know," Ben said.

"Someone close enough that no one else is surprised when he or she asks questions. It isn't anyone who works at the vet hospital."

"Why not?"

"They didn't know me before I came to Barton. All of this started originally with Doc Truman Senior then next with Marcy, but it's unlikely any of the staff would have known Truman or Marcy, except Doc Julie Rae might have known of Doc Truman professionally."

"I hadn't thought about that," Ben said.

"A relative would make sense, but the only close relative I have left is Aunt Millie."

"Would she have known Truman or Marcy?"

"Truman, possibly; Marcy, not likely."

Ben frowned. "Do you think it's possible that your aunt is the one who was pulling Eli's strings?"

"No, but I don't see how it could be anyone else that I know either."

"What else?" Ben asked.

"I'm glad Eli's going to be occupied with Marc for a while. He's been a distraction, which might have been the purpose of using him in the first place."

"Want a glass of sweet tea to go with your crossed eyes?" Ben asked. "I'll bring you up a glass then leave you to it."

Ben returned with a glass of tea and a small plate of cookies. "Mom sent cookies to go with the tea. There are six there. She'll ask you."

Riley stared at the plate of four cookies and giggled. "I've got your back, cookie thief."

"Thanks, knew you would."

When Ben bent to kiss her, she smelled the chocolate chips on his breath, and touched his top lip with her tongue. "You taste like chocolate," she said.

"You might be mistaken," Ben's eyes twinkled. "We'll have to try that again." He kissed her thoroughly then grinned. "See, no more chocolate."

Riley smiled when he whistled as he strode out of the room, After she drank half her tea, she set her plate of cookies next to her laptop.

While she nibbled on the cookies, Riley translated the names as she read. After an hour of reading, she stared at her screen. *Oh my gosh.*

"Ben!" she shouted.

"Ben's outside with his dad. Want me to get him?" Melissa called upstairs.

"Yes!" Riley continued to stare at the screen.

Melissa called out the back door, "Ben, come inside, please."

The back door slammed, then Ben raced up the stairs, two at a time. "What is it? What's wrong?" He knelt next to Riley. "You found something, didn't you?"

Her eyes were wide as she pointed to the screen. "I found invoices of drugs ordered by Doc Truman Senior with large shipments of drugs sent to Mildred Malloy in Atlanta and Miami and more large shipments sent to Peter Ainsdale in Miami."

She leaned back in her seat and exhaled. "I need to send this to the sheriff along with my cheat sheet."

Ben texted the sheriff: "R found something. Call me."

When his phone rang a minute later, Ben answered his cell then turned on the speakerphone.

"Riley there?" Sheriff asked.

"Right here, Sheriff," Riley said. "I found invoices with drugs sent to Mildred Malloy and Peter Ainsdale, also known as Preston Ansell."

"Millie? Damn," the sheriff growled. "Wouldn't the GBI have found that?"

"Not without Riley's cheat sheet to decode the Ship To names and addresses," Ben said.

"Marcy sent the invoices in an attachment to her cousin Luanne and told her I was the only one who would understand them," Riley said. "Luanne forwarded the email to me, and I still have my cheat sheet that I had created, so Marcy and I could understand Doc Truman's notes."

"Send the invoices and the cheat sheet, and I'll get them to Marc. Ben, I'll text you the email address."

After Riley forwarded the invoices and her cheat sheet to the sheriff's department, she exhaled. "And now we wait."

"We've certainly had a lot of practice in waiting, haven't we? I'm going to fill in Dad and help him with the tractor."

She turned up her face to him, and he kissed her before he raced down the stairs. Ben spoke quietly to his mom then left the house.

Riley turned off her computer then kicked off her boots, lay down on her bed, and closed her eyes. *There must be a mistake.*

Melissa came up the stairs and stood in the bedroom doorway. "Riley?" she whispered.

"I'm awake," Riley said. "I was just thinking about Aunt Millie. She has looked after me my whole life. I don't know; maybe she's a drug dealer, but I don't believe she'd ever harm me."

"I'm really sorry, honey. I know there isn't anything I can do except listen." Melissa pulled the folding chair close to Riley's bed.

"I don't even know where Aunt Millie is. She's always spent a lot of time traveling, and I know she often goes overseas. When I was little, she brought me souvenirs from Paris, London, Tokyo, and places I never heard of. She always had wonderful stories of living in foreign countries. I'd ask if I could go with her on her next trip, and she'd tell me I needed to focus on school because I was smart like my dad. She was as heartbroken as I was when Dad died. She's always been there for me." Riley sat up and shook her head in disbelief before she stepped to peek out the window. "When the Trumans suddenly closed the practice, I took Toby home with me but had to move out of my apartment and find a new job. I thought Toby and I were going to have to live in my car, but Aunt Millie told me about the vet tech opening in Barton and told me to live in Grandma's cabin. In fact, Grandma's cabin was Aunt Millie's, but she gave it to me. Helen is a close friend of Aunt Millie's and has been great finding me and Ben places to live in town. I owe everything to Aunt Millie." Riley bit her lip as tears slipped down her cheeks.

"You have good instincts, Riley. If you say Millie wouldn't hurt you, I believe it. I feel like things might not be as simple as they seem."

"I'd really like to come downstairs. Ask Ben if he thinks it would be okay if I stay away from the windows. I'll come back upstairs before you need to turn on the lights," Riley said.

"Good idea," Melissa smiled. "I'll be back."

"Thanks, Mom," Riley said after Melissa left.

"Heard that, honey." Melissa chuckled as she hurried downstairs.

Riley went to the bathroom and glanced in the mirror. *I certainly have the ugly cry look without even trying. No wonder everyone thought I was the jilted girlfriend.* She frowned. *I'm not a girlfriend, am I?* She washed her face and checked the mirror again. *Little better.*

Ben raced up the steps, and Toby loped behind him. Toby trotted into the bathroom and whined, and Riley leaned down and hugged him while Ben stood in the doorway.

"Are you okay?" Ben asked.

"I guess I've done so much weeping lately, I've got a permanent about-to-cry look, but I'm fine. It was a real shock when I spelled out Aunt Millie's name, but I talked to Mom, and she helped me remember that Aunt Millie would never do anything to hurt me. Aunt Millie may be trafficking in drugs, but she always protected me."

"By the way, Mom's excited that you called her 'Mom'," Ben said.

"I never really had one before, so it took me a while to figure it out." Riley felt her face grow warm, and Ben hugged her.

"Mom asked if you could come downstairs and suggested it might work if you stay away from the windows. What do you think?" Ben asked.

Riley smiled. "I'd love it."

As they headed down the stairs, Ben said, "I know it was your idea."

Riley tried to smother her giggle, but Ben laughed at her.

"Everybody ready for lunch?" Jake asked when they went into the kitchen.

Duffy and Finn scrambled to Riley when she answered. "I didn't realize how hungry I was."

"We're having boloney sandwiches for lunch. Fried baloney is Jake's favorite. Do you want regular or fried?" Melissa asked.

"You didn't say it right," Jake said. "It's plain, cold boloney or tasty fried."

Riley giggled. "I guess I'll have tasty fried."

Melissa glared at Jake. "If you don't like it, I'll fix you a grilled cheese sandwich, Riley."

While they ate, Melissa asked, "What do you think, Riley?"

"I love it. Why did I not know about fried boloney sandwiches?"

"We'll have to go through your grandmother's recipes. I'll bet we'll find it," Ben said.

"You're probably right. She must have called it something else because it certainly tasted like something she would have made for lunch when I was little."

After lunch, Ben and Riley cleared the table, then Jake loaded the dishwasher while Melissa took the puppies outside for a walk. Ben kissed Riley before he went outside to watch the puppies, so his mother could come in. Jake and Toby followed him.

When Melissa came inside, Riley said, "This is hard. I really wanted to peek out the window to see what's going on."

"I've got some heavy curtains for the living room windows. They are big orange flowers, and I have no idea when I ever thought they'd be a good idea, but I could put them up, so you could sit by the fireplace and read."

"Sounds great, but I'd probably come up with something else to complain about." Riley rolled her eyes. "Don't bother. I'm sure this will all be over soon. I really am grateful that I can be in the kitchen."

"I thought I'd bake some bread. Do you have a book to read? Watching dough rise isn't all that exciting."

Riley smiled. "I've got one upstairs. I'll run grab it."

When she returned to the kitchen with her book, Ben grinned as he waited for her.

"What?" she asked.

"You're really suspicious, you know that?" His crooked smile widened.

"This is my natural resting face, so tell me," she said.

"The sheriff called me. Earlier this morning, GBI arrested Preston Ansell also known as Peter Ainsdale."

"What charges?"

"Drug trafficking with murder charges pending. He had a gun in his possession that was the same caliber as the one that killed your two kidnappers. Ballistics is on it," Ben said.

"Wow. That's really good news. Am I still stuck inside?"

"I didn't think about that. I don't see why not, but let's think about it a bit."

Riley nodded. "Not my best skill, but I agree. I have my book, and Mom's going to let me watch the bread dough rise."

Ben burst out laughing. "Well, shoot; with that much excitement in here, why would you want to go outside?"

Riley grinned. "I know, right?"

"We almost got the tractor put back together. This will be our third try." Ben kissed Riley then swaggered outside.

"Don't feel too sorry for them," Melissa said. "I'm positive that after they get it back together, they take it apart, so they can hang out in the barn. Jake once told me he and Ben had their best talks in the barn during Ben's teenage years when he was going through the typical teenage angst."

When Ben and Jake came in for a break, Melissa poured sweet tea as they sat at the table with Riley. After the men drained their glasses, Melissa refilled them then put a plate of cookies in the middle of the table and smiled at Riley.

After Jake ate his second cookie, he asked, "What's your plan now that Preston Ansell is out of the picture?"

Riley and Ben stared at each other. "We could go home," she said.

"I guess we could," Ben said.

"Can I take my room with me?" Riley grinned.

"We have to find a two-bedroom house," Ben said. "Shall we call Helen?"

Riley shrugged. "I don't know. Don't you think she already has one picked out for us?"

Ben smiled. "She is amazing. She knows everyone in town and what they're doing, doesn't she?"

"You're not leaving today, are you?" Melissa said.

"No. We have to have a place to move into first. It would be nice if we could move this weekend, but we'll have to see."

"I'll call Helen," Riley said.

"I guess we better get that tractor back together, Dad." Ben grabbed three cookies from the plate.

Jake nodded then took the last four.

After they left, Riley said, "Did you notice there was no complaint when I said I'd call Helen? I guess I'm cleared to use my phone with wild abandon."

Melissa smiled. "I did notice, and you were quite smooth with that move."

Riley hurried upstairs and called Helen.

"Hi, Riley. Are you coming home tomorrow? I've got a two-bedroom house for you and Ben. Everyone knows that he was not the scoundrel that the terrible rumor claimed."

"I'm not sure yet; I'll let you know."

After they disconnected, Riley hurried downstairs.

"Helen has a house; we can discuss when we want to leave," Riley said.

"I have mixed feelings. It's been great having you two around," Melissa said.

When Riley's phone rung upstairs, Melissa raised her eyebrows.

"I should have brought it downstairs with me." Riley grumbled as she dashed up the stairs to answer it. *Claire.*

"I thought I'd be leaving a voicemail," Claire said. "You sound out of breath."

"I ran up the stairs. I'll get my breath in a minute. I can listen."

"I'm sure you've already heard that Preston Ansell was arrested. The whole town is shocked, except us of course. We're staying under the radar though, so we can crack the next case."

Riley snorted. "I think Ben is planning on no more cases."

"Probably, and Thad said the same thing about Ben. But I didn't call you about old news. I called you about more current news. It's so new that I'm not sure it's true, but I'm betting it is."

"What is it? Or do I even want to hear?" Riley asked.

"I heard on the news that hunters found the body of a young woman that had been murdered outside of Atlanta. I didn't catch everything because the TV was on in the living room, and I was in the kitchen. Thad was mowing the backyard, so he didn't hear it at all. I caught the last snippet, and I think they said her name was something Nichols. Could she have been Marcy's cousin?"

"I've got Wi-Fi access. I'll check. Thanks, Claire."

"Was it okay to call? Thad would have a fit if he knew."

"It's fine," Riley said.

After she hung up, she turned on her computer while Melissa came upstairs.

"None of my business." Melissa's eyes crinkled. "So, who called."

"It was Claire from the vet practice in Barton. She called me about Preston Ansell. She's the one who told me about Peter Ainsdale. She's awesome."

"Sounds like it. What else did she say?"

Riley's eyes widened, and Melissa laughed. "You haven't forgotten I'm the Mom, have you? Every suspicious bone in Ben's body came from me."

Riley laughed. "I should have guessed. Claire gave me a heads up about a young woman's body in an abandoned shack. I'm going to check it out online."

Riley searched the Atlanta news stations then frowned. "Luanne Nichols. The hunters found her body today, and the news channel is speculating that she was murdered yesterday. I need to talk to Ben."

"I'll call him in, but he's got Riley radar. When I open the back door, he'll come running."

"I could just wander down to the barn," Riley said.

Melissa narrowed her eyes. "Aren't we still thinking about whether you should go outside?"

Riley gazed at Melissa and frowned. "You don't think it's quite over yet either, do you?"

Melissa met her gaze. "Do you?"

"I'm not sure. I'd feel more comfortable knowing that there was plenty of time for Preston Ansell to kill Luanne before the GBI arrested him. That somehow doesn't sound right, does it?" Riley asked.

"I understood what you meant. Are you thinking there was a second killer?" Melissa asked.

"It doesn't make sense, does it? In fact, now that I think about it, we don't even know where Ansell was arrested, so he may have had plenty of time. There are too many open questions to be answered before we get too excited."

"In that case, let's go watch that bread rise, but this time, bring your phone."

After Riley had picked up her phone and they were downstairs, Ben dashed into the kitchen.

"Dad just got a text from Mr. Rowan. His truck ran out of gas. He thinks his tank might have a puncture. We'll take a can of gas, and Dad has some epoxy sealant that may work if there's a puncture. We might be a while. Will you be okay here?"

"I'll be fine," Riley said. "I have Toby and Mom, and I'll stay inside."

Ben frowned. "Maybe I shouldn't go."

Melissa raised her eyebrows. "I think you'd worry more about those two old men trying to crawl under Mr. Rowan's truck."

"You're right, Mom. I have my phone, so call me if you need me, sweetie."

"She will and take some water. Mr. Rowan may have been stranded on the side of the road for a while, and you'll need some while you're working," Melissa said.

Ben grabbed water before he and Jake left.

Riley picked up her book. "At least they can't blame Mr. Rowan running out of gas on me."

Melissa smiled as she punched down the dough then divided it before she formed the loaves and placed them in two bread pans.

"Another two hours, then the house will smell amazing. That's my favorite part of making bread. Jake's mother told me when we were first married that the aroma of baking bread makes the hardest man's heart melt and the crankiest baby smile."

CHAPTER TWENTY-TWO

When Millie's phone rang as she entered the hotel lobby, she frowned. *Why is Helen calling?* She bit her lip as she nodded at the hotel doorman and turned to hurry outside. *I'll have more privacy for a call on the street than in a quiet hotel lobby.* Millie opened her still-wet umbrella and answered.

"Is now a good time for you, Millie? I never know if I should call or not," Helen said.

"Don't be silly. I love hearing from you. Riley's okay, isn't she?"

"I should have said that first thing. Riley's fine, and they arrested the man who masterminded her kidnapping. He also was trafficking in drugs. Isn't that awful? You don't know him because he's new; in fact, he's a veterinarian from Miami who was interviewing for a position with Doc Julie Rae. Her business is booming and not just because Doc Witmer is gone."

"Oh my gosh. A veterinarian?" Millie asked.

"Crazy, isn't it? His name is Preston Ansell. I showed him a few houses and thought he was a really nice guy and a good choice to work with Doc Julie Rae, but sometimes appearances are deceiving, aren't they? I feel really sorry for his wife. She's a famous author."

"Really? Is she in town?"

"No, she's on a book tour or something. I never met her, but I understand she's delightful."

"Well, I'm glad Riley is safe. What a relief."

"She's still in Carson with Ben's family, but she'll most likely be back this weekend. I have a little house for them. Ben and Riley are very fond of each other, and Riley wants a two-bedroom house, but I'm not sure two bedrooms will be very high on their criteria soon." Helen tittered. "Young folks these days aren't quite as impetuous as we were in our glory days, are they?"

Millie snorted. "Thank goodness. It's a wonder we survived our first two years of college."

"True, but I wouldn't have missed our wild, misspent youth for anything. We certainly have the memories, don't we?"

"Don't get me started." Millie chuckled. "Thanks for calling. I love my job but hate being away from Riley so much, and I love how much you've kept me in touch with everything that's been going on."

While Millie rode the elevator to her floor, she frowned. *I need to warn Riley.*

CHAPTER TWENTY-THREE

Melissa peeked under the dish towel that covered the bread. "About an hour before it can go into the oven."

Toby barked at the back door, and Riley jumped up from her chair. "Something's wrong." She dashed to the door, and Toby stood on the doorstep and barked.

"What is it?" Melissa asked.

"Duffy and Finn have disappeared. Toby saw a car slow down on the road then a woman whistled and held out treats, and the puppies ran for their treats. She picked them up and drove off toward town."

"What? Call the Carson sheriff, and I'll head toward town with Toby. Stay here. Somebody needs to be here in case the puppies get away or something, and you're supposed to stay inside. I'll call you when we get to town."

Toby yipped and headed to Melissa's car.

"Do you think you'll be able to understand Toby?" Riley asked.

"Of course. He just told me to hurry up." Melissa grabbed her keys and purse and ran to her car.

After Melissa and Toby left, Riley called the Carson dispatcher and told them about the woman picking up the puppies and heading toward town.

Do I call Ben? She shook her head as she paced. "They're in the middle of fixing Mr. Rowan's car; otherwise, he'd have let me know they were on their way back."

I'll text him. She sent her text: "Woman stole puppies. I called Carson sheriff. Mom & Toby going to town."

When her phone buzzed a text, she frowned. *I expected to hear back from Ben. This is from Aunt Millie.*

She read the text: "Beware EA. I have to disappear. Love u 4ever, M."

EA is Evy Ansell?

Riley shifted her waistband holster with the pistol from the back to the front of her pants. *I need it to be easily accessible.*

When a puppy whined at the back door, Riley threw open the door. "Duffy! You're home. Where's Finn?"

Duffy rushed past her to the water bowl and took a long drink. Before she closed the door, Riley heard Finn yelp. *He's at the barn and is hurt.*

She left Duffy in the house and closed the door behind her before she ran to the barn.

The barn was dark compared to the bright sunlight, but her eyes adjusted quickly when a shadowy figure in the back corner moved. Evy Ansell had Finn in one hand and a pistol pointed at Riley in the other. When she squeezed Finn, he yelped.

Evy sneered as she tossed Finn to the barn floor. "I knew the mutts would bring you running. The other one got away from me, but this one squealed just fine. Too bad your dog left though. I would have enjoyed watching your face when I shot him. In fact, I considered taking out the rest of the meddlesome people who live here one by one, but my time is too precious to waste, and it was easier to puncture that old man's gas tank and grab the mutts to get the hicks out of my way. No offense meant, Riley, but you've been a royal, annoying pain."

Riley pressed her hand to her chest to feign fear while she watched Evy's face and hand. As Evy raised her pistol to aim, Riley slid her hand to her waist, then a movement in the rafters briefly caught her attention. As Evy pulled the trigger, Princess screamed and hissed as she dropped onto Evy's head while she scratched with her claws. Evy's shot went wide, and Riley felt a sting on her left arm but didn't flinch. Evy grappled for Princess, but Princess leapt out the open window.

"Damn you, Riley," Evy screamed as she raised her pistol, and Riley shot her. While the blood oozed from the chest wound, Evy dropped to her knees then raised her pistol to shoot again. Riley shot a second time then snatched up Finn, raced out of the barn to the house, and called Ben.

"We're almost home, and I heard shots. I'll be there in one minute." Ben's voice was panicky.

"Evy came here, and I shot her. She had the puppies, but I've got them now, and they're fine. I have to call Mom too."

"What about you?"

"I need to sit down." Riley sat on the kitchen floor as soon as she and Finn were inside.

I'm too close to hysterical. I'll send a text. "Puppies are home."

Melissa: "Good. Turning around."

When Riley heard Jake's truck speed down the driveway, she exhaled then forced herself to her feet and stumbled to the driveway to meet Ben and Jake before they went to the barn.

Ben threw open his door and jumped out of the truck before Jake had completely stopped. He raced to Riley and grabbed her before she fell then growled, "You've been shot."

"Where?" Riley felt her chest.

Ben pulled back Riley's blood-soaked sling and lifted her bloody left sleeve to look for the wound in her upper arm then exhaled. "It's a graze, but you're bleeding."

He examined her splint and exhaled in relief. "Good. Your forearm is fine."

He pulled out his knife that he carried on his belt and tugged at his shirt.

"Wait, use my shirt." Riley pulled out her shirttail, and he ripped a section then wrapped her wound with the cloth.

He examined her chest, legs, and back. "You weren't shot anywhere else?"

"No. Evy's in the barn. I shot her twice. After I shot her the first time, she aimed her gun at me again, and I shot her then grabbed Finn and ran to the house."

When Jake hurried toward the barn, Ben said, "Wait, Dad. I'll go; stay with Riley."

Ben pulled out his pistol from the holster and edged his way to the barn. He stood next to the doorway and listened as he held his weapon ready to fire. He whipped around the corner with his gun pointed into the barn then stepped inside.

He hurried away from the door. "Call nine-one-one; she's unconscious but breathing."

Jake held Riley while he called; after he hung up, he asked, "Do you know who she is?"

"She's Preston Ansell's wife, Evy. I don't know if that's her real name, though," Riley said.

Ben stayed near the barn doorway and watched Evy. "Do you know how her face got all scratched up?"

"Princess dropped down from the rafters onto Evy's head and caused Evy to miss with her first shot; at least, I thought she'd missed," Riley said.

Princess strutted around the corner of the barn with her tail in the air and its tip flicking in time to her steps.

"Way to go, Princess," Ben said.

Ben exhaled when a car drove down the driveway. "Mom's here. I need to call Sheriff Dunn."

Melissa parked behind Jake's truck because he had blocked the driveway then let out Toby, and Toby rushed to Riley and Ben.

"Toby's been barking at me the whole way to hurry up. I shudder to think how fast I drove to get here," Melissa said.

"Good boy," Riley cooed as she hugged Toby. "Duffy and Finn are fine. They're in the house."

The sheriff, a deputy, and the ambulance parked in the driveway behind Melissa's car; Jake talked to the sheriff while Ben accompanied the ambulance crew and the deputy to the barn.

Melissa helped Riley to the house, and Toby followed them. Melissa led Riley to the living room and pointed to the sofa. "You sit right there, and I'll get you some hot tea with honey."

After Melissa brought Riley her tea, she asked, "Will you be okay?"

"I'm just a little shaken." Riley shivered, and Melissa tossed a crocheted woolen afghan over her legs.

When Ben came into the living room, he said, "The ambulance crew loaded Evy, and they're gone. We should probably take you into town with that wound."

"Let me look at it," Melissa said. After she unwrapped the makeshift bandage and removed Riley's sling, she said, "If we wash it well and put on some antibiotic cream, it will be fine. It's a surface cut, and there's no reason for stitches."

Ben looked over her shoulder. "You're right, Mom. It looked a lot worse when I first saw it, but I think it scared me."

"I'll wash your arm then dress your wound for you. I'll make you a new sling, and your shirt is a goner, but I'm sure you knew that. Ben, you want to grab a clean shirt?"

Ben dashed up the stairs and returned with one of Riley's new shirts.

After Riley and Melissa came out of the bathroom, Riley said, "I feel a lot better."

"Good. I'll grab some muslin from my box of material in the storage closet and make you a sling." Melissa hurried upstairs.

"I called Sheriff Dunn and told him what happened. He wants you to call him when you feel up to it," Ben said.

"Was he mad?" Riley asked.

"Not at all. I think he just wants to hear everything from you."

When Riley sat on the sofa, Toby jumped up next to her, and Melissa said, "Toby earned the right to sit on the sofa with Riley any time he likes, as far as I'm concerned."

Riley called Sheriff Dunn and told him about the puppies, Princess, and Evy.

"I can just imagine Princess dropping down on your assailant's head with claws flying. She's one fierce cat, and I'm proud of you for keeping your head and not getting shot other than the flesh wound; not many deputies could have remained calm under those stressful circumstances. The outcome would have been completely different, and I don't even want to think about it, but there's a little more you haven't told me, isn't there?"

"Yes, there is," Riley said.

"Does Ben know?" Sheriff asked.

"No."

"Then make sure he can hear you and tell me."

"Ben, the sheriff wants you to hear this too." Riley scooted over to make room for Ben on the sofa to sit next to her; Ben put his arm around her as he sat.

"I got a text from Aunt Millie right before Evy showed up. The text said, 'Beware EA. I have to disappear.' I shifted my holster and pistol from the back to the front of my waist, so it would be more accessible."

After the sheriff and Riley hung up, Melissa handed the new sling to Ben and sat next to Riley to provide support for her splint. While Ben adjusted the sling, Jake and the Carson sheriff came into the house

Melissa rose and headed to the back door. "I need some air; I'll walk to the mailbox by the road to clear my head."

"Wait up, Mom. I'll go with you." Before he left, Ben raised his eyebrows as he peered at Riley. *Ben just gave me permission to skip mentioning Aunt Millie.*

"Tell the sheriff what happened, Riley," Jake said after he and the sheriff were seated.

Riley told them about the puppies, Evy, Princess, Evy's first shot, and her two shots.

"We heard the shots when we approached the driveway, and I sped to the house," Jake added.

"Wow. I've never heard of an attack cat before. Your Princess saved your life. It'll be hard to write this one up; I'll call in GBI and let them handle it. I hear Marc's in the area. He's good; I wouldn't mind having someone like him investigating this. He'll be thorough."

Riley nodded, and Jake said, "Good. Anything else, Sheriff?"

The sheriff rose. "That's pretty much it. I'll go check on our shooter at the hospital. I can't see that I'd have any more questions for you, but I'll call if I do. It was nice to meet you, Riley. You're an amazing young woman."

Riley's face warmed, and she stared at her hands.

The sheriff's phone buzzed a text, and he cleared his throat after he read it. "Evy Ansell died on the operating table. I'm sorry, Riley, but she gave you no other choice except to defend yourself."

Jake walked the sheriff out, then after he returned, he sat next to Riley. "I told Ben and Melissa about Evy. This has been rough, but especially on you. Let me know what I can do for you or Ben." He patted her hand. "Did anyone take your gun?"

Riley's eyes widened. "No."

"Good. Give it to me, and I'll clean it for you."

Riley rose and pulled out her holster and pistol. "I'm kind of surprised the sheriff didn't ask for it."

"He knows the make and caliber. If the GBI needs to verify your gun shot Evy, they can even after it's cleaned."

When Melissa came into the house, she said, "Jake, are you cleaning a gun at the kitchen table?"

"It's Riley's," he said.

"Well, okay then."

Riley smiled. *I got a Mom pass for the day, at least, and Dad knew it.*

Ben strode into the living room, and whispered, "You heard that?"

Riley nodded, and he grinned. "I've got mail for both of us."

Riley's eyes widened. "Really? Already?"

Melissa hurried into the living room. "You were supposed to wait until I was here to open it."

Jake still held the cleaning cloth in his hand as he followed Melissa into the living room. "What am I missing?"

"Both of them heard back from UGA; you said it wouldn't be long before they sent out their first batch of letters, Jake, and you were right." Melissa sat on the chair across from Riley and folded her hands in her lap. "Okay, I'm ready."

Ben gave Riley her envelope. "You first," he said.

"No, you." Riley stared at her envelope and shivered.

"I can't take it; both of you open your envelopes now," Melissa said.

After they opened their envelopes, they stared at their letters.

"Oh for heaven's sake," Melissa said. "We're not going through that again. Give them here." They handed their letters to Jake, who gave them to Melissa then leaned over her shoulder as she read.

"This is absolutely wonderful," Melissa said. "I should torture you the way you tortured me, but I'm a better person and above all that. Both of you have been accepted by UGA. Ben has been accepted into the veterinary program, and Riley is on the wait list."

"I'm not going," Ben said.

"Yes, you are," Riley said with the sound of hard steel in her voice.

Jake looked at Riley then Ben and raised his eyebrows.

"I'm not going if you aren't going," Ben said.

"I'm on the wait list. That doesn't mean I'm not going. I have five days to accept. How long does Ben have, Mom?"

"Five days," Melissa said.

"We need to accept immediately because I'm certain that will increase my chances of getting in," Riley said.

"What if you don't get in?" Ben narrowed his eyes.

"Then I'll be higher on the wait list next year, but I've been accepted by the school. I can take any required nonveterinary classes."

"I'm not going if you're not going," Ben said.

"You, sir, are a broken record, and I give up." Riley struggled to rise from the sofa, but Ben kept his hand on her shoulder.

"Talk to him, Dad." Riley glared at Ben with her eyes of fury, and he pulled back his hand and his arm and bent his elbow to rest his head on his wrist.

When Riley left the room, Melissa followed her.

"Let's check the chicken coop, Riley."

After they were outside, Melissa said, "Honey, I know he's your boyfriend, and I'm really very fond of him, but he's an idiot."

Riley's eyes widened, then she burst out laughing. "Is this how Dad is? Bullheaded with stopped-up ears and a closed mind?"

"Absolutely; you don't think Ben got that from my side of the family, do you?"

"I would have knocked some sense into him, but I might have bruised my one good hand on his hard head." Riley wiggled her eyebrows, and Melissa laughed.

When Ben came outside, Melissa smiled and went inside.

"Aren't you cold?" Ben asked.

"I'm freezing." Riley spoke between her tightly pressed lips to keep her teeth from chattering.

"I think we should sign our acceptance letters and get them in the mail right away, so we can go to Barton tomorrow."

Riley rolled her eyes. "Good idea."

"I'm sorry I forgot to listen to what you were saying." Ben tilted up her chin and kissed her gently. "I just don't want to go anywhere without you."

While Ben held Riley, a bird called from the brush beyond the barn, and Riley and Ben smiled as they gazed at each other.

"Hello, Bob," Ben said, and Riley echoed, "Hello, Bob."

Riley leaned against his chest. "You're going to make me see the surgeon next week, aren't you?"

"You got it, babe." Ben chuckled as they went inside.

ACKNOWLEDGMENTS

Huge thanks to my husband for his patience, support, talented technical expertise, and for being so hilarious.

Thanks to my editor for her entertaining non-editor editing comments and her ever-ready pocket of commas, semicolons (whatever they are), and magic word-slicing sword.

Thank you for reading. You keep reading; I'll keep writing!

What to read next?

RACE AGAINST DEATH

RILEY MALLOY THRILLER, Book 3

Riley, vet tech and dog whisperer, races with death to find a friend's husband, but is she racing to her own death? The killer waits: Riley must die.

Subscribe: to the newsletter!

Look for the Subscribe button on www.judithabarrett.com

ABOUT THE AUTHOR

Judith A. Barrett is an award-winning author of mystery, thriller, crime, and survival science fiction novels with action and adventure to spark the reader's imagination. Her unusual main characters are brilliant, talented, and down-to-earth folks who solve difficult cases and stop killers. Her novels take place in small towns and rural areas in the southern states of the US.

Judith lives in rural Georgia on a small farm with her husband, dogs, and chickens. When she's not busy writing, Judith is busy with farm chores, walking with her husband and dogs, or watching the beautiful sunsets from her porch.

Website   www.judithabarrett.com

Newsletter   *Subscribe* to her eNewsletter via her Website

You keep reading; I'll keep writing!